CORY'S SHIFT

CUTTING A NEW TRACK

SUSPENSEFUL SECRETS
BOOK 3

DAN PETROSINI

Print ISBN: 978-1-960286-18-5
Naples, FL
Library of Congress Control Number: 2023903573

ACKNOWLEDGEMENT

I would like to thank my wife Julie and daughters Stephanie and Jennifer for their love and support.
Also, a shout out to Steven Epright, Battalion Chief Collier County EMS\Fire Department, for info on drugs to quickly subdue someone.

OTHER BOOKS BY DAN

Complicit Witness

Push Back

Ambition Cliff

PROLOGUE

Pedaling in sync with a Tower of Power bass line, Gerry reached for his water bottle. Halfway through his daily twenty-mile bike ride along the East River, he sucked a sip. Addicted to exercise, he loved 'paying for his day,' especially in the four-in-the-morning solitude of the city. In an hour, cars would pour onto the FDR Drive after the city's nightly nap.

A passing van caught Gerry's attention. The only vehicle in sight, he followed it as it exited the highway. A half mile ahead, its taillights brightened. The cyclist made a quick challenge for himself and put his head down. He closed half the distance before the van raced away.

Gerry saw a shape on a park bench where the van had stopped. Shaking his head, he hoped they hadn't robbed a homeless person. Bemoaning the city's increasing crime rate, he stood, pedaling as quickly as he could.

As he drew nearer, the person struggled to sit up. Gerry blinked. It was a boy. A stocky kid.

He pulled his headphones down. "Hey! You all right?"

A moan drowned the sound from his headset. Gerry

braked, coming to a stop. He hesitated, trying to understand what the stuttering boy was saying.

"Take it easy, I'll help you."

He saw tears forming behind the kid's thick glasses. Moaning, the flat-nosed boy was clutching his abdomen. Gerry realized the kid was disabled and had some of the physical traits of Down Syndrome.

Gerry took his helmet off "What happened?"

"My . . . my belly. Ma . . . ma . . ."

Ronnie squinted in the gray light. It looked like there was blood on the kid's shirt. Had he been stabbed by the bastards in the van?

"Let me see." As the kid babbled, Gerry pulled the boy's shortened hands off his stomach. "I'm just going to take a quick look."

He lifted the kid's shirt. "What the hell?" Gauze soaked with blood was wrapped around his midsection.

"Ma . . . make, make it go away. Make it go away."

"Hold on, guy."

Ronnie tossed his helmet aside, pulled his phone out, and dialed 911. "I just found a kid, all by himself. I think he's got Down Syndrome and he's injured or something. Hurry, the kid's bleeding. We're on the Finley Walk, just north of the Queensboro Bridge." The kid tried to get up, falling onto the sidewalk. The kid screamed and Ronnie hung up to help him.

"Take it easy, my friend. Just lie there." He adjusted the band holding the child's glasses in place. "Help is on the way. You're going to be okay."

"No, no, no, no, no."

Gerry took his jacket off and folded it under the kid's head. "Did they stab you? Did those people in the van do this to you?"

The kid moaned.

"Hang in there, buddy."

As the sound of a siren intensified, Gerry wondered what had happened to this defenseless kid. How did this innocent child end up on the side of the road in the middle of the night?

1

———

Cory rushed into a small room and put his guitar case on the table. "Hey, Katie. Sorry, the session took longer than expected."

Katie Waters, a volunteer at Mount Sinai Children's Hospital, said, "No problem. Hope it went well."

Cory smiled. "It took time convincing the suits to keep it acoustic. They're always overproducing things. But it worked out."

"Hope you sell a million records."

Cory shrugged. "The kid's market isn't big, but I don't care. I love playing and making kids happy."

"You're a good guy."

Strapping on his Gibson, Cory said, "Oh, I got pimples for sure, just ask my wife."

"How many years you married?"

"Nineteen. Come on, let's go."

Cory pushed through a door. "Hey, guys!"

A roomful of kids in wheelchairs roared a welcome, except one, a boy hunched over in a wheelchair. Cory smiled at him but couldn't place who it was.

"You guys ready to have some fun?" Cory strummed his guitar. "How about I play a new tune I just wrote. In fact, I recorded it right before coming here."

Cory launched into the song. The kids were mesmerized. When he finished, they clapped as hard as they could.

"What do you say we make a new version of that one? That'd be super cool, right?"

A chorus of yeahs broke out.

"All right. On *our* song, I want the first two rows to sing the melody and the rest to sing background, something that supports the melody. Let's start with the first four bars."

Cory demonstrated what he was looking for, and all the children were excited except for the boy in the first row.

Cory walked the room through his idea. "Wow, you guys practice before I get here?"

The room exploded.

Cory said, "Let me play you another one." He dug out a sheet of paper. "Listen to how it goes. I'll play the first eight bars a couple of times." He held up a sheet. "These are the lyrics. Anyone want to try singing it with me?"

Every hand in the room shot up but one. The boy seemed to be sleeping. Cory wondered if the kid was too weak or just uninterested in music.

"Great. Everyone will get a chance. Now, make sure to listen carefully so you get the rhythms in your ear."

A handful of aides entered and stood in the rear as Cory ended the hour. "You were super amazing today. I had a ton of fun, and next week I'll see if the hospital will let me bring a keyboard and maybe a guitar or two."

As the kids were ushered out, Cory went over to the boy. "How's it going?" He recognized him. "You're Bobby, right?"

The kid had trouble lifting his chin off his chest to nod.

Cory checked Bobby's wristband. His last name was Kennedy. "Did you have fun today?"

"Uh-huh."

"It's good to see you here." Cory stuck his hand out. The kid struggled to reach it. Cory patted him on the shoulder. "I'll see you next week."

Carrying his guitar, Cory followed Katie back into the small room.

"You're, like, amazing with kids."

"Thanks. It's fun for me."

"You got kids, right?"

"Yep. Ava, she's seventeen, and Tommy just turned seven."

"Nice."

"Hey, what's going on with that kid Bobby? He seems very sick."

"Yeah, I don't know the whole story, but I heard he was on the transplant list, like, forever, and his parents took him to some other place. Like, an illegal one. And whatever they did to the poor kid, it didn't work."

"What do you mean, an illegal place?"

"I shouldn't have said that. I don't really know what happened, but he's not doing good."

"Who's his doctor?"

"I don't know."

Cory snapped his case shut. "All right, I gotta run, see you next week."

Waiting for the elevator, he checked the time. He had to move it; he had two lessons to give, and they were in Brooklyn.

As he rode down, Cory couldn't get the kid, Bobby, out of his head. He was only ten or eleven and looked like he wouldn't last another month.

The elevator opened. Cory peered into the lobby but didn't get off. He pushed number three and the doors closed.

Cory stepped on the transplant floor. He headed straight to the administrative offices, asking to see Dr. Evans.

The head of the transplant unit eyed Cory's guitar. "You get off on the wrong floor?"

"Just finished with the kids, Doc."

"It didn't go well?"

"No, it did. But a kid, Bobby Kennedy, he's real sick, and I heard something that's bothering me."

Evans's shoulders sagged. "You know I'm not supposed to discuss a patient's case."

"I know, but he was here waiting on a transplant, right?"

"He was on the kidney list and receiving nephrology treatment."

"His parents took him out?"

Evans nodded.

"Why? Where'd they go?"

"We don't know for sure."

"What happened to him?"

He lowered his voice. "You didn't hear it from me, but it was a botched transplant."

"What?"

"Shush. I can't say anymore."

"Come on, man. You're telling me his parents took him to some place that wasn't a hospital for a transplant, and they screwed it up?"

Evans frowned. "I don't know where this took place, but whoever performed the surgery either never screened for HLA matches or thought they could get away with it."

"HLA?"

"Tissue matching. Kennedy has strong antibodies that are

reacting against the donor's HLA. He's in critical rejection mode."

"Can it turn around for him?"

"We're doing the best we can, but he's likely to suffer irreversible damage."

"How the hell does something like this happen?"

"People get tired and sicker as they wait for an organ. It forces them to consider options that are unconventional at best and dangerous."

"You've seen this before?"

"Unfortunately, incidents like this are increasing."

"Who's in charge of shutting these types of places down?"

"It's not something the authorities focus on. It's relatively low on their radar. They're focused on the opioid epidemic, Medicare fraud, shootings, and the like."

"That's crazy. They should see this kid."

"I agree, but it's a matter of priorities."

"If there were enough organs, nobody would have to do whatever Bobby went through."

"That's probably true."

"Who can I report this to?"

"We filed a malpractice complaint with the New York Medical Board."

"The guys doing it are doctors?"

"We don't know."

"How did you file a complaint then?"

"We advised them of the neglect. We hope they'll investigate the particulars and shut the operation down."

"You don't seem convinced."

"We can only do what we can do, and that's report the incident."

On the way to his lesson, Cory couldn't shake the circumstances of Bobby's condition. As the subway rounded a turn, Cory imagined the hopelessness that forced a parent to go outside the system to save their child.

It wasn't a stretch, as he and his wife had been down the same path trying to save her mother. They'd paid a hundred thousand as a down payment to get Linda's mother a kidney. Like many things the last couple of years, it involved Barney Tower.

He remembered going to the attorney with the cash. The crooked lawyer was part of the problem, he thought, before realizing that he and his wife were just as guilty.

If no one was willing to go to the black market for an organ, facilitators wouldn't exist. He wondered how many other children's lives were damaged or lost because desperation forced them underground.

Why wasn't the press exposing these nefarious operators? For that matter, why didn't the media encourage people to donate their organs? If there were enough organs to satisfy demand, there'd be no room for backroom surgeries.

Walking up the subway steps, Cory knew he had a responsibility to say something. He was no longer a pop star and didn't have the platform he once had. But he could still make some noise.

2

———

Cory put his guitar case down and closed the door.

"Hey guys, I'm home."

Tommy came running to the door. "Hi, Dad, how was the record you made?"

"It went super. How was school?"

"Okay."

"Just, okay? Come on, you got to do better than that."

"But—"

"No buts. Wasn't there something good today?"

"Uh, yeah, I was the only one to get the math problem Mrs. Green gave us. And I made a dish in ceramics."

"Wow. You're smart. What kind of dish?"

"I'm going to get it to show you."

Tommy ran out as Linda came in. "How'd it go today?"

"Good. It was touch and go, but I'm super happy the way the recording came out. We did it acoustically."

"That's what you wanted. You didn't go to the hospital?"

"No, I went. It was a total downer."

"Why? What happened?"

"There was this kid, he's just a couple years older than Tommy. He's in bad shape."

"What happened to him?"

Cory filled Linda in on Bobby Kennedy.

"That's horrible. The poor kid. His parents must be beating themselves up."

"I want to talk to them."

"About what? You couldn't say anything; we did the same thing for Mom."

"I know. I just want to find out who they dealt with. These guys got to be shut down."

Linda kissed Cory. "I love your intentions, but stick to making music. You're not a private investigator."

"I'm not investigating, I just want to shine a light on this crap. People need to know how dangerous this is."

"Then write a song about it."

"Not a bad idea, but—"

"Look, Dad." Tommy held up a blue dish.

"You made this?"

"Yeah."

"I can't believe it. You can do anything."

"You too, Daddy. You can do anything if you set your mind to it, right? You always say that."

Cory looked at his son, wondering if he had a sixth sense. It was good advice, but acting on it, especially exposing a wicked illegal transplant ring, seemed out of reach. "Yep. If you try hard enough, you can do anything."

Cory had no idea what to do, but he had an idea of where to start.

IT'D TAKEN Cory a week to get in to see his nemesis. He only agreed to meet after Cory said he had compromising material he wanted to hand off.

Cory was shown into the lawyer's office. He smelled a hint of cigar smoke in the air. Barney Tower had lost thirty pounds, and there was a gray cast to his skin. He'd swapped out wearing three-thousand-dollar suits in favor of baggy lounge wear. He moved slower, but his eyes still projected confidence and power.

Tower cleared his throat. "Mr. Lupinski. We meet again."

Cory nodded. "How are you feeling?"

He waved Cory off. "What did you want to discuss?"

"Getting an organ transplant."

"I suggest you visit a hospital in the area that specializes in transplants."

"I want to know about who you worked with when we asked for help for my mother-in-law."

"I have no idea what you're referring to."

Cory took a shot. "Look, I have the refund check, and it's marked transplant reimbursement."

Tower's eyes widened. "Transplant? No, that was a refund of legal fees."

"I hear you need a heart transplant."

"The doctors debate whether that's the best course of action."

"You're a smart man, and I know you're always prepared."

Tower smiled. "I try to see around as many corners as possible."

"So, you've had to do your homework on the factors of a successful transplant. You know, the surgeon, where it's done, the screening process, matching, etcetera."

"Improving the odds."

"I assume you wouldn't entertain an unconventional way to get a transplant. Someplace outside the system."

"I haven't given it any thought."

"Oh, come on. You had to. Anybody waiting for an organ looks at every option, especially somebody like you."

"I agreed to see you because of the information you alluded to."

"Look, you know what I know about you."

Tower's ears flattened.

"I said I'd keep it private and haven't said a word, not even to my wife, the lawyer Worth, or anyone. After what you did to me and my family, you owe me."

"Owe you?"

"That's right. All I want is some help understanding how these places work. Kids are dying."

"You're very dramatic. The system is simply unable to meet the demands, and the market steps in to fill the void. My advice is to forget about all about it."

"Killing people—"

"Don't get so sanctimonious. While rates of mortality are slightly elevated, it offers those in need a chance at life."

"Would you go to one of these places for a heart?"

"Today, no. However, if my condition worsens and there is no other option, I'd give it serious condition, like any reasonable person would."

"I wouldn't do it. It's not right—"

"Is it right to leave your kids without a father? Your wife a widow?"

"I get it, but what about the donor? It's okay to kill him or her?"

"The vast majority of off-market organs are kidneys and liver sections, as they regenerate. Lungs, hearts, and pancreases are another matter."

"Where do they do these transplants?"

"Most times, surgicenters."

"Legit surgicenters? Why would they risk it?"

"Money. There are no insurance companies to deal with, and they get paid retail rates. The paperwork doesn't reflect the actual procedures, and with their own team and confidentiality laws, it flies under the radar."

"But don't they need to be hospitalized?"

"They usually stay a night or two, and when stable, they're moved to a rehab facility. A private nurse accompanies them, monitoring their condition."

"How many of these kinds of operations are there?"

"More than you'd believe. There are scores of organ brokers. This is a highly lucrative business, and it's global. There's no shortage of players."

"It's that widespread?"

"Yes."

"Give me an idea. Say in the New York area, how many operators are there?"

"Ten or so."

"Ten? That's crazy."

Tower nodded.

"Where do they get the training?"

"Most are trained surgeons. You ever go to one that didn't want to perform surgery on you? They love cutting, and with this, they earn extra money. Big money."

Cory never had gone under the knife, but he'd heard it was true: surgeons want to do surgery.

But would they stoop to doing them illegally? Risk the years of schooling and internship for more money? It didn't make sense. There had to be another angle to this.

3

———

Cory stood at the head of the room, beaming. "Well, you did it again. I didn't think you guys could be better than you were last week, but you were amazing today. I couldn't get the hospital to move the keyboard up here, but they promised it next time. And I'll have a surprise next week."

The kids shouted, "What? What? Tell us."

"I'm going to bring in a small PA system. We'll have a mic and speaker. Maybe we'll record something you can have your families listen to."

A chorus of yays broke out.

"See you next week."

Cory carried his guitar behind Katie, who said, "I remember going to see Raffi when I was, like, eight, and you're miles better."

"I don't know about that."

"You should do concerts. It'd blow up your career."

"I used to do some, but the traveling kept me away from my family. And I wouldn't be able to do this."

"You really enjoy working with kids, don't you?"

He smiled and put his guitar into its case. "I learned a

while ago, and it wasn't an easy lesson: helping kids, especially sick ones, is more important than any career. We can't put making money ahead of curing cancer or getting a kid the organ he needs."

"I know, it's crazy, right. You know, sometimes, when I'm home, especially at night, one of the kids pop into my head and I'm, like, sad, you know? I'm here, like, every day, and it still bothers me. I bet if people came here, they'd change their minds."

Cory shrugged. "You're right. Maybe it was the roller-coaster I was on. It opened my eyes—all the money, and people fawning over you like you were some kind of god. Everybody has to do what they feel they gotta do, but it didn't work for me. I got to do something meaningful, something with a higher purpose."

"The world needs more people like you."

"I'm no angel. Say, how's Bobby doing? He wasn't here today."

"They said he was going for some nuclear test."

"I hope he's doing better. See you later."

Cory took the elevator to the nephrology floor. An anti-septic smell strengthened as he found Bobby Kennedy's room. The kid's parents were sitting at his bedside. Cory knocked on the open door. "Hi, just stopped in to see how Bobby is doing."

Eyes on Cory's guitar, the father stood. "I'm John, Bobby's dad."

"Nice to meet you. I'm Cory. I volunteer here."

The woman stood. "Hi, I'm Valerie. Bobby told us about you. You're a big star."

Cory shook hands and said, "Hey, Bobby. How you doing?"

"He's tired from the test. They injected him with nuclear material to see how the kidneys are doing."

"Oh. So that's why you're glowing."

Bobby managed a weak smile.

"We missed you today. I just wanted to say hello."

The father said, "Thank you for stopping in."

Cory said, "No problem. I'll see you, buddy."

The father walked him to the door, and Cory said, "I know it's none of my business, but I get what you did."

"What are you talking about?"

"Going outside the system for a transplant."

"We didn't—"

"Look, I would've done the same thing if it were my kid. In fact, we tried to do it for my mother-in-law, but she died before we could get one for her."

Kennedy hung his head. "It was a fucking mistake, they almost killed him."

"Don't beat yourself up."

"Yeah? You see him now? And it's all my fault."

"You took action. At least you weren't waiting years, watching twenty percent of the people on the list die each year."

He frowned. "We didn't know what to do."

"It's a big mess."

He shook his head. "And to think I paid a hundred grand . . . what a fool."

"The transplant system is broken. I'm no expert, but I've been volunteering at Mount Sinai for five years, and the numbers aren't good here, or anywhere, for that matter."

"When they first said he needed a transplant, we went right to the Internet, and it was shocking. Over a hundred thousand people waiting for organs, and twenty people a day dying, day after day. I didn't want Bobby to be one of them."

"Look, I want to use whatever status I have, get a few people in the music business on board as well, and get the word out about the need to donate organs. You don't hear anybody talking about it. It's never in the news. I bet if people could see what kids like Bobby are going through, they'd think about donating. That's what got me to be a donor."

The father hung his head. "You're right. I'm part of the problem too. You'd think I'd be the first one to sign up as a donor."

"That's my point. We can do better, and we will, if we get the word out."

"I hope it's not too late for Bobby."

"It's not. In the meantime, we got to try to shut down some of these butcher shops before they do more damage."

He nodded.

"How did you find out about who you went to?"

The father looked at the ground but said nothing.

"Look, I'm just curious and want to help. And you know, like I said, when my mother-in-law was sick, we got in touch with a lawyer who made the arrangements. It was double what you paid."

"Yeah, well look what the cheaper price got me."

"Who'd you go to?"

"I didn't go anywhere; they came to us. This woman approached us one day as we came into the hospital. She said she was with the International Association of Transplants."

"I never heard of them."

"They don't exist. It was a cover."

"Who was the woman?"

"We never saw her again. She gave us a number to call that's now disconnected. And this Asian man told us to go to this place on Baxter Street in Chinatown. It was like being on a spy mission. Another lady took us in a Lincoln to the W Hotel, where we met with this guy, Chou. He was slick, now that I think of it, but reassured us everything would go well."

"How did they handle the payment?"

"They sent somebody to the house. On a motorcycle, if you can believe it. We gave them half and then when they picked us up—"

"They picked you up?"

"Yeah, the day we took Bobby out of Mt. Sinai, they came over right after, in a van. They took us to this surgery place."

"Where was it?"

"No idea. We couldn't see anything, and while the surgery went on, we had to stay inside this room, no windows or anything. We saw Bobby after. He looked okay. They took us home. We didn't want to leave him, but that was the deal. They came back the next day and he seemed all right, but the day after, we knew he was getting worse and they knew it too. So, we took him back to here."

"And you have no idea who they were or where you were?"

He wagged his head. "No. It makes me sick that I was so frigging naive. Man, I'd like to get these bastards."

4

Cory stepped into the apartment. The aroma of cumin was in the air. He put his guitar in the studio and headed to the kitchen.

"Hey, Linda, I'm home."

"Hi."

"Making tacos?"

"Yep. How was your day?"

He shrugged. "Remember that kid with the botched transplant?"

"Of course."

"I talked to the father—"

"You did what?"

"Bobby wasn't in the rec room today, so I went to see how he was doing, and his parents were there."

"How is he?"

"He had a nuclear test today and was beat. Anyway, the father told me all about what went down. It's like a horror flick."

"What do you mean?

He filled his wife in. Linda said, "Don't get involved, Cory. These people are dangerous."

"I guess so."

"Guess so? They're switching locations, hiding people in vans, picking up money on a motorcycle? It's a Hollywood movie, and somebody always gets killed in them."

"I feel bad for the parents. It's sad they're so desperate. They were willing to pay, and it backfired."

"Where do these people get the organs from?"

"Evans, he's the big shot in the Mount Sinai transplant unit, he said with kidneys they prey on the poor. Like that *60 Minutes* show we saw on India's black market."

"That was Americans and British going to India. This is happening here?"

"Yeah, it's crazy to think we got Americans who need money so bad, they sell a kidney."

"It's horrible."

"Maybe there's a way to incent people to be donors."

"You mean pay them?"

"Why not? Come up with a system, say, pay people a thousand dollars to become a donor. Make it so that you couldn't back out unless you paid it back. Can you imagine how many would sign up?"

"It would solve the shortage right away."

"Not immediately. You'd have to wait for people to die and weed out organs with disease and stuff."

"It's still a good idea."

"Or what about taking people sixty-five or so and healthy. They figure they got another twenty years to live and need money. Maybe they can be paid a chunk of dough to give up a kidney."

"What?"

"It would give them money for their retirement, and

they'd recover. They could live the rest of their life with one kidney."

"That's still taking advantage of poor people."

"I don't think it's as bad. They'd have to wait until a later age to do it."

"I don't know."

"It'll buy time before they figure out how to grow organs in some lab."

"Ow. That sounds like Frankenstein."

"It's no different than using a human organ."

"You think they'll be able to do that?"

"I saw something on the web about it; they're working on it."

"Can you imagine what they'll be doing in twenty to thirty years?"

"We may benefit from it, but anybody on a waiting list will be dead in five years."

"That's terrible."

"It is, but what's worse is going off-line to one of these black-market places for a transplant. It's all about the money. People are getting maimed, killed, and nobody is stopping them."

"It's not your job to fix it—"

"I know, but the kids . . ."

"You're not a cop."

"I'm just going to see if me and a couple of others can get the message out about how dangerous these places are and ask people to become donors."

———

Linda was watching the news as Tommy built a Lego building. She stood. "Oh my God. Cory! Come here."

"What's the matter, Mommy?"

Cory ran into the family room. "What's going on?"

She pointed to the TV. "A boy was kidnapped, and they took his kidney."

"That's crazy."

The newscaster said, "It's the city's second case this month. Authorities have launched an investigation into these bizarre cases."

"I never heard anything about the first one. Did you?"

"No."

"Mom! What's wrong?"

"Sorry, sweetheart. Something very bad happened to a boy."

"What happened?"

"He was kidnapped at the park. That's why we always tell you not to talk to strangers."

"He was talking to a stranger?"

"Yes. Do me a favor and clean up your room. I have to vacuum, and your toys are all over the floor."

"But I'm building something."

"If your toys disappear into the vacuum, they'll be gone forever."

Tommy huffed and ran off.

Linda said, "This is so creepy. It's like a horror movie."

iPad in hand, Cory said, "Look at this. Reuters has an article on it, 'Police Suspect Organ Theft.' It says they believe it's related to a New Jersey case where a kid with Down Syndrome was kidnapped and left by the East River. The cops originally thought it was related to a satanic cult active in Trenton. Now they suspect there's an organ ring operating in the Tri-State Region targeting kids with Down."

"Oh my God. That's horrible."

"You see how heartless these bastards are? They're kidnapping kids, with Down, to steal organs."

"How can they get away with it?"

"How? The cops can't stop people from shooting each other."

"What do you mean?"

"I'm just frustrated, that's all. It's hard to believe this is happening here. But you know, I got a feeling kidnapping kids is going to backfire on them."

"You think?"

"Kids are vulnerable. Everybody knows we got to protect them; they have to do something about it. I gotta do something about it."

"Don't get involved, these people are dangerous."

"Trust me, I know, but I can't just sit around."

5

———————

Cory sat in the waiting room. His mind was spinning over the kidnappings. How could something like this happen? He stood when he saw Dr. Evans get off the elevator.

"Hi, Doc, you have a couple of minutes?"

Evans raised his eyebrows. "Not really."

"I'll make it quick."

"I can only spare five minutes."

He followed Mount Sinai's head of transplants into his office.

"What's on your mind?"

"This kidnapping ring."

Evans bit his lip. "It's concerning."

"I don't get it. I mean, how do they use the kidneys? Don't they need to match and have a recipient standing by?"

"We'd hope they screen the victims. It's my belief they're sedating these children and screening for blood type at a minimum. Ideally, they'd run HLA testing, but based upon what we see with the Kennedy child . . ."

"How do they get it done so fast?"

"The first kid was released four days after he was taken,

the second in five days. Either there was a complication with removal, or they needed a day for the recipient to be in position."

"Where do you think they're keeping these kids?"

"It could be anywhere. I think they're sedated and brought in for surgery, maybe into a surgi center or, God forbid, a hospital."

"You think they do it in a real hospital?"

"I doubt it, but I didn't think anyone would harvest organs from a kidnap victim."

Cory stood in front of a podium in Mount Sinai's lobby. Behind him were ten well-known musicians, an aging movie star, and a handful of hospital staff.

He smiled at the reporters as they positioned their microphones. As they backed away, Cory said, "Okay, looks like we're ready to go." He shifted his weight. "A couple years ago, I stood here asking for help in the fight to cure childhood cancer. I didn't just ask. I tried to do what I could by committing the lion's share of the royalties I earn to Reach for the Stars, the trust I set up to research cures and make the lives of our children a bit better.

"Fortunately, many of you responded to my plea. Actually, my wife says it was begging, but I'm cool with that."

The gatherers laughed. "Today, I want to talk to you about something you probably just heard about. And that's illegal organ transplants. These poor kids who were kidnapped, right here, not in some third-world country, but in New York City.

"As disgusting and shocking as it is, illegal organ transplants have been going on in the United States for years. It doesn't get much attention from the press, but it should.

These dangerous transplants prey on the poor and sick. But to me, it starts with the demand. With people wanting them so badly, they'll do anything to get one.

"It sounds crazy, right? People going to the black market for organs. Most of these illegal operations use second-rate surgeons and do them in places less than ideal. Why would anybody do that, you ask?

"It's simple; the waiting list for organs is too long. About twenty percent of the people on the list, including many children, die each year. Being on an organ list is as close to a death sentence as you can get."

Cory wagged his head. "People feel they don't have a choice, and go outside the system. But instead of saving their lives, they're putting them at risk while enriching criminals. For those thinking about selling your organs, I beg you not to do it.

"Now, what can we do? You knew I was going to have an ask for you, and the good news is you don't have to pony up any money this time. I have two requests: the first is become a donor. It's a simple thing that costs nothing and will save lives. Where else can you have an impact like that? It's an easy process, and you can do it at organdonor.gov.

"We also need you, especially the media, to spread the word against illegal transplanting. We need to raise public awareness about this practice and pressure law enforcement to shut down these operators.

"What kind of society can't protect its children from being snatched off the streets for their organs? We got to fix this, now. There's no time to waste. So, become a donor, and spread the word. Thanks for coming today, please do your part."

Cory hung around for an hour talking with the press and friends. The vibe was good, but a question his buddy Donny posed haunted him: If people stop selling their organs, the black-market supply would go down, so, wouldn't that force the operators to resort to more kidnapping?

CORY CAME out of the study. "Man, must be a slow news day or something. I just hung up with the *New York Post*, and before that it was the *Daily News* calling."

"That's what you wanted. It was on the news two times already."

"Wow, I'm surprised at the attention this is getting. I'm not exactly a chart-topper anymore."

"I hate to break it to you, but it's not you, it's the Down Syndrome kids these animals are kidnapping."

"Yeah, I know. It just feels weird to get all these calls."

"Give the press a day and they'll move on to the next story."

"I don't think this is going away so fast."

"Why's that?'

"If another kid goes missing and—" He pulled out his phone. "It's probably *The Times*, they're the only one left."

"Hello . . . What the hell?" Cory raised his voice. "Who is this?"

6

Cory stared at his phone. Linda asked, "Who was that?"

"Nobody."

"Nobody? It didn't sound like nobody."

"Just a nut saying something stupid."

"What'd he say?"

"For me to keep my mouth shut."

"About what? The illegal transplants?"

"Yeah, he said if I kept going to the media, I'd regret it."

"He threatened you?"

Cory nodded. "He's just a lunatic."

"No, maybe not. I told you these people were dangerous."

"Don't get carried away."

"You've got to report this to the police."

"That's ridiculous."

"Are you crazy? These people kidnapped kids, innocent, disabled children. They're the lowest thing on earth."

"What are they going to do? Kidnap me?"

Linda bored her eyes into Cory. "You forget you have kids of your own?"

"Of course not."

"These people are savages; you can't tell what they'd do."

"Take it easy. I'll stop. Okay?"

"Please. We can't take a chance, not with Tommy and Ava."

"I doubt anything would happen, but I'm done."

"Good."

"I can't get over this guy called."

"You should report it."

"The cops will say it's nothing. If he calls again, I'll take it to the police."

"What did he sound like? Was he, like, mean?"

"He had a Chinese accent."

"They're Asian, like that kid's parents said?"

"I guess it could be that guy, uh, Chou, they dealt with. I think that's what they said his name was."

"You think it's the same man?"

"I doubt it. It'd be too risky for him to be making calls. He probably has somebody do his dirty work."

"How big a gang do you think they are?"

"Tough to say, but you need a lot of people involved to pull it off. Somebody has to find the kids to kidnap and watch them. Then they got people to sedate them. It's got to be someone who knows medicine."

"Maybe a nurse."

"Could be. They also need people to deal with the family of the recipient. Plus the doctors to do the operation and keep an eye on the recoveries."

"It's got to be highly organized."

"It doesn't get more complicated than a transplant."

"We've got to tell the police. Maybe they can trace the call."

"He probably used a burner phone, so it can't be traced."

"Maybe he didn't. It's worth a try. We've got to do what we can to stop this."

"You just told me to back off."

"Yeah, that's right. Stop talking to the media about this. All I'm saying is tell the police about the call."

"All right. I got to finish mixing that jingle I'm working on. Can you find out what precinct or detective is dealing with this?"

When he was finished working on the radio ditty, he called Brooklyn's Seventy-Fifth Police Precinct. There was a lot of background noise when the call was answered.

"Detective Belfi."

"Hi, Detective, my name's Cory Lupinski."

"The singer-songwriter?"

"Yeah, you saw the press conference?"

"I did, but my daughter was a big fan a few years back."

"Cool."

"What can I do for you?"

"I got a strange call and figured you should know."

"Tell me about it."

"Well, I've been trying to get the word out about people becoming organ donors and how dangerous this illegal ring is, and some guy called and threatened me."

"How so?"

"He said if I didn't stop drawing attention to the kidnapping of children for organs that I'd regret it."

"Did he make a direct threat?"

"No, just that I better stop, or I'd regret it. You know, I've got two kids and I, well, you know, can't take any chances."

"Certainly not. Was there anything about the man you can tell me?"

"He was Chinese for sure. He had a Mandarin accent, so probably from China."

"How do you know it's Mandarin and not another dialect?"

"I make my living with my ears. I spent a lot of time as a kid in Chinatown. I can tell the difference."

"Interesting."

"What do you mean by that?"

"Well, it lines up with what we've been hearing about a ring out of China."

"Wow. What do you know?"

"Can't discuss an active investigation. Now, this Asian man probably used a burner, but if you'll allow us to check, we might get lucky."

"Whatever you need."

"You'll have to sign off on an authorization for Verizon to release your phone records. It'll be limited to today."

"No problem. Happy to help. I want to shut these guys down."

"We all do. If this guy or anyone for that matter, contacts you again, let me know immediately. Don't do anything stupid. We don't know much about this gang, but what we do know is they're ruthless."

7

———

Cory came out of the vocal booth. He'd laid down six tracks of the new tune. He thought the second take was the best but looked forward to listening to all of them and choosing.

The sound engineer stuck his head in. "Hey, Cory!"

"Yo, what's up?"

"You better call your wife. She called three times."

"You got it." He took his cell phone out of his backpack. Linda had called five times.

He punched in her number. "Sorry, I was—"

"Is Tommy with you?"

"Tommy?"

"Do you have Tommy?"

"No, I've—"

"He's missing."

"What?"

"I went to pick him up at Taekwondo, and they said he left with a man."

"How could they just let him go with a stranger?"

"It was a new girl, she thought it was you."

"How the fuck could they do that?"

"Who could've picked him up? You think it was Donny?"

"No, I saw him this morning. He was going to the Van Gelder Studio in Englewood."

"What should we do?"

"Call the police. I'll meet you at home."

Cory grabbed his stuff and ran out of the studio.

A PATROL CAR was double-parked in front of his building, and Cory took the stairs two at a time.

Cory burst into the apartment. Mascara was running down her face as Linda talked to two officers.

"Any news?"

Linda embraced him. "My Tommy. Where is he?"

"We'll find him. Don't worry."

He walked her to the couch and asked, "What's being done to find my son?"

"We've interviewed the woman at the Taekwondo place, and she's working with a sketch artist for a rendering of the man your son left with."

"How long is this going to take? We can't wait for a picture—"

An officer held his hand up. "The studio didn't have any cameras, but we have someone going to the surrounding businesses to see what kind of CCTV footage there may be."

Cory said, "What else?"

"We've issued an Amber Alert and are monitoring the bridges and tunnels."

"Call Detective Belfi. He's with the Seventy-Fifth Precinct."

"What's his involvement in this?"

"Just a hunch. I was threatened a week ago by this Chinese guy because—just call him, he has to know. This may be related."

Linda said, "Oh my God, you think they took him?"

"Who, ma'am?"

"The transplant ring."

Cory said, "Call him, will you?"

An officer stepped into the kitchen and called the detective. They spoke for a few minutes, and the cop came back in.

"Belfi doesn't think there's a relationship. The phone was a burner, but they used cell-tower location data to place the call from somewhere in Chinatown."

"It's got to be them."

"We're going to check into every possible cause, but we can't discount the possibility he wandered off."

"But they said a man took him."

"We're going on the assumption it might be an abduction, but we have to organize a search party to walk the streets in the area in case he's lost. Okay?"

"All right."

"We need a family member or friend we can trust to organize people who know your son."

"I'll call Donny and Margaret."

"Good. We also need to organize a press conference."

"What?"

"We need your son's face on the news. If somebody remembers seeing him, it'll help."

"We should get posters made. Ava can do that."

Linda's cell phone rang. "It's the Taekwondo studio!"

The officer said, "Answer it."

"Hello?"

"Is he all right?"

"Oh my God. We'll be right there."

"We'll drive you, ma'am."

LINDA AND CORY rushed into the studio. Face pressed against the glass, Tommy was watching a class of white-robed kids being led through movements.

"Mom, Dad!"

The parents embraced their son. "Why's the policeman here?"

Linda's voice cracked. "Because we were worried someone took you."

"Don't cry, Mommy. He was a nice man."

Cory said, "We told you never to go with a stranger. Didn't we?"

"Yeah, but he said Mom was hurt, and he was going to take me to the hospital to see her."

"Never, ever, do that again. No matter what they say, don't believe them. Never go with anyone unless it's a neighbor or one of our friends. Okay?"

Tommy nodded.

"Promise."

"Yes."

Cory said, "What else did this man say?"

The police officer stepped forward. "Hi, Tommy. I'm Officer Salvitti. You gave everyone a good scare."

"I didn't mean to."

"It's okay. I have a couple of questions. You think you can help the police catch this man?"

"Like in the movies?"

"Yep. Only this time for real."

Salvitti crouched down. "What did the man look like?"

"He had black hair and was Asian. He was nice."

"Was he tall, short, or in the middle, like me?" Salvitti stood.

"Like you."

"Did he have any scars or tattoos?"

"I didn't see any."

"Did he tell you his name?"

"Joe."

"Where did you go?"

"We went that way." He pointed left. "To the park."

"He told you that your mother was hurt?"

"Yes, and we were going to see her in the hospital."

"Did he say anything else?"

"That he told Daddy that bad things would happen."

"Do you know what he meant by that?"

"I don't know, just figured when somebody tells you not to do something and you do it anyway, you get hurt. Like the time Mommy told me not to skateboard on the stoop and I fell on the stairs."

Salvitti asked a couple more questions and finished with, "How did you get back here?"

"The man said he got a text and that Mommy was okay and we started walking back. He said he had to go when we got to the corner over there and he left."

"What corner?"

"The one by the bank."

"Okay. You've been very helpful, Tommy. On behalf of the entire police department, we thank you. Now, remember what your mother said about strangers; never go with them, no matter what they say or give you. Can you do that?"

"Yes."

"Great. Thanks again."

He turned to Cory and Linda. "I'd like to come by with a couple of books of photos. See if your son could pick out this man."

Cory said, "Okay, but you got to tell Detective Belfi. I'm telling you, this is all connected."

8

Linda turned off her nightstand lamp. Cory crawled into bed. The coolness of the sheets felt good. "Man, I'm shot."

"Me too, it's the stress."

Cory sidled over. "We had some scare today. It can't get worse for a parent."

Linda sniffled. "I was so frightened, I kept seeing him being chained in a basement."

Cory brushed a tear from her cheek. "He's safe now. And he knows never to do that again."

"I hope so."

"What the hell was that idiot at the studio thinking?"

"It's scary how quickly things like this happen. They probably didn't train her right."

"It doesn't matter, she should have known. That 'mommy's hurt' bullshit is the oldest scam in the world. I get Tommy buying it, but not a twenty-year-old. She should have known better."

"What kind of world are we living in?"

"One with a shitload of maniacs."

"It's that transplant ring, isn't it?"

"It looks like it."

"I told you to stop."

"I didn't do anything. I bet it has to do with tracing the call. Belfi said he sent a couple of officers to canvass Chinatown. The word probably got back to them."

"How can they get away with this?"

"The cops can't be everywhere."

"Well, they should be."

"They're doing what they can."

"How can you say that? Our son was kidnapped. Other kids had their kidneys cut out of them."

"So, what do you want me to do? You want me to keep pushing the subject? Keep it front and center?"

"No, no way. Stay away. I'm just frustrated, that's all."

"Don't worry, I'm done. It's not worth the risk."

GETTING OUT OF A CAB, Cory's phone rang. "Hello."

"Cory Lupinski?"

"Yes, who's this?"

"Marty Breem, I'm with an independent film production company. We mainly work with Amazon. You may have seen one of our pieces, *Surviving Death*."

"Oh yeah, the one where people came back after being declared dead."

"That's it. You liked it?"

"The first part I did. But the other episodes, there was too much about mediums. What can I do for you?"

"We're always on the lookout for a subject we can serialize, and this organ-theft story caught our interest."

"It's unbelievable it's happening in America."

"It's in the exploratory stage, but we're white-boarding ideas for a possible series. You know, maybe start off following someone on the waiting list, then one on the state of transplant medicine, another on the world-wide market for organs, one on the effort to grow organs in a lab . . . But this story where kids are kidnapped could be the pilot, you know, the episode that hooks viewers."

"And what does this have to do with me?"

"You'd add to the human-interest component; a former pop star who volunteers, working with children on the waiting list, and you urging the public to become donors. I mean, it's unselfish and ties beautifully into the unselfish act of becoming a donor."

"I'm glad you're thinking about doing it, but I can't be involved."

"What's your objection?"

"I'm too busy. Don't have the time."

"If I were you, I'd make the time. This hits, like I think it might, exposure will be off the charts. You could relaunch your career."

"I'm not interested in that. I'm happy doing what I do."

"We could do a lot of good with this series. It'll open up eyes and doors."

"I'm sorry, the timing isn't right for me."

"Look, this wouldn't be something demanding, especially right now. These projects take time, and most of them never end up airing."

"I don't know."

"All we need at this point is a commitment. We tell Almighty 'Zon the whos and whats, and they'll decide whether to green-light it."

Cory wanted to do it but said, "I'll think about it, but at this point count me out."

———

CORY PLUGGED the drum machine in. "All right. This is going to be fun. Last week, we had a tiny problem keeping everybody together. So, I brought this in. I'll set it at a simple rhythm, all quarter notes. And at the first beat of every measure you're going to hear a big cymbal crash. Listen."

Cory hit play. "So, everybody can hear that, right?"

A sea of heads nodded.

"Now if you get lost, you'll know where the next measure starts."

He turned the drum machine off. "Today we'll start off with "Sunflower." It's the song we worked on the last two weeks."

As Cory instructed the kids on the parts they'd each play, he scanned the room. Bobby Kennedy wasn't there.

After finishing the session, Cory asked Katie, "What's going on with Bobby?"

She frowned. "I heard he's not doing good."

"What's going on?"

"A bunch of things, from the operation he had."

"I'm going to see him."

"He's in ICU."

Bobby Kennedy's mother was holding her son's hand. His father sat stone-faced. Neither had slept in days. Cory nodded at the parents and whispered, "How's he doing?"

The father shrugged. "They induced a coma to try and get the septic under control."

"He has an infection?"

"From the surgery."

Cory shook his head. "These guys are butchers."

"I can't believe we did this to him."

"Don't blame yourself, you were trying to help."

"Biggest mistake of my life."

"He'll be okay. Keep the faith."

9

Cory returned from giving lessons to his paying students. "Hey, tiger, how was your day?"

Tommy said, "Okay, Dad. The policeman came and showed me so many pictures."

Linda had filled him in on the phone. "Did you see the bad man?"

"No. I couldn't find him."

"That's okay. You still helped the police."

"I did?"

"Yes, they now know all the pictures you looked at weren't the bad guy, so they won't waste time on them."

Tommy smiled. "That's good, right?"

"Yep. You have homework to do?"

"Yeah, I have to make up a story and write it down."

"That's fun. Go get started, and if you need help, let me know."

Cory pecked his wife's cheek. "He doesn't seem fazed by all this."

"I hope not. But we'll see."

"Did the police say anything about seeing this bastard on any surveillance cameras?"

"He said they checked everything in the area. They have one from the jeweler who they think is him, but it's only his back."

"Man, we need a break."

"That'd be nice. How was your day?"

"Pretty good, except I'm super bummed over that kid, Bobby Kennedy."

"What happened?"

"They put him in a coma. He's got a bad infection."

"Poor kid."

"They probably didn't sterilize something."

"Ugh."

"You should've seen his parents. Like zombies. I couldn't stay in the room more than five minutes."

"It's horrible having a sick child."

"I hope he pulls through."

"Yeah, and they better catch these guys doing this."

"What time is Ava getting home?"

"She said she'd be back around four."

"We got to leave by five thirty latest. They want me there early to take some pictures."

THE MAN at the podium had silver hair and wore a royal-blue suit. Smiling, he looked over the ballroom. "It's life-affirming to see so many supporters here this evening. As our chairwoman stated, the challenges that face us and our children are formidable. But that reality shouldn't deter us from our mission. We'll keep pressing and making progress for our children."

A burst of polite applause petered out and he continued, "Tonight, as we continue the fight against childhood cancer, we take time to honor someone who not only has donated his treasure to the cause but graciously gives him time. Earlier, he warned me about reciting his biography, and I'll honor his wish. Ladies and gentlemen, please welcome CURE's man of the year, Cory Lupinski."

Cory squeezed Linda's hand. He rose, kissed both his children, and made his way to the stage. As the applause died down, he gripped both sides of the lectern.

"Thanks. When John asked me to come this evening, I wanted to say no but realized whatever publicity we get, it helps drive donations, and that is the fuel we're using in this battle. Everyone here tonight probably knows that childhood cancer kills more children than any other disease. Think about that.

"How many people do you think know that sad fact? I had no idea until I joined the fight. Tell your friends and family. See if they'll help kids battling cancer. Ask them to help us save kids' dreams by finding a cure to childhood cancer."

He held up a plaque. "Thank you for this, but it's not about us, it's about the kids. Enjoy your dinner."

Cory left the stage to a standing ovation. He settled into his chair.

"Yay, Dad. You did good."

Cory tussled his son's hair. "You think so?"

"Yeah."

Ava said, "I'm proud of you, Dad."

"Thanks, honey. I'm trying."

"You're doing better than trying, you're leading people by example."

"I hope so."

"You're the least selfish person I know, Dad."

"Thanks, hon. It took me a while to make whatever progress I made."

As the servers laid down dishes of pasta, a woman, press credentials hanging off her neck, said, "Mr. Lupinski, I'm Sandra Wells from *New York One*. Can I have five minutes?"

Cory rose. "Sure."

Linda said, "Make it fast, your macaroni is going to get cold."

They stepped to the side of the room.

"Thanks, I just wanted a couple of quotes for an article I'm doing."

"Fire away."

"How much money has your foundation donated to finding a cure?"

"Oh, I should know this but don't. It's been about seven years, so, I'd say it's more than three million dollars."

"That's a significant sum of money."

Cory shrugged. "We need a heck of a lot more."

"Is there anyone else raising that kind of money?"

"Oh, there's a lot of people helping. Some big organizations like Brave Hearts and Alex's Lemonade—"

"I was referring to an individual giving their own money."

"It's not something I focus on."

"How does it feel to be one of the most selfless people around."

"This isn't about me, Sandra. It's about the kids."

"Is any of your generosity an attempt to make up for some of the trouble you've been in?"

"Like most people, I've made mistakes, but my involvement has nothing to do with anything like that."

"Where does it come from?"

"Most people go through life trying to find something that

makes them feel fulfilled. I've been lucky to have two things that light me up: music and helping kids."

"You have two children of your—"

"I'm sorry, but I don't talk to the press about our children."

"I understand. You recently waged a campaign to elevate awareness about the need for organ donors."

Cory nodded.

"Would you like to say something about that?"

"Since we're here, let's keep the focus on childhood cancer."

"Fair enough, but could you say something on the recent kidnapping of Down Syndrome kids?"

"What's to say? It's disgusting. We have a responsibility to protect the most vulnerable, and we're failing. Miserably."

10

Cory stood in front of the room and put his guitar down. "I thought it'd be fun if we played around with using just our voices to create a rich, layered sound. Let me play you an example of a group of people singing without musical accompaniment. It's called 'a cappella'. You might have heard about this group, they're called the Pentatonix."

He played a sample of a song. "Isn't that cool? You can hear them singing the different chord tones." He took a step toward the kids. "Let's go around the room. I'd like each of you to sing one line. How about 'Happy Birthday to You'? I want you to hear the different qualities of each of our voices. They're all good, and when combined, they're amazing. Okay. How about you start it off, Brian?"

The kid sang and Cory said, "Excellent. Everyone hear how deep and sonorous his voice was?" As the kids nodded, Cory said, "His voice is what is called a baritone."

A girl went next, and Cory said, "We got lucky. Brian was a baritone, singing at the low end, and Beverly sings in the high range; she's called a soprano.

"Check out this." Cory sang "Happy Birthday" in an

unnaturally high voice. "I'm sure you've heard that before. It's called falsetto. It's where you sing higher than your normal voice." Cory sang it within his normal range and then falsetto.

"Let's all do that. Sing it normally, then in falsetto."

The room erupted in a cacophony of voices. "Wow. You guys are super amazing. Let's get back to having everyone sing 'Happy Birthday.' I'm betting we'll find some tenors and altos out there."

After the last kid sang, Cory said, "I'm psyched. You guys sound super. Everybody here like Taylor Swift?"

Most of the room yelled out a yes.

"Cool."

Cory broke into one of her biggest hits, perfectly emulating her voice. The kids went wild.

Cory smiled. "That's 'Shake it Off.' What I'd like to do is take it and see if we can sing harmonies on it. Here, let me cue up the part of the song where there's more than one voice singing the line. Let's have a listen."

After playing the song, he said, "Everybody hear that? The two voices?"

Everyone nodded.

"Now, what I'd like to do is start simple. I'd like someone I said was a soprano and one who's a baritone to sing the line together. That way we'll have the high and low ends covered. It will sound cool."

CORY WAS PACKING his guitar up when Katie came in. "Hey, Cory, heard you guys had a blast today."

"Yeah, it went good. It always amazes me how quick kids learn. They're sponges."

"That's because they got a great teacher."

"Nah, that's got nothing to do with it."

"No way. I remember this math teacher, he talked like a drone. Almost half the class failed."

Cory spoke in a monotone voice, "Two plus two equals nine."

"Close."

Cory laughed. "Say, how's Bobby Kennedy doing?"

"About the same."

"Damn. What a shame."

"Did you hear about that poor kid they found?"

"What kid?"

"A cop found a boy dumped in an alley on Eleventh Avenue."

"Don't tell me he was another Down Syndrome kid."

"I don't think so, but they took most of his liver out and—"

"Another transplant?"

"I guess so."

"They botched it?"

"I don't know. He's in ICU. I heard he's not going to make it."

He put his guitar down. "I'll be back for my ax."

Cory waited for Evans to get off the phone. He knocked on the window and cracked the door open. "Sorry, Doc. I need five."

"I'm sorry, Cory. It's a madhouse."

"I heard they brought another kid who was butchered for his liver. Is that true?"

"Close the door."

Cory shut the door. "Is it true?"

"You know I can't say much about a patient."

"Come on, Doc. Is it true or not?"

Evans nodded.

"What happened?"

"We don't know exactly. When he was brought in, he was unresponsive. He'd lost a lot of blood and was bleeding from a wound in the abdomen. The emergency room originally thought it was a knife wound."

"But it wasn't. It was another botched transplant."

"An MRI revealed that a large segment of his liver was removed."

"What the hell is going on?"

"If I had to speculate, I'd say it went into a recipient."

"This has got to end. How old was this kid?"

"I believe he's twelve."

"How's he doing?"

"Critical. We're doing our best to save him."

Cory's stomach dropped. "Save him?"

"He's vitals are unstable. The prognosis isn't good."

"Why?"

"From what we can tell, the segmentation of the liver was done well. It appears to have been performed by a qualified surgeon."

"Then what the hell happened?"

"He began to hemorrhage. I don't know if they were under a time constraint or perhaps were interrupted, but the suturing was either rushed or done by someone other than the surgeon who removed the liver section."

"Damn it. What about his parents? Do they know what's going on?"

"We were able to locate them, and they're here now."

Cory exhaled. "This makes me sick."

"It's never easy to lose a patient, especially a child."

"What's the kid's name? I want to go to the chapel to pray for his recovery."

"Nathan Hendry."

Cory took the elevator to the Intensive Care Unit. He checked the board. Hendry was in room 7B. He turned down a corridor and stopped in his tracks. A man and woman were sobbing outside of the kid's room.

Cory leaned against the wall. A nurse came out of the room and walked his way. Her eyes were red. Cory said, "Nate didn't make it?"

She shook her head and hurried away.

Cory's heart broke for the parents. He needed to talk to them. But now wasn't the time. He went back, got his guitar, and left.

On the subway ride home, the kid's death weighed on him. He tried to shake the blues, telling himself he didn't know the Hendry boy. But it didn't matter.

You didn't have to personally know someone to realize the magnitude of their death. He tried to keep it in perspective, but the reality that defenseless children were being treated as disposable was making him physically sick.

11

Outfitted in a green scrub suit, Park Shu entered the room and examined the man on the gurney.

"The donor is partially anesthetized. Start an IV with anti-rejection drugs. Put him completely under in half an hour."

The aide said, "Yes, Dr. Shu."

"Put your mask on properly. There is a serious risk of infection during these procedures."

The woman's hands trembled as she fitted her mask over her nose.

Shu said, "This your first time?"

"Yes."

"In your first year?"

"Yes, the CUNY School of Medicine."

Recalling his own difficulties, he said, "The second is exponentially harder."

"That's what I'm told, sir."

"You're from Shantou?"

"Yes, the center of Shantou."

"You're going to be placed in Xiamen, where you'll be near family."

"I was lucky."

"Luck? Your father is the deputy of the Niwan Residential District."

"He is."

"And your sister, I understand she's stirring up trouble in Hong Kong."

She stared at her clogs. "We're shamed over her activities."

"Disgraceful."

"She's a good person."

"Now, today's procedure will prove to be an invaluable experience for you."

"I'm eternally grateful."

"This is a highly confidential matter. Breaches are dealt with harshly."

"I understand."

His droopy eyes bore into her. "We wouldn't want things to get difficult for your sister."

"Oh no, sir."

"I'm needed inside."

"Are you performing the removal surgery?"

Shu turned around, saying, "Not today. I have other responsibilities requiring my attention."

He put a fresh mask and gloves on and stepped into an adjacent room. It wasn't a hospital-grade operating room, but Shu was thankful for the proliferation of surgical centers performing outpatient surgeries. It was a serious upgrade from some of the exam rooms the organization had used when starting out.

Three monitors, displaying the donor's vitals, were positioned at the head of the gurney.

A man and two women in surgical gowns were hunched

over the patient. Shu sidled up. "Everything under control, Doctor?"

The man said, "Yes, Dr. Shu. Will you be observing?"

Shu nodded.

The nurses finished cleaning the patient's abdomen with an iodine solution, and the doctor said, "Scalpel."

Shu felt a rush of adrenaline as the doctor made an incision. He watched the doctor apply clamps to slow the bleeding. This doctor wasn't doing anything special, he thought.

The surgeon opened the abdomen, exposing the kidney. "Be prepared with the clamps. I'm going to start cutting the arteries."

He made three quick cuts, and blood began to spurt. Shu stepped back. It was the same point where Shu had panicked while in the Beijing School of Medicine.

It still amazed him how someone who wanted to be a doctor couldn't get used to seeing blood. The doubt that he could control the bleeding had made his hands shake.

Shu took a step closer. He stared at the doctor's hands. Rock-solid and moving without hesitation.

Everyone had their gifts, Shu thought. He did what had to be done to protect the enterprise he'd built with authorization from the director of the Central Committee. Once a path was decided, he acted. There was no nervousness or hesitancy.

Shu observed the surgeon, believing there was no difference between how the doctor and he performed their duties. The difference was the respect a doctor was given. It wasn't fair, but in order to do his job he needed respect, and if it meant telling people he was a doctor, so be it.

After an hour, the doctor said, "We're thirty minutes from removal. We'll need to wheel the recipient into position."

Four hours later, Shu took a piece of gum out of his mouth before stepping into the room. The doctor stitching up the recipient didn't raise his head.

Placing a valise in a corner of the room, Shu said, "The donor is stable. He'll stay overnight before moving him to Sunny Palace Rehab."

"I'd recommend a minimum of two, if not three nights for the donor."

"He'll be leaving in the morning."

"His blood pressure is low, it—"

"Is the closure complete?"

The surgeon pulled a suture away from the incision. "Two more to go."

"Excellent. I'll send someone to notify the wife."

"He did well, but we'll need to monitor for signs of rejection. The HLA matching wasn't optimal."

"He'll be fine. The human species is stronger than most believe."

"The probability of rejection—"

Shu slid the briefcase closer to the doctor. "This is for you."

"Thank you."

"Seven p.m., Tuesday. Every Day Urgent Care, One Hundred Seventy-Third Street."

"I have office hours on Tuesdays."

"Cancel them. Be there Tuesday."

"Okay."

"Exit the usual way."

Shu took the loading dock exit and got into his Honda SUV. He took a phone out of the glove box and sent a text to his underling, Mak.

"Recipient in urgent need. Small-framed, male, type AA. Bonus offered. Double the usual fee."

A text pinged in: "No problem. Will advise."

Shu watched two of his men climb the stairs to the loading dock. They'd keep an eye on both patients and help move them into the van in the morning.

He unwrapped a stick of gum, popped it in his mouth, and drove off.

12

———————

CORY WAITED FOUR DAYS TO APPROACH THE HENDRY FAMILY. The story had died faster than Cory expected, reinforcing his belief he had to do something.

A strong sun countered the wind blowing off the Hudson River. The Hendrys lived on the fourteenth floor of a Battery Park City building. When the father opened the door, Cory expected a flood of light to pour into the hallway, but the apartment was darker than the hallway.

"Hi, I know how hard this is for you. I'm a father of two and can't imagine what you're going through."

The lines on the man's face made him look twenty years older. He exhaled, "My wife doesn't want to talk, but I, I don't know, I feel like I got to do something to keep Nate's memory alive."

"I understand completely. It was senseless and barbaric . . . uh, I'm sorry."

"It's okay. I got nothing left at this point."

"Like I said, I'm just a guy, a father, who wants to do his part, you know? I'm no saint, but I've been working to help kids."

"We know all about what you've been doing. You're a good man."

"Ever since the Down Syndrome boys were kidnapped for organs, I've been trying to keep this in front of the public. I mean, this stuff has to end."

"Nate was treated like a science experiment. The wound . . ." he winced, "it looked like a ten-year-old sewed it up. I took pictures." He dug out his phone and paged through five images.

Cory gasped, "Oh my God. I'm so sorry."

"Who knows if Nate felt anything? I asked if he had anesthesia in his system, but the hospital never tested for it."

Cory doubted that had transpired, but said, "I'm sure your son was out when, when they, uh, did it."

He shook his head. "They didn't do this kind of shit in the medieval days."

"I know this is going to sound weird, and it's okay if you don't want to, but would you mind sending me the pictures?"

"What for?"

"Only if you say it's okay, but I think if we can get these out there, people might rally around them. We've got to keep organ theft in the news. It's out of control."

"If it'll help, but I don't want my son being used by the media."

"Look, I get it. I've got a son and daughter of my own. I was planning to keep the identity anonymous. They don't need to know who it was done to, just that something like this occurred should be enough."

"I hope you're right."

"Can you tell me what happened?"

"We don't know. Nate never came home, and"—he swallowed hard—"and then we got the call."

"Where do you think he was abducted?"

"We're thinking either at the park or on the way home."

"What park?"

"The Tribeca Skatepark."

"He went there a lot?"

"Oh yeah, he loved skateboarding. He was there every day."

"He went by himself?"

"No, a group of friends." He hung his head. "I know it sounds terrible, but why him? Why'd they take my Nate?"

"It had to be random. Just bad luck."

"It doesn't get worse than that."

"And nobody saw anything out of the ordinary?"

"No. The cops say they talked to everybody, and they have no leads."

"They're still investigating?"

"They say they are, but this city is a frigging mess. It ain't safe anymore, and I'm not just talking about what happened to Nate."

"I know, things feel like they're spiraling out of control."

"You know, I lived here my whole life. I was born at the old St. Vincent's Hospital and never thought I'd leave. But now?" He shook his head. "I can't see myself staying."

"A change of scenery might help."

"I know, too many memories."

"I'm sorry. I don't know what to say."

"There's nothing anybody can say, we just got to nail these bastards, make them pay for what they did."

LINDA WAS on the couch leafing through a magazine. Cory came in after helping Tommy with homework.

"Man, they're teaching kids computer science at his age?"

"You're going to have to know how to program to get a job."

"They should teach them how to communicate. Everybody has their faces glued to their phones. Some kid was riding on his bike in the street earlier and texting. I told him to be careful, and he gave me the finger."

"That's terrible. Everybody wants immediate answers to meaningless questions."

"You got that right. Half the time, I'm using my phone to see how old someone is."

"Are you okay?"

"Yeah, why?"

"You seemed off when you got home, but I was distracted with Tommy, and you went into the studio."

"I talked to Mr. Hendry."

"The father of that poor kid?"

"Yeah."

"Why did you do that?"

Cory shrugged. "I just felt like I had to. This crap has got to stop."

"Don't get involved."

"I can't—"

"You want something to happen to Tommy or Ava?"

"Take it easy. I'm just saying we can't sit around. Nobody is safe, not our kids or anybody if these bastards are left to do what they want."

"I'm worried about Tommy and Ava."

"I get it. But if we can't protect the most vulnerable, then nobody is safe."

"It's not your responsibility. Let the cops deal with it."

"I know, but I feel like we got to do something. The cops are dealing with regular crime. This is outside their zone."

"Then it's the FBI or CIA or whatever."

"Let me show you something." He pulled his phone out.

"Oh my God."

"See? That's what these butchers are doing to our kids."

"That's horrible. How can this happen? In New York, no less?"

"This is the fourth kid in a month, and Kennedy and Hendry don't have Down."

"Is the whole world corrupt? How else could this be happening if they're not paying people off?"

"There's a ton of money involved. Look, we were paying two hundred grand for your mother."

Her shoulders sunk. "We were part of the problem."

"I know. But now we can be part of the solution."

"I'm worried about the kids."

"Me too. But we'll be super careful. I'll stay out of the limelight. We just need to get people motivated, and they'll have to shut down."

13

———————

Cory closed the door to his studio. He looked up a telephone number and dialed.

"*New York One News*."

"I'm looking for a reporter. I met her at the CURE childhood cancer event about ten days ago. I'm pretty sure her name is Sandra."

"That would be Sandra Wells. I'll put you through."

"Hey, Sandra, this is Cory Loop. We met at the CURE dinner."

"Oh, hi. You ready to talk?"

"Yes. I have something that needs to get out."

"I'm all ears."

"It's super powerful, but I can't have my name associated with it."

"What are we talking about?"

"And you can't reveal the name of the person in the photos."

"Hmm. What do you have?"

"Promise me you won't reveal my name or the kid's."

"You have my word. Tell me what you have?"

"Photos of the kid who was abducted and left to die."

"What kind of pictures? We're not the *Enquirer*."

"Did you know they harvested his liver?"

"What? That's gross."

"They butchered the poor boy. I have pictures of the wound. It looks like it was stitched by a five-year-old."

"Oh my God. That's terrible."

"Now, I'll send them to you, but you can't say who it is, and you can't say you got them from me. What I think you should do is focus on what happened with the Down Syndrome kids. You can say this is another example."

"I get the family's privacy, but can't we use you as a source? You've already gone public about this."

"No. These people are dangerous. The police think they could have been the ones who sent someone to pick up my son."

"Really? Because you said something?"

"It has to be."

"Seems like a stretch."

"Look, I don't care what you think about it. My name doesn't go in the news, or you don't get the pictures."

"We'll quote it as an anonymous source. You don't have to worry about the boy. We never use the name of a minor without the parents' permission."

"Super. What's your cell number? I'll text them over."

SHU POPPED a piece of gum in his mouth and closed the door to his office. He went to the stereo and pulled out an album. He put "Plum Blossoms" on the turntable and dropped the needle.

As the sounds of the traditional seven-stringed instrument

filled the room, Shu slid behind his desk. The ancient song from the Jin Dynasty was the perfect soundtrack to Shu's life. The theme of the three-part movement was praising the gritty spirit of the plum blossom which bloomed in the severe winter.

Shu logged on to a server located in Shanghai and put in his credentials. He opened a double-passworded spreadsheet and scrolled to the bottom.

Ten new contacts had been made with possible recipients. Li had graded six of them as likely to close within two weeks. The 60 percent rate had been constant. It wasn't bad, but Shu would push to see if they could raise it to 70 once he added another surgeon.

Shu's mood took a dive when he viewed the donor stats. Three people they considered sure things had moved to the unlikely column. Money was a lever to increase supply, but that hit margins.

Shu signed out. He closed his eyes. It was time to get creative.

14

———

SHU PUT DOWN THE *NEW ENGLAND JOURNAL OF MEDICINE*. The article on using artificial intelligence to perform surgery fascinated him. While wondering if the advancement would enable him to do the surgeries he desperately wanted to perform, there was a knock on his door.

Cooke Tay stepped into the room. "Come in."

"Dr. Shu, we just got word that a complication arose in the Goldfarb transplant."

"What happened?"

"Details are sketchy, but during the sectioning, the donor started to hemorrhage, and Dr. Fung decided to concentrate on the recipient."

"How is the donor?"

"Fung didn't think he was going to make it."

"What did he do?"

"They left him in an alley."

Shu bolted out of his seat. "They did what?"

"Fung was concerned about what to do with a corpse if he died."

"So, he left a patient to die? How could he?"

"I'll get more information."

"I want to know how he is and what we can do to save him."

"No problem."

Shu shook his head. "Fung panicked. Why didn't he call?"

"I don't know, sir. Anything else?"

"How is the recipient?"

"They said the transplant of the liver portion was uneventful, and the patient is stable."

"Make sure Edgar's team keeps him an extra day before moving him. We need to ensure he makes a full recovery."

"Will do, sir."

"And find Li. Tell him I need to see him—now!"

Shu collapsed into his chair. They'd gone to Beijing Medical School together, and he had doubts about Dr. Fung. It was tough to admit, because they were similar.

They both wanted to be doctors, to cure sickness, and be a force for good. But what bonded Shu and Fung was their shared anxiety that overwhelmed their intelligence.

He recalled taking a leave of absence, telling Fung and the others he was going to get treated for a neurological disorder that led to his shaky hands and paralysis.

It took Fung an extra year of residency to become a doctor. Shu assumed he'd mastered his nerves, but should have known better. The bottom line was the Party kept its best in China.

Shu paced the room. Fung was out. He'd have to find someone to replace him. Recruiting doctors for their business operation was not only difficult but critical to their success.

Surgeons were in a class of their own. Shu tried to remember who'd said surgeons were like gunslingers. It was true, they were a cocky bunch. Even with the quietest of them, the god complex would seep out. People excused them, believing you had to be arrogant to think you could cut someone open and put them back together again.

He pulled up a list he'd received from Deputy Director Gao. He'd organized the inventory of prospective doctors recently, putting a few he'd met at the top, and now clicked on the first row.

The biography of Richie Ho opened. Thirty-four and single, Ho had served as the only surgeon in a small-town hospital outside of Xi'an.

Shu wanted to visit Xi'an to see the army of terracotta warriors that had been buried for centuries. Maybe he'd go there on his next trip to China. He'd mix a little pleasure in when he couriered cash to his partners.

He pulled out a burner phone and was punching in Ho's number when Tay entered.

"What did you find out?"

"The donor died at Mt. Sinai."

Shu's shoulders sagged. "Terrible news. What was Fung thinking?"

"Li is on his way to see him, and then he'll meet up with you."

"Fung discarded the boy like an animal carcass. We're here to give life. This is an unspeakable breach of the oath he took."

"The recipient is doing well. And Edgar's been told to keep him an extra day."

"This is a stain on what we do. We can't tolerate this kind of attention. It will destroy all the hard work we've done."

"What can I do to help?"

"We're going to need our friends in the media to plant an alternative story or two."

"Good idea."

"Give me a minute to think it through, but something along the lines of a cult. Maybe something with voodoo, a sect that feasts on organs."

"I like that. The Americans will love the story."

"I need time to think."

As Tay retreated, Shu slumped in his chair. What was he doing, making up outlandish stories? People like Fung were a liability. They endangered the progress he'd achieved. He couldn't let people like Fung make him go from a rising star to a fool in the Party's eyes.

Shu recalled suggesting to Gao the idea to start a transplant operation in the States. It was a perfect way to stay close to medicine. If he couldn't practice medicine himself, Shu could still save lives and advance the techniques used.

It had been a success from the start, helping the sick with the added benefit of burnishing his reputation with the Party. There was no way anyone was going to disrupt his operation.

15

THE RESTAURANT ON MOTT STREET WAS JAMMED AND LOUD. Shu tipped his chin toward an elderly man at the register and made his way to a private room in the rear.

Dr. Richie Ho rose as he entered. "Mr. Shu, how are you?"

Shu wanted to correct the salutation, but Ho was friendly with Dr. Fung and knew Shu didn't finish medical school. "Sit, sit. You ever been here before?"

"No, first time."

"You'll love it. Some of the best Szechuan in the city."

"I'm in your hands."

Shu waved the waiter over and ordered in Chinese.

"Ordered a taste of a couple of their best dishes."

"Sounds perfect."

"Let's get the business part out of the way. Shall we?"

"Sure."

"Last time we met, I mentioned the transplant operation we started about a year ago. It's an excellent way to gain experience for a young surgeon like you. It's really a one-of-a-kind opportunity."

Ho lowered his voice, "Are you still operating in the black market?"

"Black market? I believe that's an unfair characterization of what we do."

"I'm sorry, but how else can it be characterized?"

"Filling an unmet need. Some people need organs, and others, money. It's as perfect an exchange as they come. Our role is to make sure the donors and recipients are as safe as possible."

"Paying people for their organs is unethical."

"And watching people die as they wait for one is not? And what about the fact we're helping a donor with a payment that elevates their lifestyle and reduces financial stress?"

"I see the possible benefits for two willing parties, but I've heard there are, uh, unwilling donors."

"Sometimes it's necessary to use unconventional means to save a life."

"Unconventional?"

"We're no different than the traditional organ supply system. We both have shortages, except, when we do, we take remedial action."

"But it's illegal. I'd be risking my license."

"The Party understands the delicate nature of the opera-tion and rewards those who help, handsomely."

"I understand, but—"

"This operation is overseen by the Central Committee, and they consider it an important project."

"I could go to jail."

"That's extremely unlikely. The American authorities are not interested in us. Besides, if a serious investigation were to take place, anyone in danger would be flown out of the country."

"How could they do that?"

"There are many avenues to use, but the Party has used diplomatic immunity in the past when a loyal member is scrutinized. There is nothing to worry about."

"I don't know. I appreciate the offer, but it just doesn't feel right for me."

"Are you positive?"

"Definitely."

Shu stood. "That's unfortunate. I'll advise Beijing immediately. They demand to know bad news as soon as possible. They're not going to take the refusal lightly."

"What does that mean?"

"Their reaction is out of my control, but those who've refused in the past . . . well, let's leave it that there are consequences for them and their families."

"My family? What do they have to do with it?"

"I'm not involved in their decisions, but they believe those who have benefited from the Party's greater vision must show gratitude."

"I am, but—"

"You could be stuck in the backwaters of Xi'an, yet here you are in New York, performing surgeries. You think you achieved this on your own? If the Party hadn't chosen you to attend better schools, where do you think you'd be? Consider if they hadn't allowed you to go to medical school or obtain the visa to come to America." Shu snapped his fingers. "And just like that, it can disappear."

"Hold on. Sit down a minute. I wasn't thinking properly. I understand the Party has assisted me; I'll do whatever they need."

Shu smiled and sat down. "Excellent. You've made a wise choice."

"I hope so."

"You're going to love the hotpot here. It's the best outside of China."

SHU WAS BEHIND HIS DESK, scouring the Internet for the latest information on guided, robotic surgery when Tay came in. He picked up the TV remote and navigated to the news.

"Sorry, but you need to see this."

A newscaster was standing in front of Mr. and Mrs. Hendry. She said, "We'll keep you informed on the investigation into this heinous crime. Live from Battery Park, I'm Chelsea Sonos."

"They went on TV again. I thought they wanted to stay out of the limelight."

"Cory Lupinski has been to see them. He's the one who got them to start talking again."

"Are you certain?"

"A hundred percent. We've been told he's behind the pictures getting out."

"Fung. Damn it! We can't have the parents running around in the media. It makes it too real. It'll generate too much sympathy, and the authorities might be forced to act."

"What do you want me to do?"

"Perhaps we can start an anonymous fund for the parents. No, let's make a large, anonymous donation to the United Network for Organ Sharing. Make sure to have our media friends make a big deal of it. Play the good-comes-out-of-bad angle, you know, the money wouldn't have come if not for the tragic—etcetera, etcetera."

16

———————

Shu put the menu aside. A server poured tea for him and Li. When she left, Li said, "What are we going to do? The heat is too high to continue. We'll have to shut down for a while."

Shu shook his head. "We're certainly not taking a breather. We have a backlog of clients to serve."

"But we have to wait."

"We wait, they die"—he let it hang before continuing—"and we make nothing."

"We should ask for more money upfront."

"I tend to agree with you. But Beijing believes it would cut into the number of recipients. They have a point; these patients are skeptical and ill. We don't need to present an additional hurdle for them."

The waitress set down a plate of dumplings and hurried away. Li inhaled deeply. "Smells good."

"Best in the city."

"What do you want to do about that bigmouth?"

"This Lupinski is quite surprising. He's still a professional musician, isn't he?"

"Yes, but he's one of those activists when it comes to children. He's trying to cure cancer and—"

"Ah, another American superhero." Shu speared a dumpling.

Li laughed. "I'll have Eng and his guys stuff his cape down his throat before we throw him in the East River."

"As good as that would feel, we can't risk igniting a firestorm. The last thing we want to do is make him a martyr."

"Agreed. So, what are you thinking of?"

Shu grinned. "Something he wouldn't expect. Why don't we have a little fun with this? I have a plan in mind that'll ensure this gnat minds his business."

"Sounds good. Just give the word and I'll get it done."

"I want to wait a bit. Let's see if this dies down on its own."

"Okay."

"Now, I'm losing patience with Mr. Wong. I believe another visit needs to be made. We need sites to replace the Green Tree facilities."

"He's been a problem. How hard should I push?"

"We don't have time."

"Don't worry. Wong will see the wisdom of doing business with us."

"Offer him an extra ten thousand per procedure. If he doesn't come around, press until he caves. When he does, tell him the extra money is off the table."

SHU SLAMMED THE PHONE DOWN. Two of five prospects they'd been courting decided against a transplant. He muttered, "Fools, they'll both be dead in a year."

He placed a piece of gum in his mouth, contemplating whether the Hendry news had scared them. Or were they taking the moral high ground to their grave? Shu grabbed the phone and buzzed Tay.

"Tell Li I need to see him. Immediately."

"I just saw him on the camera, pulling into the lot."

"Perfect."

A minute later, Li walked into Shu's office.

"You needed me?"

"Have a seat. We need to be ready to deal with Cory Lupinski."

"No problem."

"We've got to be careful but effective. He must understand we can't tolerate meddling in our affairs."

"What do you have in mind?"

"It's a delicate maneuver, one that will probably bring more media attention in the short term but will convince Lupinski to back off completely."

Li moved to the edge of his seat. "Sounds interesting."

"You'll need your best men. No hiccups will be tolerated. We must have plausible deniability."

"Tell me."

Shu leaned over his desk and whispered the plan he'd concocted. Li smiled. "That's as good as it gets."

"Wait for the go-ahead. But make sure your best team is in place and ready."

"I'll get it organized today."

Li left, and Shu ran the possible reactions and outcomes of his plan through his mind. It was dangerous, but he knew the best rewards always came from bold action.

Shu swapped his chewing gum for a fresh piece and picked up the *Journal of Heart and Lung Transplantation*.

The organs represented the most difficult operations and had troublesome survival rates.

When he'd started out, Shu assumed heart transplants had the worst survival rates but learned lungs had higher mortality rates. After three years, only 60 percent of the recipients were alive compared to 75 percent for those receiving a new heart.

Shu wondered whether the practice Chinese doctors got on prisoners was improving the odds of living longer with someone else's heart.

It was an important program started by Shu's business partner Gao, who had encouraged his interest in medicine. When Shu expressed an interest in transplants, Gao permitted him to observe transplants on inmates.

Shu recalled the first time he witnessed the removal of a prisoner's heart. It was the ultimate example of the power over life which surgeons wielded. He'd envisioned himself in the doctor's shoes, but it was not to be.

He wondered whether advancements in artificial intelligence would present another chance for him to become a doctor and decided to search the web for new information.

Shu opened his browser as his phone rang. It was Tay. The news was bad. Shu called Li to activate his plan.

17

THE PIZZERIA WAS NOISY AND HOT. CORY SAID, "TOMMY, you want the last slice?"

"No, I'm full. Can I get a spumoni?"

Linda said, "You still have the one from last week in the freezer."

"Is it still good?"

"Yes, it's ice cream."

"Can I have it when we get home?"

Cory reached for the last piece as Linda said, "Sure."

Cory took a bite and said, "Go wash up."

Linda watched Tommy go into the bathroom and took her phone out. "She still hasn't called or answered my text."

"She's probably got her headphones on."

"It should go through them."

"Maybe she's in the shower."

"Probably. I'm gonna order a calzone to take home for her."

Cory carried the bag of food up the stairs. He moved the bag from hand to hand. "This is so hot, it's crazy."

Linda opened the door and Tommy hurried to the kitchen. Linda called out, "Ava! Ava, we're home."

Cory said, "I'll set the table for her."

Tommy had a spoonful of ice cream. "Mom, you want some?"

"No, honey. Ava's not here."

"Maybe she's at Skylar's."

"She better not be with Bruce. She said he's home from college."

"Take it easy. Call Skylar's house. I'm going to put the calzone in the oven to keep it warm."

Linda came back into the kitchen. "Skylar said she's not there, that Ava told her she was going home to finish a history paper that's due tomorrow."

"Where the heck is she? You got this kid, Bruce's, number?"

"No. But his mother is friendly with Rosalie."

"Call her."

Linda made the call, got the boy's number, and called him.

"Bruce? This is Linda, Ava's mom. Is Ava with you?"

"Uh, no."

"Are you sure?"

"Yeah, I've been home all day. I twisted my ankle playing basketball."

"Did you talk to her?"

"Not today."

"Do me a favor, save my number. If you hear from her, call me."

CORY CAME into the apartment and shook his head. "I went to the park, the diner, and basketball courts; she's not there."

"Oh God, Cory. I've called everybody. No one knows where she is."

"It's ten o'clock. If we don't hear from her in an hour, we call the police."

"I can't wait an hour. What if she's in trouble?"

"Don't get excited. She could be at a movie or—"

"Then why doesn't she answer her phone?"

"I don't know. Maybe the battery's dead."

"She'd use a friend's. Something is wrong, Cory."

"All right. I'll call the police."

An hour later, Cory was looking out the window as a squad car pulled up. "The cops are finally here."

Linda and Cory told the uniformed officer what they knew. He said, "You checked with her friends?"

Linda said, "Yes, first thing I did."

"Does she have a boyfriend?"

"No."

"Is it possible that she's run away?"

"No, never. Besides, all her stuff is here."

"Has she ever been in trouble?"

"You mean with the law?"

"Yes, or at school."

"No. She's a good kid. I know everybody says it, but Ava really is."

"Okay. Chances are she's just being a teenager, but since she's a minor, we can't take a chance. I'll need some pictures of her. They have to be current."

Linda said, "I'll get them."

"And if she has a laptop or tablet, anything with data on it. If you allow us to access it, and her phone records, we might get a valuable clue."

"She has an iPad. I'll get it."

"Good. The way kids are with social media, we might find something."

Linda left the room and Cory said, "You know, about a month ago, our son was picked up by an Asian man at his Taekwondo studio. We never found out who it was, but there's a chance it was this Chinese gang that does illegal transplants."

"You mean organs, like a kidney?"

"Yeah, I'd been vocal about the whole thing, and somebody told me to lay off, but I didn't, and next thing we know, Tommy went missing."

"How long was he gone?"

"Like, under an hour."

"You called it in?"

"Yes, a Detective Belfi knows all about Tommy and the transplant ring. He's with the Seventy-Fifth Precinct."

"As soon as I'm done here, I'll call him."

"Good. Are you going to organize a search party?"

"We'll get an Amber Alert out and circulate her picture. I'll call the station and see what resources we can get out on the street. It'd be good if you got ahold of some of your friends and organized a search."

"No problem. I'll start making calls."

CORY PICKED up a hundred posters of Ava and walked out of Staples. He handed a stack to three friends, and they left to distribute them.

Rush hour was underway. Cory scanned the street, wondering where the hell his daughter was. As he headed home, he rolled around whether a lunatic had snatched his daughter or whether it was the transplant gang.

After Tommy's misadventure, Cory had kept a low profile. The pictures of the Hendry kid had garnered considerable coverage, but they'd kept Cory's name out of it.

Was there a way these bastards had discovered his involvement? It seemed remote. He had to be careful, or he'd make them into superpowered bad guys.

At this point, he just wanted his daughter back. Let those animals do whatever they were doing. His daughter was all that mattered.

Cory checked his phone again, no messages. He was worried about Linda. They were scheduled to do a press conference in an hour. He hoped she'd hold up. She didn't want to do it, but Cory knew the reach of the media.

Many times, journalists misused their power, but there was no better way to get the message out about Ava's disappearance. He hoped whoever had taken her would reconsider after seeing them plead for her return.

18

———

Cory looked out the window, and about forty onlookers were crowded around two reporters and their cameramen. There was a knock on the door. "Mr. and Mrs. Lupinski? They're ready for you."

Cory said, "We'll be right down."

He went into the bedroom. "Come on, hon. Let's get this over with."

Linda said, "I don't know if I can do this."

"You don't have to say anything, I'll handle it."

Linda stopped in her tracks when she saw the crowd. Cory took her hand. "It's okay. The more people this gets out to, the quicker Ava gets home."

Detective Grillo looked at Cory, who gave him a thumbs-up. Grillo nodded to the reporters. "Two days ago, Ava Lupinski went missing. She's seventeen years old, and this is a recent picture of her."

Grillo held up an eight-by-eleven photo. "We're asking the public for help in returning Ava safely to her parents. Time is critical in these types of cases. If anyone has any information about Ava, please call 1-899-800-1000."

"This hotline number is completely confidential. You don't need to identify yourself during the call. We only want to know whatever you know or believe happened to her."

Grillo repeated the number and his plea for help and said, "Ava's parents would like to say a few words." Grillo stepped to the side. A distant siren wailed as Cory squeezed Linda's hand. Stepping forward, they approached the microphones.

"My wife, Linda, and I thank everyone for their thoughts and prayers. What's happened to us is a parent's worst nightmare. Our family is sick with worry over what happened to Ava. She's a good girl, and we need your help getting her home. Please call the hotline with anything you saw or heard. The littlest thing could be the key to her safe return."

Cory paused and looked into the camera. "To whoever took our daughter, my wife and I beg you to let her go." Cory sniffled. "We don't care who you are or why you did it, we just want Ava to come home. Thank you."

A reporter asked, "Mr. Lupinski, do you believe your daughter's disappearance is related to your public appeals over illegal organ transplants?"

"We don't know why anyone would do this to Ava. There's no reason on earth. She's an innocent seventeen-year-old getting ready to go to college."

Grillo stepped up. "The Lupinskis need your help. Here's the hotline number again: 899-800-1000. It's completely confidential. Thank you."

The detective led the Lupinskis back into the building. "Well done. Let's hope it generates hard leads."

Linda said, "Do you think it will work?"

"These pleas always generate responses. Some are real, some are well-intentioned people who want to help, and others . . . are a bit kooky."

"What about looking into what that reporter said? Cory

and I talked about it but didn't think there was anything to it. But now that she brought it up, what do you think?"

"We look at anything and everything. I've talked with Detective Belfi, and they're exploring the possibility of a connection."

Inside the apartment, Grillo said, "If you don't mind, I'd like an article of clothing that Ava wore recently. Preferably something not washed."

"Why?"

"We're bringing the canine unit in. You never know where they might pick up a trail. We'll start them from the dance studio where she was last seen."

Linda said, "I have a couple of things that have to go the cleaners. I'll get something."

As Linda left, Cory sidled up to Grillo. "Does this mean you think she's, uh, not alive?"

"No. Not at all. We're just pulling out all the stops. If we lost her trace, say, by a grocery store, we'd try to find who was there and if they remember seeing Ava. We'd check their CCTV footage."

"Okay. You had me worried."

"I know it's impossible, but try to relax; we're doing everything we can to find your daughter."

Grillo promised to call with an update and left with a blouse Ava had worn.

Linda stared out the window. Cory said, "Why don't you take a nap? You haven't slept in two days."

"I can't sleep when she's out there. We have to do something."

"Donny got about twenty guys we've played with over the years doing a search. They got five different groups checking around Brooklyn."

"We need to see if anybody saw her in the city."

"Silvertone Studios is handing out flyers all over the city."

Linda started crying. "Where is she? Where's my baby?"

Cory embraced his wife. "She'll be home soon. I can feel it."

"Why would anyone do this? It's crazy."

"There's a lot of lunatics out there."

"He better not hurt her."

"Ava's smart. I really think she'll be okay."

"I swear, I'll get whoever did it."

"Take it easy. Go eat something."

"I can't eat."

"You have to have something. Have a piece of toast. I'm going to call Belfi."

Cory punched a number in.

"Detective Belfi."

"Hi, Detective, this is Cory Lupinski."

"Hello, Mr. Lupinski. What can I do for you?"

"Did you talk to Grillo?"

"Not today. Why?"

"The more I think about it, maybe it is the transplant ring that took Ava."

"What makes you believe that?"

"To get back at me. You know, to make me keep my mouth shut. Don't forget, they warned me just before they took Tommy."

"We don't know if it was them who took your son."

"Oh, it was them. I'm positive. You got to get on them before they do something to Ava."

"We're gathering as much intel as we can and notified the FBI as well."

"You need to get out there and find my daughter! Sitting behind a desk isn't cutting it."

"Rest assured we're doing everything we can to locate your daughter. I realize for you it will never be fast enough, and I understand that."

"You understand? I don't want you to understand, I want you to find my daughter!"

Cory hung up and Linda said, "Don't get the police mad; they won't look for Ava."

"Don't worry. They will, but I just got an idea."

19

Linda said, "What are you talking about?"

"We got to call Mr. Black. He'll find Ava. I don't know why I didn't think of it earlier."

"How's he going to do that?"

"I have no idea, but he's got all kinds of underground contacts."

"But he double-crossed you with Tower."

"I know, but—"

"But what? We can't trust him."

"How's he going to screw with us? Ava's missing. We need all the help we can get."

"Okay, okay. Call him."

"I want to think it through a minute. Why don't you go down to Mrs. Murray's and see how Tommy's doing?"

Linda left and Cory paced the apartment. He never confronted Black when the operative betrayed him. He was pissed, but the reality was Tower had a lot of people under his thumb.

The crafty lawyer worked hard to collect whatever he could to get someone to do what he wanted. If there was nothing compromising, Tower would revert to bribes or entrapment.

Cory didn't think Black could be bought. It had to be something else that had turned the facilitator against him. He wondered what Tower had over Black.

Cory palmed his phone. There was no need to be anything but direct, he thought as he dialed. As expected, it went to voice mail.

"It's Cory Lupinski. We need help. My daughter's missing. Please call me ASAP."

***

CORY WAS a life-long New Yorker who lived in Manhattan when he'd been at the top of the charts. But he still had to look up the place where Black said to meet. Twenty-Four Sycamores Park was just off the East River on Sixtieth Street.

Cory walked under the Queensboro Bridge and into the square-block park that was filled with mothers, strollers, and kids on playground equipment.

Cory started counting the trees to see if there were twenty-four, when he spotted Black. The operative was sitting on a park bench under a red erector-set-like pergola.

"Thanks for seeing me so fast. We need help."

"Sorry about your daughter. What can you tell me?"

A red Roosevelt Island Tram car passed overhead as Cory filled Black in. Black nodded when told about the possible connection to the illegal organ transplant operation.

Cory said, "You know something about them?"

"I've heard things."

"They got my daughter?"

"Not about your kid. About the syndicate running it."

"Syndicate?"

"I don't know much more than the organization has been around awhile, and based on what I hear, they've stepped up their activity."

"My gut's telling me it's them. I mean, with the threat and Tommy getting taken, it's got to be them."

"It could be, but these people are low-key. They have to be to do transplants and avoid detection. We're talking about something that requires a lot of people and days if not weeks to pull off."

"I know, you'd think this couldn't be going on. But it is."

"It's all about demand. Over the last ten years, I know two people who died waiting for a transplant."

"Yeah, the lack of donors is a problem, but now all I care about is getting Ava home safely. Can you help?"

"This isn't going to be easy."

"We'll pay whatever you say."

"With your kid missing, I couldn't take your money. You take care of whatever expenses there are, and we'll call it even."

Cory wondered if Black was giving him a break to make up for double-crossing him or if he was sympathetic. "Thanks. I appreciate it. You have kids?"

Black nodded. "A son, but we're not close."

"It's never too late."

"Maybe someday. Look, don't expect too much here. I'll check around, see what I can tap into."

Without saying goodbye, Black stood and walked away.

Cory's eyes followed him out of the park, catching a glimpse of the bumper-to-bumper traffic crawling over the Queensboro Bridge. He was sure no one in all those cars had a kidnapped daughter.

Cory closed the door and stripped his sweater off. Linda was on the phone. She hung up quickly.

"What did Mr. Black say?"

"Said he was going to check around, see what he could find out."

"That's it?"

"What did you think? That he knew where Ava was?"

"No, but . . ."

"He's on it. Let's give him some time."

Her face crumpled. "Ava may not have time."

Cory hugged her. "Take it easy, it's going to be all right. The police are working on it, and now we have Mr. Black on the case. Oh, and guess what?"

Linda broke the embrace. "What?"

"Black isn't going to charge us. I think he may actually have a heart."

"I don't care about money. I want my Ava."

"Me too."

"What are we going to do?"

"Let me call Grillo and Belfi, see what's going on with them. Why don't you take Tommy to the park for half an hour?"

"I can't."

"He needs you. We have to pay him some attention."

"All right, but just for a little bit."

Cory kissed his wife's cheek as she put a jacket on. "See you later."

He dialed a number.

"Detective Grillo."

"Hi, it's Cory. I'm checking in."

"Hello, Mr. Lupinski. How are you?"

"Not good. What's going on with the case?"

"Well, we're running down the hotline leads, but at the moment, nothing has panned out."

"But you still got more to check?"

"One or two."

"What about her computer? Did you get anything off it?

"Forensics went over it thoroughly but didn't find anything that raised a flag."

"What about her social media accounts?"

"They were clean. Normal teenage stuff. A lot of dance stuff and her girlfriends."

"What about that kid, Bruce?"

"His alibi checked out."

"So, there's nothing?"

"At the moment, we don't have a definitive lead on your daughter's whereabouts."

"What about the transplant gang?"

"That's being handling by Detective Belfi."

"Great. My daughter's missing, and you guys are screwing around with bureaucracy."

"I'll reach out to him and—"

"Forget it. I'll call him myself."

20

———————

"DETECTIVE BELFI, THIS IS CORY LUPINSKI."

"Mr. Lupinski, how are you?"

"Not good. I just talked with Grillo and he's gotten nowhere. I asked him about the transplant gang, and he said you're handling it."

"That's true. I realize it's frustrating—"

"You have no idea what it's like with your kid missing, so, don't tell me you do."

"I understand, sir, I was only trying to express my sympathy about the situation."

"I don't want sympathy, I want to know what's going on with the situation, as you call it."

"Detective Grillo is in charge of your daughter's case."

"I know, but he told me you're handing the transplant gang. Where are you with them?"

"We continue to investigate the alleged transplant operative—"

"Alleged? Tell that to the Hendry parents or the parents of the Down Syndrome kids."

"Let me rephrase that. Clearly, we're aware these crimes

have been committed. But we're uncertain the same group is responsible for them."

"Oh, come on, how many people do you think are doing this?"

"Unfortunately, the FBI has evidence there are several groups operating in the United States."

"What about the one right here in New York? The one that threatened me? The one that took my son? Why aren't you going after them?"

"It appears they are operating across state lines, and it may be an international ring. As such, the FBI has jurisdiction."

"I don't care about jurisdiction, I want to know what they're doing about it."

"I can't share much about an ongoing investigation."

"And you expect me to be satisfied with that answer?"

"I wish I could tell you more, but I'm unable to. I'd be happy to provide the contact information for Agent Knox. She's the lead on the investigation."

"If you're not going to help me find my daughter, give me someone who will."

Cory hung up and made another call.

"Jennifer Knox."

"Miss Knox, this is Cory Lupinski. My daughter has been kidnapped, and I want to know what the FBI is doing to get her back."

"Mr. Lupinski, I believe the NYPD is handling your daughter's disappearance."

"It's not a disappearance. She was kidnapped."

"While that may be true, I don't believe NYPD has evidence to support an abduction."

"Are you frigging kidding me? My daughter was walking

home and vanished. What do you think, she beamed herself up to some alien ship?"

Knox remained silent and Cory said, "You're handling the transplant ring, right?"

"Yes, I'm leading the investigation."

"They got my daughter."

"What evidence do you have?"

"They threatened me, and then they took my son. What the hell more do you want? Storm wherever they work out of and save Ava."

"We're moving as quickly as the law allows. We can't go barging in without evidence."

"What exactly are you doing to find her?"

"We're working across agencies to determine the scope of and any illegalities of the purported ring."

"What the hell does that mean?"

"It's early, but we believe there is an international component—"

"You should've asked me. The Chinese are behind this, right?"

"I can't confirm that at this point."

"What the hell can you confirm?"

"That we're working with the DEA—"

"The drug agency? What do they have to do with this?"

"If in fact they are performing organ transplants, the drugs used to both anesthetize and prevent rejection had to originate somewhere."

"You're going after illegal medicines?"

"It may sound like a disconnect, but ultimately it may be easier to interrupt their scheme by identifying and shutting down the supply of these drugs."

"I get it, and it's a good idea, but how is that going to get my daughter home? Drug cases take too long."

"Every effective investigation requires an investment in time. Bulletproof evidence, especially when dealing with sophisticated rings, must be developed."

"What about my daughter?"

"As I stated, NYPD is leading that case. We're involved, but on a periphery basis."

"Why can't the FBI get involved? You're supposed to be the best. You got resources nobody has."

"We're examining everything we have on this group. Rest assured, if we find a connection, we'll move on it."

"I can't rest. If I've got to find my daughter on my own, I will."

"You don't need to, Mr. Lupinski."

"Well, it sure as hell feels like it. Goodbye, Miss Knox."

Cory hung up. What was he going to tell Linda? That Ava was caught in some jurisdictional mess? He thought over what Knox had said about the drug angle. It made sense but didn't help.

The thought that building a case against the gang was more important to the FBI than getting Ava home safely hit him. Hard.

It was crazy, but it was something the authorities did all the time. They'd let criminals go to pursue the top dogs. There was no way he was going to let his daughter become collateral damage.

The problem was he didn't know what to do. Maybe he'd hold another press conference. They needed help from the public, and that was the quickest way.

All they needed was one good tip. Then the nightmare would be over. It'd been three tortuous days since she vanished. As Linda swung open the door, Cory was hit with the realization that with each passing day, the odds of her returning alive lessened.

21

Cory's feet were sore. He'd walked from Prospect Park to Marine Park. He should've taken an Uber but wouldn't give up the chance of randomly seeing Ava.

He cut down Kings Highway and saw a girl with the same build and hair color as Ava. She was alone. Cory crossed the street, jogging toward her. "Ava? Is that you? Ava!"

The girl looked over her shoulder and began running. Cory stopped; it wasn't Ava. Cory continued walking on Kings Highway and made a right onto Coney Island Avenue.

The street's name reminded him of taking Ava to the historic amusement park. He could see her squeezing the pole as she rode a pink pony on the merry-go-round.

Approaching Avenue M, Cory's phone rang. He hoped it would be Ava. It wasn't. Mr. Black was calling.

Red Hook, one of Brooklyn's oldest neighborhoods, was bustling. The gentrification of the shipping yards and waterfront had transformed the area.

Cory walked toward the water, passing small restaurants, edgy bars, and an art gallery. He saw Black standing in a Court Street doorway. Black was talking to someone that a casting director would put in a gangster movie.

Black jerked his head toward the water, patted his companion on the shoulder, and joined Cory.

"You know where my daughter is?"

"No."

"Damn. What do you have?"

"Given the situation, I wanted to update you."

It wasn't like Black to be considerate. "Thanks. What's going on?"

"It's sketchy, but it looks like the transplant ring is run out of China."

"China. That fits with what the FBI said."

"What did they tell you?"

"Just that it was an international ring. Did you get anything else?"

"State-sponsored rings are tough to crack. They're well-funded and use diplomatic status to cover problems. There was a recent buy of pharmaceuticals that could be traced to them. There were opioids in the mix but also a stash of prednisone. It has a couple of uses, but it's also an antirejection med."

"You know who bought it?"

"I'm working on it. These guys are sophisticated; there's a web of head fakes."

"Man, you find that, and we're on the way."

"We got nothing."

"But you said—"

"I didn't say much. So, don't get your hopes high."

Cory shrugged. "This is so screwed up, man."

Black nodded. "I heard something, but it could be nothing."

"What? What did you hear?"

Black lowered his voice. "They may be using trucks as mobile hospitals."

"Holy shit. That makes sense. They can drive them around. Maybe the police can put up roadblocks and—"

"Don't tell anyone. And I mean it. You start mouthing off, and I'm done. You hear?"

"Yeah, sure. I'm sorry."

"You start blabbing like the last time, lose my number."

As Cory started to say sorry, Black walked away.

Riding an Uber home, Cory kept his eyes peeled for his daughter. He thought about Black and the way he was. Cory reasoned he had to be tough and unemotional, otherwise he'd be ineffective.

He remembered what Black had said when he asked him why he never wore a heavy coat or hat when it was freezing. Black said he blocked out the cold. When Cory questioned him, he said you had to train your mind.

Cory had read how people were able to teach themselves to compartmentalize. He wondered if his ability to focus on music, no matter what else was going on, was something he could build on.

When he played or even composed, he was able to concentrate so intently that people told him he was in a trance. It wasn't something he was born with.

Cory recalled struggling to focus when he began playing. He was easily distracted by what others were playing and the doubts in his head over how he sounded.

He remembered how hard it was playing in the high school big band, where others were playing different lines.

He made a ton of mistakes. It was frustrating, but instead of quitting, he forced himself to focus.

Climbing the stairs to his apartment, Cory wondered about the difference between the training Mr. Black mentioned and the concentration Cory was able to attain.

Cory stepped into the apartment. It was quiet. Where was his wife? He hoped she was sleeping. He checked the master bedroom. It was empty.

He went into the kitchen to get a bottle of water and heard something. He checked Ava's room. Linda was curled up on her daughter's bed, sobbing.

Cory crawled beside her. "It's okay. She'll be home soon."

As he spooned his wife, she said, "She's not coming back. I can feel it."

22

The vehicle was slowing down. She wondered if they were stopping again. The engine shifted into a lower gear, and it felt like they were climbing uphill.

She squinted and tried to see through the sleeping mask they'd put on her. She'd tried to keep track of the days, but between the constant darkness and the drugs, it was impossible.

It was hard not asking what was going on, but if she spoke, they'd put her under like they did the two times before when she tried to talk. There were voices. People talking. She strained to hear what they were saying.

Were they talking to the boy in the vehicle? It was impossible to understand what they were saying.

They switched from English to what she thought was Chinese. The voices got louder.

Two pairs of footsteps approached. They stopped where she was lying. The man with the deep voice said, "All right now. We're going to get you up."

Her anxiety rose as they grabbed her ankle and put something on her feet. They were her shoes. She hoped it was a good sign.

"Get ready." Hands snuck beneath her shoulders. "Here we go. Nice and easy."

She moaned as they helped her into a sitting position.

"Take your time, it's just some stiffness. I'll get you something for the pain, but you can't speak. Okay?"

She nodded.

"Open up."

Opening her mouth, two pills hit her tongue.

"Here's some water."

Water dripped down her chin as he placed the bottle to her lips. The smell of latex hit her as she took two gulps. She nodded and he pulled the bottle away.

The vehicle slowed to a crawl. A woolen hat was pulled over her head.

"We're going to put your jacket on."

Her heart began pounding. "I'm going outside?"

"No talking!"

She nodded.

They put something in her jacket pocket. She used the inside of her elbow as a probe. It felt like a handful of small bottles.

"Don't be afraid. I'm going to tie your hands behind you. You'll be able to wiggle them free in a couple of minutes. Okay?"

Her fear growing, she nodded.

As they bound her hands, the deep-voiced man said, "Don't try to remove your mask. If you see us, we'll have to do something we don't want to. You understand?"

She bobbed her head.

They chattered in Chinese. The vehicle ground to a stop.

The other man said, "Okay. Let's get going."

Two hands snaked under her armpits and set her on the floor. She muffled a groan.

They walked her ten steps and stopped. A quick command in Chinese was given. She heard a door open.

"There are three small steps. One foot at a time."

Inching her foot forward, she tipped it over the edge and probed for a landing. "That's it. Go ahead."

She crept down the two other steps and landed on a hard surface. Was it asphalt? The hum of traffic made her wonder if she was near a highway.

"We're going straight ahead."

The men led her a dozen paces, and the ground under her feet turned softer. Her body stiffened.

"It's okay. We're going to sit you on a bench."

They walked her five steps and turned her around. As they eased her onto a bench, the deep voice said, "Now, don't do anything stupid. Sit here and count to two hundred before you try and untie your hands. You understand?"

She nodded.

"Remember, we're watching you. You don't follow instructions, you'll regret it."

She heard them jog away. Seconds later, the closing of a door sounded. Counting, as the vehicle's engine accelerated, she began crying at twenty-three.

She listened but could no longer hear the vehicle. Wrestling her hands back and forth, the rope loosened. Slipping a hand out, she pulled her mask off.

The flood of light stunned her eyes. She clamped them shut and freed her other hand. She opened her eyes to a slit. She was at the edge of an expansive parking lot.

Squinting, she made out a building in the distance. It looked like a rest area off a highway. She stood, clutching a hand to her belly. It hurt. She was puzzled by the padding.

She clawed her sweater up. What had they done to her? She tried to recount being swept off the street. Someone had put a smelly cloth over her mouth and nose.

She remembered consciousness slipping away. Before everything went black, there was a man in a white van. He'd reached out, pulling her inside.

She searched her memory; had she banged into something when they stuffed her into the van? The only thing that came to her was the cool feeling of the metal floor.

Though doubting it'd be there, she patted her pockets for a phone. Getting up slowly, she scanned the area. The highway's off-ramp access to the rest area was a football field away.

The building was farther and an uphill walk. She took a series of small steps and paused. Her legs were weak. A car came up the ramp.

"Help! Help me!"

The hum of the sixty-mile-an-hour traffic drowned her plea and the car kept going. Realizing she was too far to be seen, she took a deep breath and broadened her gait.

Each time a car exited the highway, she flailed her arms and screamed as loud as possible. She was getting closer. Shuffling toward the ramp, a white van left the highway.

She backpedaled, hiding behind a tree. The vehicle zoomed by, and she resumed her struggle to reach help.

A red pickup truck exited. She ambled to the side of the road. She waved her arms. "Stop. Please. Help."

The truck passed her by. "Oh! Come on."

The pickup slowed down. It pulled over.

"Help me. Please."

White taillights came on, and she prayed the truck would back up.

23

───────

Cory weaved in and out of traffic. He kept replaying what Detective Grillo had said, 'We found Ava. She's alive but has been wounded.'

He'd asked what kind of an injury, but Grillo couldn't provide details. As he exited the Henry Hudson Parkway, Cory questioned whether the detective had held back. Did he know about his daughter's condition but was afraid to say?

Cory and Linda jumped out of their car, running past the parking attendant into Columbia Presbyterian Hospital. They went straight to the elevator bank.

Cory pushed the button. "Come on. Hurry up!" He pecked the button repeatedly. "The hell with this. Let's take the stairs."

They bounded up to the second floor. The nurse's station directed them to a room. A police officer was standing outside the door. He put up a hand and Cory said, "We're Ava's parents."

A nurse was changing an IV bag as they stormed in. Linda said, "My Ava. What have they done to you?"

The nurse, whose blond hair was piled on her head, said, "She's resting. I wouldn't wake her right now."

Linda sobbed as she kissed her daughter's hand. Cory asked, "What happened to her?"

"Let me get Dr. Simmons."

The nurse hurried out, and Cory sidled up to the bed. "She looks good. Don't you think?"

Linda wiped her nose. "I thought we'd never see her. I really did."

Cory put his arm around his wife. "She's going to be fine. Let her rest. We'll go see the doctor."

"I can't leave her alone."

"She's safe. Come on, we have to talk to the doctor."

Cory pried his wife away, and they stepped into the hall. A doctor in green scrubs and red clogs approached. "Mr. and Mrs. Lupinski?"

"Yes."

He extended a hand. "Dr. Simmons. I'm taking care of Ava."

Cory took his soft hand. "What happened to her?"

"It's hard to believe, but she had a section of her liver removed."

Linda wailed, "Oh my God."

Cory put his arm around her waist. It was the organ transplant gang that took his daughter. "They butchered her?"

"Actually, and I don't mean to condone this, but it appears whoever performed the surgery was highly skilled."

"How can you say that?"

"The MRI of her liver is already showing new growth, and there are no signs of bleeding or infection. The incision and suturing also show signs it was executed by a professional."

Linda said, "Is she going to be normal. Doesn't she need a full liver?"

"Fortunately, the liver regenerates. Given it appears that the surgery was performed professionally, I'd expect her to make a full recovery."

"Thank God."

"She'll have to be monitored. We'll continue giving her antibiotics but wean her off pain medications."

"They gave her pills?"

"Yes, it's critically important with a surgery of this kind to avoid infection."

"Did she suffer when they did it?"

"I don't think so. I don't know where the surgery was performed, but they seemed to have followed all recommended protocols."

"When can she come home?"

"We'd like to keep her for another couple of days as a precaution. She's really doing fine, but given the circumstances, I'd like to closely monitor her to make sure she fully recovers."

"Of course, whatever you believe is best."

Linda said, "I'm not leaving this hospital."

"I understand, and that won't be a problem. We'll make it as comfortable as we can. Besides, Ava will be glad to have your company."

"Can we wake her up?"

"I don't see why not. It'll be good for her to see you."

Linda headed in before the doctor finished talking. Cory said, "Thanks, Doc," and followed her.

Linda was at Ava's bedside, stroking her face. "Honey? It's Mommy."

Ava's eyes slowly opened. She blinked. "Mom?"

"Yes, honey. We're here now. You're going to be all right."

Cory swallowed. His voice cracked when he said, "Hey, Ava. How are you doing?"

"She's doing great. Look at her."

Cory had seen it before; Linda was a wreck but pulled it together better than he did when the kids needed her. It reinforced his belief that there was nothing like a mother. They were filled with love and patience and were selfless when it came to their children.

"What did they do to me?"

"You're going to be fine."

"But, but what happened?"

"Don't worry about that. Just get better so we can go home."

"Where's Tommy?"

"He's with Mrs. Murphy. If we would've known you were doing so well, we would have brought him along."

Ava's eyes teared up. "I miss him."

"He was worried about you."

"I can't wait to see him."

"We'll get him here later. You need to rest."

"No. I'm fine. I want to know what they did to me. Why isn't anyone telling me what happened?"

Cory looked at Linda and said, "Okay. But it sounds worse than it is."

"Tell me."

He told her they'd kidnapped her and taken part of her liver. Ava placed both hands on her abdomen. "Oh my God. I'm gonna die."

"You'll be fine."

Her eyes welled up. "Am I going to be disabled?"

"No, you're going to make a full recovery."

"You're just saying that."

"No. It's true. Livers regenerate. The doctor said yours is growing back already."

She searched his face. "Really? Is that true?"

"Of course it is. We wouldn't lie about something like that."

Ava's ears flattened. "Why are these people doing this to us?"

"Don't worry about that. Your job is to get better. The police are going to get these people. And even the FBI, they're involved as well."

"This is scary, Dad. It's like a science fiction movie."

"I know."

"Can they get me in here?"

"Who are you talking about?"

"The people who kidnapped me."

"No. Don't worry."

"Are you sure?"

"Yes. There's even a policeman outside your door."

"Oh, good."

Linda said, "You're safe now. How about we brush your hair?"

There was a knock on the door. Standing in the doorway was Detective Grillo.

"How is she?"

"Good."

"I know the timing seems bad, but the sooner we talk to her, the better our chances are."

Cory said, "Ava, Detective Grillo wants to ask you some questions. Do you feel up to it, or should he come back?"

"I'm okay." She propped herself up.

"Great." He turned to Cory and lowered his voice. "She's

a minor and you're entitled to stay, but it may be easier for her to talk alone."

"Uh, okay. Look, honey. Mommy and me are going to get a cup of coffee. You want anything from the cafeteria?"

"I'm not hungry."

"Okay, see you in a bit."

Cory and Linda stepped into the hallway. Linda said, "She looks good, don't you think?"

"Oh yeah. To tell you the truth, I didn't know what to expect. I thought it was going to be a lot worse."

"I know, but can you believe this? They took our daughter's liver. What kind of animals are these people?"

24

———————

Grillo took a seat and pulled his Moleskine out. "Don't feel any pressure to recall every detail. Just say whatever you remember about what happened."

"Okay, but can those people get me again?"

"Don't worry about that. You'll never see them again."

"You sure?"

"Cross my heart." Grillo smiled. "You ready to tell me what you recall?"

She nodded. "I was on the way home, walking on Prospect Avenue. There's a Walgreens there, and a little past it a van slowed down and pulled over."

"What color?"

"White."

"Did you notice the license plate?"

"No. I should've—"

"That's fine. Go on."

"I kept walking, but a lady said, 'Excuse me.' She was driving the van. I figured she was lost or something and went to the passenger window. She just started asking me if I knew where a bakery was, and out of the corner of my eye I saw someone. A man. He reached around my head and put a cloth over my face. It smelled gross and I got all dizzy. The next thing I remember was, like, being on the floor, or I think it was the floor, but I remember it felt cold."

"So, the driver was a woman?"

"Yes."

"And the person who used the cloth, he was a man?"

"I'm pretty sure."

"Was there anybody else inside the van?"

She shrugged. "I really don't know."

"That's okay. What do you remember next?"

"Waking up in a bed, but my eyes were covered, and I couldn't move my hands."

"They were tied? To a bed railing?"

"I'm pretty sure."

"Okay, you're in a bed and can't see or move your hands. Where do you think this was?"

"A truck."

"What makes you believe it was a truck?"

"Because it sounded like a truck or bus. And it moved around. Not all the time, but it was definitely moving every now and then."

"Any idea where they might have gone to?"

She shook her head.

"Was anyone in the truck with you?"

"Yeah, at least two guys. One had a real deep voice. They were Chinese."

"How do you know that?"

"Because they talked in Chinese."

"Are you sure it wasn't Japanese or—"

"No, it was Chinese. My friend Crystal, her parents were born in China, and the men in the truck talked the same way."

"All right. What did these men do?"

"They didn't want me to talk. The two times I did, they put me to sleep with drugs."

"With a needle?"

"Yes."

"How did they treat you?"

"They gave me food and water and made me get up, but I felt sick, like nauseous, you know. Most of the time, I was like, groggy."

"Did you hear them speak to anyone in English besides you?"

"No, I don't think so. I was, like, out of it. My stomach hurt. You know, I didn't know what they did to me till my parents told me. I was, like, wondering why my side hurt so much."

"Do you think the men were doctors?"

She shrugged. "I don't think so, maybe, like, nurses or something."

"Was there anyone else in the truck?"

"Oh yeah, there was a boy. I'm pretty sure it was a boy."

"Any idea how old?"

"No."

"Do you know his name?"

She shook her head. "Sorry."

"It's fine. You're doing great. Let's talk about the Sloatsburg rest area where they dropped you off. Tell me how you were released."

Ava recounted being told to be quiet and how she was helped out of bed and off the truck to a picnic table in the rear of the lot.

"You said there were stairs and a door."

"Yeah, I mean, I didn't see them, but I went down them."

"Did you feel like it was the back of the truck? You know how they have those two big doors at the rear?"

"Hm, I don't think so, but I was so scared . . . I really don't know."

"That's fine. Now, you said they left you there, threatening to come back if you said anything."

"They wanted me to count to two hundred, but I heard the truck leaving, so I freed my hands and took off the mask."

"When you first took it off, did you see the truck leaving?'

"No. Where I was was in the back, to the right side, and the road kind of bends, so I couldn't see it."

"Any other vehicles? Maybe a car that could have been connected to them?"

"Not that I saw."

"Then you walked to the access road, and that was where the pickup truck stopped for you?"

"Yes. He was such a nice man."

"Okay. If you feel up to it, I'd like to go over this one more time."

Cory waited outside his daughter's room. When Grillo came out, he asked, "How did it go?"

"Okay."

"Get anything useful?"

Grillo exhaled. "Tough to say. It looks like they're Chinese, and she might have been in a truck of some kind."

"A mobile operating room?"

"Maybe."

"What else?"

"Not much more. She was out of it most of the time. I'm hoping she remembers more over the next day or two."

"These bastards got to be hung."

"I'm with you, but we have to catch them first."

"They should have been nailed as soon as those Down

Syndrome kids were taken. I don't get why you guys can't get them."

"We will, it'll just take us some more time. But we'll nail 'em."

As Grillo walked away, Cory steamed. How many more kids would get cut open before the authorities shut them down, if they even could?

Did another kid have to die before they did something? Cory remembered petitioning the traffic department to put a light at the intersection by their apartment. He hounded them for two years, but they did nothing until two kids were killed in an accident.

It was unacceptable, but so was putting his family in harm's way. He had to do something. But what?

He pulled his phone out and called Mr. Black.

25

———

Shu scrolled through pictures of his family. He loved the picture of him sitting on his mother's lap. He was about seven years old at the time.

His mother's smile made his heart ache. Everyone commented on her beauty. He knew she could've been a movie star, but all that mattered to her was him. It went beyond the cultural reverence the Chinese have for firstborn males. It was a selfless love.

Her devotion to Shu never wavered, even when her kidneys were failing. He'd found out she'd missed dialysis twice to attend a school play and a science fair he'd participated in. Both times, she ended up hospitalized.

It pained him to know she'd suffered to support him. He swiped to another photo and winced. His mother's blouse hung off her bony shoulders.

While bemoaning the primitive nature of transplants forty years ago, there was a knock on his office door.

Li said, "Sorry to disturb you."

"Come in."

Li took a seat. "Are you all right?"

Shu shook his head. "Just thinking about my mother."

"Sorry. I remember how close you were growing up."

"The good old days. So, how did it go?"

"Excellent. It went as planned. She was left at a rest area."

"And her condition?"

"Excellent. Her vitals were strong, and she was moving well."

"I understand she's at Columbia."

"Yes. Her parents and that detective, Grillo, were up there as well."

"Any press?"

"None."

"I expect that'll put an end to his meddling."

Li smiled. "It was an excellent plan."

"We'll see. Are our media friends ready to help if needed?"

"Yes."

"Good. We're going to be busy. When will the new RV be outfitted?"

"A shipment of equipment is arriving at JFK tonight. Dishi thinks he can have it installed in three days."

"I'd like you to take a ride to New Jersey. Go to Freehold. They have a large population of illegals. Gauge the level of interest in that community."

"Sounds like a good idea. Make the usual offers?"

"No. Offer forty thousand for a kidney or liver section."

"That seems high."

"Our backlog has grown. We'll pass the extra cost onto the recipients."

"Okay."

"Don't take anyone with you. You identify those interested and hand it off to Ming. She'll take it from there."

"You got it. I'll let you know how it goes."

Li got up to leave. Shu said, "Close the door behind you."

Shu signed into Alibaba's document cloud in China. He entered his password and punched in the two-step verification code he received on his cell.

He pulled up an encrypted spreadsheet and typed another password in. Shu scanned the waiting list of recipients. They'd added two kidney requests and a liver in the past eight days.

Shu unwrapped a slice of gum. Beijing was pressuring him to expand the operation. The demand was there, but supply, as well as surgeons, presented challenges.

The Party could twist arms to get doctors to participate, but Shu preferred surgeons who were passionate about doing transplants. He would have to talk to Gao. He had an idea to offer prized positions to surgeons who agreed to work with Shu's American operation for two years.

It was a way to get quality surgeons that he hoped would work. Success in the field would lead to more satisfied customers and more lives saved.

The cycle would create a growth spurt, presenting a quality alternative to dying on a waiting list. Americans liked to espouse lofty ethical positions, but Shu believed his results would change minds.

Shu would no longer authorize harvesting organs from unwilling donors. It wasn't the money that made him do it. People would have died without a transplant. He couldn't allow that to happen.

The problem was it distracted from the larger goal. The way to prevent it was to build a roster of donors ready to donate when needed.

He hoped his outreach idea would provide a steady stream

of healthy illegals willing to trade an organ for life-changing money.

Shu checked the time. Gao's nephew was on the 1 p.m. Acela from Washington. He had to get to the safe deposit box at Chinatown Federal Bank before they closed.

He went to the closet and pulled out a leather valise. Shu set it on the desk and opened a drawer. He reached under and pried off the key taped to its bottom.

Shu headed to the parking lot. After he handed off the cash, he'd feign a stomachache. There was no way he was going to be trapped in a fancy whorehouse while the diplomat got his rocks off.

As Shu got into the back of his car, he had a thought. "Ling, stop at a Duane Reade or some other drug store. I need you to buy a bottle of Brioschi."

"Okay, sir. No problem."

Shu smiled. Every time he took the lemon-flavored effervescent, it made him burp for an hour. It'd be proof he wasn't feeling well.

As they pulled out of the garage, Shu thought over the plan he'd begun forming last night. The Freehold excursion would test people's willingness to participate, but the real goal was larger. Much larger. Logistically, it posed problems, but geographically it offered anonymity. Shu considered it the best idea he'd ever had.

A large pool of illegals was living in the shadows in the Southwest. Most were new arrivals with meager means. Shu's team would have to screen their health, but the big challenge was getting them to the New York area.

Shu considered establishing a Southwestern outpost, but they hadn't yet developed a pool of recipients. They had demand in the tri-state area, which meant they'd have to move the donors to the Northeast.

Stopped at a light on Sixty-First Street, Shu saw a tractor trailer off-loading onto the sidewalk. He gave a passing thought to outfitting a truck. He decided it would be too stressful for the donors, possibly affecting the quality of the organs harvested.

Flying was too risky. Papers were easy to get, but there were cameras everywhere. As the car lurched forward, Shu settled on sticking with RVs.

They were self-contained. No need to stop for food or the bathroom. He'd use a double team of drivers to speed the ride. It'd add costs, but those in need would pay.

Shu felt himself nodding. RVs made good mobile hospitals, and now they'd transport donors.

26

AS THE SUBWAY SLOWED TO A STOP, CORY REALIZED HE hadn't been to Central Park since moving back to Brooklyn. It seemed crazy, as he'd spent hours walking Ava around the eight-hundred-acre park.

Cory exited the Seventy-Second Street station and crossed Central Park West. It was a small detour, but strolling through Strawberry Fields was his homage to John Lennon.

A handful of people were gathered around the mosaic tribute to "Imagine." The Lennon composition had become a utopian anthem for many. He remembered watching home videos as Lennon shaped and recorded the tune.

The Beatle had no idea of the lasting effect the song would have on the Western world. He'd even discounted it, calling it a pop tune.

Cory hummed the tune as he headed to the lake. He felt the song was a force for good, a guiding principle for unity, and considered creating something with a similar message for children.

He crossed the Bow Bridge, vowing to take Tommy to the

park. Maybe they'd build a model boat and sail it on the pond with the children's statues in it.

Cory dodged a taxi while crossing East Drive and cut across a vast lawn. He saw Black sitting on a bench near a large statue.

The bronze sculpture of Alice, the Mad Hatter, and the White Rabbit had been Ava's favorite. He wondered where she'd put the collection of Lewis Carroll books they'd accumulated.

Black stood and Cory followed him, walking deeper into the park. They circled around three men kicking a soccer ball back and forth.

Black said, "Everybody needs a place like this."

"Yeah, it's a great spot, so much to do here."

"It's got nothing to do with the physical. You're missing it."

"Missing what?"

"An inner sanctum. People don't understand, they're always looking for something external to distract them. We don't need to come here or anywhere; we have space inside of us."

"You mean like meditation?"

"There's a relationship if you're looking to settle your mind. It's useful and it helps some to focus. But for me, retreating internally, blocking out pain, difficulty, the world for that matter, frees me to pursue a goal."

"You said something a while ago about training your mind. Is that what you mean?"

"The ability to control your consciousness is the most powerful tool man has."

"I don't get it. Isn't that like your awareness?"

"Not exactly, but since you mention awareness, how

much better would we be if we could block out fear, pain, the elements?"

"Man, that's hard."

"All it takes is discipline. Discipline equals freedom."

"I like that. I tell my kids all the time, the price of discipline is always less than the cost of regret."

Black nodded. "Your daughter still doing good?"

"She seems to be. The doctors say she'll be back to normal in a month or so."

"I hear these guys are using real surgeons."

"Yeah, Columbia said whoever did it was a pro."

"Between what your daughter described and I can piece together, it looks like they're using mobile units as hospitals."

"That should make it easy to nail them."

"These Chinese are too smart. Normally, I'd look to follow the equipment they'd need, but they've been importing all kinds of contraband without detection for years."

"Bastards."

"It's like drugs. The fact they're illegal has nothing to do with it. You can't stop it if people want them."

"That doesn't mean we shouldn't try."

"Of course not, but you've got to know it's an uphill battle. These guys have plenty of money and have thought this through. They must threaten the recipients to keep them quiet."

"Why do you say that?"

"No one has come forward."

"The donors made a lot of money, and the recipients got an organ. Why would anyone say something?"

"Because people talk."

"You think they killed someone for talking?"

Black stopped in his tracks. He turned to Cory. "You're incredibly naive. They kidnapped your daughter for her liver and left another kid to die. What makes you think they wouldn't kill?"

"I guess . . ."

"I gotta go."

Cory watched Black walk away, and he was right; these guys would kill if threatened. As he headed out of the park, Cory realized that trying to shut these guys down was too dangerous to pursue.

A step away from Ava's room, Tommy broke into a run. "We're here, Ava!"

Cory said, "Be careful. Don't jump on your sister!"

Linda said, "Hi, honey, how are you today?"

Ava shrugged. "All right, I guess."

"What's the matter?"

"Nothing."

"You sure?"

"When did the doctor say I can come home?"

"A couple of more days."

Ava frowned. "I want out of here."

"You can have your friends visit now."

"So?"

"Don't you want to see your friends?"

She shrugged. "I'm not ready to see anybody."

"What do you mean? You're fine, the doctors said it'll be good for you."

"I don't want to!"

"Okay, honey, take it easy."

Cory opened the blinds.

"Leave it!"

"It's dark in here."

"No, it's not."

Cory saw the pained look on his wife's face. He closed the blinds. "You tell me when you're ready to see your friends, I'll drive them up."

Tommy said, "What's the matter, Ava? You don't want us here?"

"I'm just tired, okay. Everybody is always asking how I feel. I'm sick of it."

Cory said, "I need a cup of coffee. Let's leave Ava alone for a while."

As they filed out, he looked at his daughter. Her life had been interrupted in the most brutal way. They'd been so focused on her physical recovery, they'd never given thought to the mental scar of being snatched off the street and having part of her body stolen.

It was a violation that was simply unheard of. The trauma from being raped permanently damaged women. He shuddered to think this might be worse.

Cory felt she'd rebound, but it was no sure thing. Would she live in fear the rest of her life? It was a possibility, and it shook him. Who were these bastards who did this to his little girl?

27

Staring at the ceiling, Cory bounced between bouts of rage and fear. He slipped out of bed. Checking the clock, he shook his head—3:19 a.m. It was the second night that he'd been unable to sleep because of what Ava had gone through.

Cory trudged into the studio, softly shutting the door. He clicked on the keyboard and put his headphones on. Looking at the sixteen bars he'd composed last night, Cory hummed the melody. It needed work but was catchy.

He placed his fingers on the keys and found a triplet figure he liked. He took it down a step and repeated the three notes. Cory played it twice more before jotting it on manuscript paper.

Cory played the entire melody and smiled. It sounded good. He explored ideas for the bridge. Nothing was particularly interesting, so he did what he did when stuck: he shifted to writing ideas to lyrics.

Rhymes were an important musical device, especially in music for children. While erasing a line, there was a knock on the door. Linda stuck her head in. "Good morning. How long you been in here?"

Cory pulled his headphones down. "What time is it?"

"Six ten."

"Wow. Couldn't sleep."

"You've got bags under your eyes."

He shrugged and held up his composition. "At least I got some good work in."

"Grab a nap. You've got an hour before Tommy gets up."

"I'll try."

As soon as Cory lay his head on the pillow, he started thinking about Ava. He tried to think about Tommy but kept seeing her on a gurney.

He tried to picture the surgeon. Was he a doctor somewhere and did this on the side? How many physicians worked for the illegal operation? And what about nurses? They probably recruited their medical staff from foreign countries.

He settled on people who couldn't pass the rigorous requirements the United States had. Cory wondered if a nurse had comforted Ava. She must have felt so alone. When he thought about them slicing into her, he swung his legs out of bed.

It was no use. He went into the bathroom wondering if he should try a pill to sleep. He'd heard melatonin worked on some people. Passing the studio, he realized he'd been able to shut down the preoccupation when music was involved.

It wasn't always that way. He remembered getting distracted in the early days, but he'd learned to focus. It was an acquired skill. Could he learn to quiet his mind? Control it like Mr. Black had said?

Black didn't seem the teaching type. If he wouldn't help, Cory would find a way to learn it himself.

CORY HUGGED the wall as two officers walked an intoxicated man to booking. It was the first time he'd been inside a police station not under arrest. With three experiences as a hand-cuffed prisoner, he couldn't understand why the place felt so chaotic.

He wondered whether being in shock from an arrest dulled what was going on around you. Cory scanned the photos of the wanted persons and missing children.

It was a grim picture of the New York he loved. Wondering what level of crime was acceptable in a city with more than eight million people, he heard his name called.

Detective Grillo was standing in a doorway. He waved him over. "Sorry, Mr. Lupinski. It's a little crazy here today."

"I can see that."

"We'll go to my office."

Cory followed him through a bullpen area packed with desks. This was one place where real landline phones still played a role.

You couldn't park a Mini Cooper in the space Grillo called his office. He took a stack of files off a chair. "Have a seat."

The detective squeezed behind his metal desk. "What brings you here?"

"You never returned my calls. I know you're busy, but I called a couple of times."

"I'm sorry." He swept his hand over the stacks of files. "As you see, we've got a lot going on."

"I'm sure you do, and I don't want to seem selfish, but all I care about is getting the guys who took Ava. I want an update on the case."

"I understand your concern. I'd feel the same way."

"And? What's going on with it?"

"Unfortunately, not much. We're trying to identify the location or locations where they do what they do."

"They're using trucks."

"We're not sure of that."

"What do you mean? Ava told you she was in a truck or some kind of vehicle."

"Yes, but we believe she was transferred to be dropped off."

"Are you sure?"

"We've talked at length with medical professionals, and they don't think these kinds of surgeries can be successfully performed in a truck."

"I'll ask the people at Mount Sinai. They do a lot of transplants up there."

"Any and all information is useful." Grillo reached for his ringing desk phone. "Excuse me a second."

The detective promised someone he'd be there in five minutes and hung up. "Sorry, another emergency just cropped up."

"What else are you doing?"

"We've got our network of informers looking for information."

"Why isn't anyone talking to the patients on waiting lists? If they weren't willing to buy an organ, these guys would be out of business."

"That may be true, but we just don't have the resources to do that, besides, it's not the role this office plays."

"I don't get it. What you're saying is, you wait until some kid dies or is mangled to get involved."

"That's not the way it is."

Grillo's phone rang again. He put up a hand and picked up the receiver. "Yes, sir. I'm on my way."

28

Cory passed Petrarca Cuisine and Vino, wishing he were lunching at the Tribeca eatery instead of where he was going. He turned onto Franklin Street and steeled himself when he saw the sign for Aire Ancient Baths.

Cory changed into a bathing suit. Towel and phone in hand, he walked down a hallway. He slowed as he approached the brick-lined walls of the cold-plunge room.

The pool was empty. It made him wonder just how bad an idea it was. Cory dipped a foot in the fifty-degree water and yanked it out.

This was crazy. Couldn't he get a heart attack from the shock of such cold water? He rummaged through his mind, trying to recall the warnings he'd read.

He considered leaving. He hadn't told anyone he was coming, not even Linda. It'd be a waste of money, but what else was new? Cory slung the towel around his neck and headed out.

He paused, realizing it was all about Ava. What would he say to her or Tommy about doing something you didn't want to?

He told himself that wasn't it, it wasn't about anybody else. It was about him, about trying to control himself.

Cory turned around. Dropping his towel on a bench, he stood by the pool stairs. He took deep breaths. Better to go in all at one shot, not like some old-timer on Miami Beach.

He counted, one, two, three. Here we go. Cory stepped down, drawing and holding a gulp of air. His toes hit the bottom and he paused. The water was ice-cold. It took his breath away.

Cory held his phone over his head and bent his knees. The water encircled his chest. Breathing rapidly, Cory took a couple of selfies. He popped up and rushed to the stairs.

Foot on the first stair, he stopped. He slid his phone away from the edge and turned around. He'd done it. Now, he had to do it again and stay under for a while.

Cory lowered himself. The cold stung but he did his best to keep his mind on breathing the way Wim Hof had done on YouTube. Hof had set records for withstanding the cold, even scaling most of Mount Everest in shorts.

Forcing himself to stay submerged, Cory thought of Hof and Black. They were proof you could control your mind, evidence of a mental strength that made focusing easier.

Cory rose, climbing the stairs out of the pool. He smiled. He'd done it. He couldn't wait to text Black the photos.

He considered it proof he could do anything.

LINDA PEELED HER JACKET OFF. Shaking his head, Cory hung up the phone. She asked, "What's the matter?"

"I'm pissed. I called Grillo for an update, and he was like, short with me."

"He's probably busy, that's all."

"Nah, they're doing nothing about what happened to Ava."

"They have to be doing something."

"Yeah? You know what he said about the Hendry kid? He said they don't think it's the same gang. He said it was a copycat thing."

"He did?"

"Yep. They're burying their heads in the sand. It's frigging ridiculous. These people work for us."

"I hate to say it, but they're way too busy. There were five hundred murders in the city last year, and we're going higher this year."

"So, hire more cops then. What are they going to do, let this city turn into a war zone?"

"You know, I was thinking; maybe we should consider moving to the suburbs or someplace safer for the kids."

"No place is going to be safe unless we make it safe. Crime spreads as quick as fire does."

"Look what happened to us, to our kids. Now, you want to be a vigilante?"

"No, that's not what I'm saying. All I'm saying is we can't just run from every problem.

"Why not? I don't want my kids to grow up in fear."

"I know, but I'm sorry. It's too late for Ava. I'm really worried she's scarred by all this."

"And you think sticking around the city where it happened is okay?"

"All I'm saying is we can't cut and run. We should be a part of the solution."

"You want to do patrols? Get a badge or something?"

"Oh, come on now, Linda. That's a stupid thing to say. Besides, where are we going to move? Westchester, Jersey?"

"I don't know. Maybe. Or Long Island."

"Yeah? And how am I going to work? Everything I do is in the city."

"You could build a nice studio if we had a house or something."

"I can't isolate myself. I won't get any studio sessions, and what about my students?"

"You can't always think of yourself."

"You're calling me selfish? How does worrying about providing for my family make me selfish?"

"I didn't say you were. Look, let's just forget it, okay?"

"No, I can't leave it like this. This family means everything to me."

"I know it does. I'm sorry, I just thought a move might be good for everybody."

"I get what you're saying, but it wouldn't work. Besides, you know what they say, you can run, but you can't hide."

"I know, but I don't want you to turn into one of those crusaders against crime or something."

Cory grabbed his jacket and headed for the door. "If you call wanting justice for what they did to Ava being a crusader, then I'm okay with it."

He walked along Bedford Avenue searching his soul. Was he being unreasonable for wanting to punish those responsible for taking his daughter's liver? No, every parent would demand the same. It was a normal reaction.

But was it justice or revenge that he desired? He admitted wanting them to pay for it, but digging deeper, he didn't want any child or person to be used for parts.

The cops didn't seem to want to put the resources into shutting down the group. It didn't make sense. Did the authorities think illegal transplants helped solve the organ shortage?

He couldn't buy that as the reason. It had to be they were

overwhelmed and had to concentrate resources on killings and rapes.

He understood to a degree but remembered what a high school teacher had taught him about Alexander Hamilton. One of the nation's Founding Fathers had said: *If you don't stand for something, you'll fall for anything.*

He'd come back to that quote many times over the years. It was one of the sayings he invoked when people questioned his decision to donate most of his royalties to fighting childhood cancer.

It was speaking to him again. Cory had to find a way to do something.

29

———————

Shu turned the lights on and put a kettle on the stove. He looked forward to talking to his old friend but needed a jolt of caffeine to start the day.

He steeped his pu-erh tea, watching the water turn inky black. Shu went into his den, slipping behind his desk.

He took a sip and palmed his new Solarin. The sleek, Israeli-made phone was the world's most secure. He appreciated the Party's fascination with security as the clock ticked toward the appointed call time.

He missed seeing Gao. Shu was one of the few who felt he had a genuine friendship with the Party leader. Maybe it was because they knew each other as kids. As the grandchild of a politburo leader, Gao had risen through the ranks.

Gao was feared by many, but Shu believed he was misunderstood. His initiatives were necessary to forge China into the world's leader. Those opposing Gao's programs had enriched themselves running state entities and were unwilling to take risks for the greater good.

The leader believed technology and medicine were the

areas that returned the most on the public relations front. It was a door opener and eased other nations' concerns about freedom. Shu smiled, knowing that when your life was on the line, you didn't care about freedom of speech or what kind of a government ruled you.

Shu's friend had appointed him to oversee an experimental program that had considerable opposition. Looking back, Shu was glad he'd put his reservations aside.

What was learned from operating in the Uighurs had proven invaluable in advancing transplant surgery. It was a brilliant plan: harvesting organs from dissidents detained in internment camps.

The region was a hotbed of anti-China sentiment, and though the leaders were concerned resistance would spread, they opposed Gao's plan. Shu wasn't there during the debates but heard Gao sealed it by pointing out they were having dissidents 'disappear,' so, why not get some value out of them?

The Party was steadfast in its denial the experiments were taking place, but the rumors circulated, helping to tamp down a Turkestan independence movement.

It was the stepping-stone to Shu's other success, the prison program. The pair of wins made Shu's idea to create a program in the United States an easy one for Gao to sanction.

At 5:30, he finished his tea and made the call.

"How are you, my dearest schoolmate?"

"Very well. Getting ready to have dinner with Chan. We're going to the old neighborhood, to Mama Xian."

"Ah, brings back many memories."

"Next time you're in, we'll go back together."

"I'd like that. Remember the time we drank that entire bottle of baijiu?"

Gao laughed. "I still can't drink it without recalling that day."

"Me either. My mother was so angry with me. I was punished for a week."

"I was lucky my father was in Shanghai. My grandfather never said a word. He asked me if I'd learned a lesson; he should only know."

"He was a good man."

"Indeed. How are things in America?"

"Very well."

"What about the expansion?"

"We're taking it slow."

"We agreed to a ramp-up."

"I know, it's just the incident created by Fung has me believing we should proceed cautiously."

"Let me remind you of the proverb our ancestors built this great nation on: *A man grows most tired while standing still.*"

"Don't misunderstand my caution; we're moving ahead."

"It's my belief we must adhere to the plan, including the timeline. We have no time to waste."

Shu wanted to remind his friend of another Chinese proverb—*a little impatience will spoil great plans*—but said, "I understand and will make sure we get back on track."

"Excellent. Now, tell me, are you in a relationship?"

"No, been too busy to even think about it."

"Make time. You're the only one in your family. Who is going to carry on the family name?"

"It'll happen when it does; I can't force it."

"Nothing happens by chance. We must impose our will to secure what we want."

"I was hoping for a relationship you'd see in a China-wood film."

"It sounds like my friend is turning into an idealist. Perhaps you're spending too much time in America."

Shu snickered, "I just don't want an arranged marriage."

"You say it as if people were miserable. You learn to care for each other and build a life together. Do you know marriages brokered by the families end in divorce ten times less than a so-called marriage for love?"

"That's interesting. Speaking of statistics, I must commend you on your initiatives. China now has the shortest wait period for an organ."

"China has shown the world what is possible. Everyone touts the American system as the benchmark, but we've driven wait times down to under two months. In America, it is over three years."

"A laudable achievement. I was honored to play a small role in your plans."

"Shu, you've contributed a great deal. You'll be rewarded when you return home."

"No reward is necessary. I believe in advancing the transplant cause. And uh, um, show the world that China is a capable leader."

"Good, but the Party insists it show its gratitude."

Shu knew the money and positions they gave were more like bribery than a thank you, but said, "I'm grateful for whatever may be bestowed."

"Chan is pointing at the clock. We must get going. It was good to catch up. When can I expect an update?"

"Uh, a couple of days at most. Give my regards to Chan."

Shu took the SIM card out of the phone. It had taken him four years to get where they were. The first year they performed fifteen transplants; the next year they reached twenty-seven. In year three it rose to forty-nine, and this year they were on track to break a hundred.

He'd encountered bumps, but excluding a couple of missteps, their survival rate eclipsed many American hospitals. They hadn't attempted heart or lung transplants, but their unconventional setup had patients being released earlier from less-than-stellar surroundings.

Shu was wary. A significant ramp-up could jeopardize his accomplishment.

30

Cory walked through Little Italy and turned onto Lafayette Street. A plaque proclaimed a small park, Lt. Petrosino Square. Cory thought it was odd. The SOHO refuge was triangular. He saw Black studying passersby from a bench.

"I lived my whole life in the city; where do you come up with these places?"

Black shrugged. "The story behind this one is damn good. Petrosino was a fearless New York City cop in the early nineteen hundreds. He was the first Italian detective on the force, and he tangled with the Black Hand."

"The Black Hand?"

"It's what they called the mafia back then. Petrosino developed a lot of techniques to fight crime they still use today. He even started the city's first bomb squad."

"Wow. What happened to him?"

"He was set up and killed in Sicily. He was getting evidence against scores of convicted criminals who'd moved to America. He's still the only New York cop killed outside the States while on duty."

"They set him up?"

"Yeah. Someone in the department tipped off the mobsters, and they shot him dead. The city gave him some funeral. A couple of hundred thousand people came into the streets to pay their respects."

"Wow. That's incredible."

"He looked out for the regular guy. The store owners were getting shaken down, and he put an end to a lot of it. You should check him out online; nobody could scare him off."

"I will."

Black stared straight ahead but said nothing.

Cory waited ten beats before breaking the silence. "Take a look at these."

Black took Cory's phone. "What temperature?"

"Fifty."

Black handed the phone back. "Not bad."

"I didn't take a shot of it, but I stayed under for a good minute, probably two."

"Told you the breathing works."

"I know, it only felt like fifty-five."

Black smiled. "You can get used to thirty. You just have to work at it."

"I know you don't think I can focus, but playing music requires a super amount of concentration."

"I'm sure it does, but beating the elements, or another man, is another matter."

"Teach me."

"You?"

"Why not? Tell me how to get better control of my mind and emotions."

"You're a musician. The type of stuff you're talking about will kill your creativity."

"It won't. I've been playing music since I can remember. Wrote my first song at nine, for my mom."

"Why would you want to try and learn what I do?"

"It's a good thing to know."

"It's not like learning to skateboard."

"I get it."

"In what I do, it's the difference between life and death."

"Teach me."

"It's a way of life, a state of mind. Like you with the music, I've been doing it forever."

"I'm not looking to get to your level, but I want more control."

"It's not about control. You can only control so much; the key is your reaction."

"Like not being afraid when you're in a dangerous situation?"

"The difference between being a coward or a hero isn't that you don't get scared. It's what action you take while being scared."

"I can do that. It's different, but being on stage is frightening. But you got to do the show."

"Goes way beyond that. It's about saying less, revealing little, giving yourself wiggle room in a jam to disappear when you have to."

"Not trusting anyone."

"Bingo. You can only rely on yourself. Everyone else is a leak, a threat, a potential problem."

"Even family."

"Uh-huh. It's just what it is."

"I really regret calling my wife when you said not to."

Black nodded. "And telling me where you were hiding out."

"Yeah, but it worked out."

"Maybe, but by saying too much, you blew your cover."

"I know. I got lucky."

"Luck is bullshit. What makes the difference is preparation, seeing around corners, and especially, developing sources for info."

"How did you find out about paying illegals for organs?"

"It just made sense. They need the money, and they're invisible."

"You just thought it up?"

He nodded. "You put yourself in their shoes. What would you do if you were them?"

"But bringing them up from the border is risky."

"It's manageable. Any downside is offset by the fact these people need money. Something goes wrong, they aren't going to tell the cops; they'll fade away. Life is cheap where they come from."

"Now they got all the supply they need."

"Looks that way."

"What would you do to shut these guys down?"

"I don't know that you can stop it. If people want something, they'll find ways to get it."

"I get it, but these bastards kidnapped Ava. They took a piece of her liver. I got to do something."

"The best thing you can do is to let it go."

"I can't. I tried, but you know what? I'm her father, I'm her protector."

"I told you from the get-go, these people are sophisticated."

"Tell me what you'd do."

"You've got to get inside the organization. That's the only way to get enough evidence to bring them down. I'm not saying they won't regroup, but it'll put a big hurt on 'em."

"You mean going undercover?"

"Yep."

"How could you do that?"

"It would take time. You'd have to identify someone affiliated with them, gain their trust, and find a position with them."

"They're probably all Chinese. We'd have to find an Asian."

"Or a doctor or nurse."

"You think a doctor would do something like that?"

"Or someone pretending to be a doctor."

"But what if they made him or her do a surgery? They'd have to run."

"A nurse then. Or someone with good medical knowledge of transplants."

"Maybe I could get a nurse from one of Mount Sinai's transplant teams."

"Good idea. They could say they were looking to make extra money."

"Yeah. That would work."

"It'll take time to get them to accept someone from the outside, but once they're in, they'll do damage."

31

———

Cory turned off Avenue A onto East Ninth Street. The heart of the East Village pulsated with activity. Cory patted the money Black had told him to bring. Black was his cryptic self, making Cory excited but nervous over what the operative had planned.

He stopped in front of the Sullivan Street Bakery and checked the storefront's address. They were meeting in a bakery? As a customer left the store, Cory was enveloped in the comforting aroma of bread.

He grabbed the door before it closed and stepped in. Holding a gym bag, Black was talking to a bald man in a full apron. Black pointed to a stairway at the rear of the store.

Cory was halfway up when he heard Black's feet hit the treads. Cory turned around. "This place makes me hungry."

"It's the only place I get bread."

"Everybody says New York has the best bread because of the water."

"Up for debate. The watershed is in the Catskills. During the months-long journey to the city, it picks up a lot of minerals. Some say that's what it is, and others claim it's the production method. I don't care, I just know I like it."

Cory stopped at the landing. Black inserted a key and swung open a door to a room dusted with flour. Cory followed Black down an aisle of supplies to a room with a pair of green-felted tables.

Cory thought about the large sum of money he was carrying. He wasn't a gambler. "We going to play cards?"

"No. Sit in the armchair." Black opened his bag, taking out a small machine with a bunch of accessories.

Cory pointed to a cuff and hose. "Is that for blood pressure?"

"Yes. You need to learn to control your physical reactions." Black took Cory's hands, putting a rubber cap on a finger and pasting a sensor on his other palm. "A good place to start is fooling a lie detector test."

"You can beat those?"

Black nodded as he put two devices on his body and fitted the blood pressure cuff on Cory's upper arm. "It's about measuring your blood pressure, breathing, pulse, and sweat glands. When you lie, they ramp up. The key is to confuse your responses to control questions like what day it is. You need to have your body react like you're lying when you tell the truth."

"How do I do that?"

"There are a couple of ways. The pros bring a stressful situation to mind, increasing their blood pressure and sweat excretion. Others do it by counting backward by sevens. The idea is to control your responses."

"But I'll never have to take a lie detector test."

"Probably not. But I've been forced to when undercover. Either way, you'll learn how to focus, not on what's happening, but your reaction to it."

Black began asking questions, and the machine spit out graph paper with jagged lines. He stopped the test. "You're not trying hard enough. Focus, focus, focus."

Cory failed again. Black said, "Try this." He pulled out a thumbtack. "Put it in your shoe and press your foot on it when answering a control question. The pain will trigger elevated blood pressure and breathing."

"Like they did in *Ocean's Eleven*?"

"I don't watch TV. You could also bite your tongue, but it has to hurt."

"I really don't feel like stabbing myself in the foot."

"It's never a matter of feelings. Emotion kills. You have to do what you have to."

Cory wanted to leave. It didn't seem relative to the seed of an idea he had on stopping the gang.

"Let's go. We have work to do."

Cory slipped a foot out of his sneaker and fingered the tack.

"Put it in next to your big toe."

"Damn!" Cory jabbed himself putting his foot back in.

Black rolled his eyes. "Can't be crying."

Cory wanted to stick the tack in Black's eye. "Go ahead, ask your questions."

"Do you have children?"

Cory lifted his toe and pressed on the tack as he answered yes. Suppressing a grunt, he saw Black nod slightly.

"What month is this?"

Cory repeated the stab.

"Have you ever ridden on a bus?"

"I get the point. I don't want my damn toe to become Swiss cheese."

"Now, try to emulate the reaction without stepping on the thumbtack."

They ran through a series of questions and Black said, "Not bad for the first go-round."

Though his toe hurt, Cory felt a surge of pride. "What else you have planned for me?"

"Let's take a ride to Times Square."

"That where we're going to need the money?"

Black shook his head. "The ten grand was a test, to make sure you were serious."

The sidewalks were packed at the Forty-Third Street and Broadway intersection. Black headed north on Broadway into a sea of people. Cory tried following him.

The operative was a city block ahead when Cory lost sight of him. Cory bounced into a linebacker-sized man. "Sorry, man," he said and saw Black standing outside the Disney store off Forty-Sixth Street.

Cory hugged the building. "How'd you get through all that?"

"Focus on the spaces."

"What?"

"Don't look at anyone, just find the space and go to the next one."

"You didn't bump into one person?"

"Not really, brushed by a couple. Let's do it again. Don't follow me. Focus on where people aren't, and no matter what, don't get distracted."

Black melted into the crowd. When he disappeared, Cory stepped into the flow and headed for the spaces between people. He got half a block without a problem, but when he thought about it, banged into someone.

Cory stepped aside and regrouped before plunging back in. Black had a smile on when Cory emerged at Forty-Third Street. "You're getting the hang of it."

"I guess. It's weird that it works."

"The great race car drivers focus on the spaces between the cars."

"Never thought about it that way."

"The other thing you've got to do is visualize. It's practicing for success."

"You know, when I had to audition for Jay Bird, and he was way at the top then, I was nervous like never before. Then I saw an interview with that skier Lindsey Vonn. She talked about visualizing the ski run before a race. Said when it came time to go, she felt like she'd been on the course a hundred times."

"Yep. You create a reality in your head, and it'll come true."

Cory recalled the audition. He'd imagined doing well over and over, and when it came time to play for Jay Bird, he killed it.

Could he visualize a world without suffering children, without cancer, or illegal organ harvesting? It was unrealistic, he reasoned.

But he could visualize the idea he had to shut down the bastards who kidnapped and maimed Ava. It was dangerous but doable.

32

Cory was shown into Dr. Evans's office. The head of Mount Sinai's transplant unit smiled. "You made a proper appointment. Should I be worried?"

"No. What I want to talk about is super important. I wanted to make sure you had the time."

"Have a seat."

"Mind if I close the door?"

Evans arched an eyebrow. "Go ahead."

As Cory sat, Evans asked, "How is Ava doing?"

"Physically she's doing well. She's going back to school next week. I hope it improves her mood."

"I'm sure it will. What did you think of Dr. Illardi and his team?"

"We liked them, and Ava seems to like them. It makes doing what they tell her easier to swallow."

"In that regard, teenagers and those in their eighties are similar."

"Too young to listen and too old to be told what to do."

"I think that's it. But give Ava some time, she's been through a traumatic experience."

Cory exhaled. "You ain't kidding."

"It'll get better. She needs more time."

"I hope you're right, but she's not herself."

"Keep me apprised. Maybe I can help."

"Thanks."

"What's on your mind?"

Cory filled him in on Black's idea.

"Interesting. I wonder if the police are considering infiltrating the gang."

"I doubt it. The agent running the FBI's investigation said their focus is on following the drugs they use."

"The G-men caught Al Capone for cheating on his taxes."

Cory leaned forward. "What do you think of using one of your doctors or nurses?"

"To go undercover?"

"They're experienced. I bet these guys will jump at the chance."

Evans shook his head. "That's an absurd idea."

"Why?"

"Because they're medical professionals. They don't have the training for a clandestine operation."

"But—"

"No buts. Look, I'm sorry, but there is no way I, or the hospital, could take part in something like that."

"How are we going to stop the butchering?"

Evans exhaled. "Keep doing what you were doing to increase the donor pool. If the wait times come down far enough, no one would take a chance, they'd come inside the system."

"But there's a limit to how many will volunteer."

"A few years ago, I participated in an effort that explored incentives to boost the donor pool."

"I bet it came down to money."

"Outright payment for an organ is illegal, but we came up with some novel ideas. One was having the government offer lifetime Medicare or make a deposit into a retirement account for a donor. Even issuing tuition vouchers for a donor's child was discussed."

"All good ideas. Where did it go?"

"The Feds nixed it. We were surprised, since paying for dialysis treatments has higher long-term costs than a transplant."

"That's the government for you. What other ideas did you come up with?"

"Most were controversial, but one I liked, and I'll deny saying it, was using inmates."

"Forced harvesting like they do in China?"

"No. Hypothetically, say someone is incarcerated for a twenty-year term for robbing a bank. If they're in good health, why not offer a reduction in their prison term, say, cut it down to five years if they agree to donate?"

"Wow. That almost makes too much sense. They pay their debt to society, but with an organ, not by doing time."

"Exactly. You'd have to exclude people like murderers and rapists, but we have about two million people in correctional facilities. It would have had a significant impact on wait times, but it went nowhere."

"It'd be voluntary. What was the argument against it?"

"An old, reliable one—the slippery slope."

"I can see the objections, but something like this should be aired out in public."

"I agree, but unfortunately, the organ shortage is not a priority."

"Until some big-shot politician needs one."

"Maybe."

"I guess we're going to have to wait until we can figure out how to grow organs in a lab."

"There are efforts in that direction, but it's going to take a significant amount of time to become a reality."

CORY WAS HANGING HIS JACKET. Linda sidled up. "Ava's been in a terrible mood."

"All day?"

"Yup."

"Hopefully she'll cheer up when she goes back to school."

"She doesn't want to go. Said it's too early."

"What did these bastards do to our Ava?"

Linda hung her head and Cory embraced her, whispering, "She'll be okay."

"I'm worried."

"This may sound crazy, but it might help if we can get her to visualize herself as she was before all this happened. Visualizing something is a real powerful tool. I use it all the time."

"Since when?"

"Since I started playing. I never thought about it until recently. You know, we should be telling Tommy as well. It really helps. It makes achieving things easier if you can see yourself doing it."

"I heard of that, but I'm not sure how it will help Ava."

"She has to get back to thinking she's normal. How you see yourself is super important."

"I know. I'll work it into a conversation, maybe after dinner."

"Try to use an example of what you did when you were around her age."

"You a psychotherapist now?"

"I hope we don't need to take her for therapy."

"This goes on any longer, we're going to have to."

"If we got to go there, Dr. Bruno is the one. She's the best."

"We'll see."

Cory headed to the studio. "I gotta get moving."

"What are you doing?"

"Gonna do a lesson via Zoom."

"A video lesson?"

"Yeah, a friend of the kid, Reggie, lives in Canada and wants to take lessons."

<hr>

CORY TURNED off the lamp and crawled into bed. "What the heck was Ava crying about?"

"She doesn't know. She said she feels bad. I think it's depression."

"This is frigging crazy. It's not bad enough she was kidnapped and cut open? Now, she's got mental problems?"

"If you remember, Dr. Illardi said it was a possibility. He said she'd get over it."

"Take her to Bruno."

"We need to talk to her about it. Together."

"Okay."

"Good night. I'm beat."

"'Night, love you."

Cory stared at the ceiling as Linda's breathing slowed. How did you start a conversation with your daughter, telling her she needed therapy?

He turned on his side, wondering how the hell this happened. The daughter he knew was drifting away, and it was the gang's fault. The need for revenge quickened his heartbeat.

What could he do? He wanted them dead or behind bars for the rest of their miserable lives, but how?

Though it would take time, Cory felt Black's plan was solid. Having someone inside made a lot of sense. But Evans had shot down the idea that would have provided the police with irrefutable evidence.

Cory rolled Black's scheme around. It was likely the FBI had agents who were doctors or could fake it. Why hadn't they thought of this? Reasoning they had and passed, Cory cycled through options.

Linda moaned in her sleep. Cory gently nudged her. He hoped she wasn't dreaming of Ava, then an idea hit him. Considering the notion, he propped himself up.

He thought it through and swung his legs off the bed. It was dangerous, but he'd do it.

33

SHU OPENED AN INCOGNITO TAB AND PLUGGED AN URL IN. IT routed him to a monitoring station in North Station controlled by China. The video captured by the satellite was first-class and had been stolen from the US military.

He zoomed in on the RV traveling north on Route 95. The vehicle was just outside of Washington, D.C. Shu checked the timeline. The expected arrival time was 3:05 p.m.

Shu smiled. The long journey from Spotford, a small town forty miles from the Rio Grande River, had experienced no delays or unusual activity.

He had three hours to get to Trenton. Though he'd seen pictures of the donors, Shu wanted to personally eyeball the men riding north. The quality of the donors played a critical component in the success rate. Though blood panels were revealing, Shu couldn't take chances.

The next load of donors was originating farther west, from Las Cruces, New Mexico. The coyotes who shepherded people over the border said those crossing at New Mexico were less likely to be from Central America.

That made geographical sense, but what interested Shu was the general health differences.

He sent a text, and a minute later, Li knocked on his door.

"What can I do for you?"

"They're due in three hours. Let's go to lunch before we head to New Jersey."

"Sounds good."

"Bring the car around."

"Will do."

"And release the second load. I want them on the road."

<hr>

"THEY'RE HERE."

Standing behind a one-way window, Shu watched the garage door grind its way open. The light flooding into the warehouse cut down as a gray RV inched in.

The driver got out, unlocking the RV's side door. He stepped up and guided the first donor off. Shu studied the blindfolded man. He was lean but moved purposefully. Though his face had been aged by sun exposure, Shu knew he was around thirty years old.

Shu thumbed through a handful of papers and found the one with a picture matching the man: Eduardo Jimenez, a thirty-two-year-old.

Claiming to be from Mexico City, Jimenez was five feet six inches and had type O blood. Shu marked him as a possible kidney donor, pending HLA comparisons with a recipient.

A second man was led past the window. A scar ran down the muscular man's face. It was Ricardo Vasquez. Shu was glad to see he was fit. Vasquez also had type O blood.

Shu studied the four other men. His people had followed instructions. Shu wanted men in their late twenties and in good health, but even more desirable was having type O blood.

The most common blood type meant they could donate an organ to anyone regardless of the recipient's blood type. It streamlined the process, and Shu was feeling good about the quality of donors.

As a precaution, Shu waited as the men were examined by a physician and underwent MRI imaging. Informed there were no red flags, he gave the go-ahead.

Separated into two groups of three, the men were guided toward two black RVs. As the men were loaded onto the mobile surgical units, Shu and Li left.

Li pulled out of the parking lot. Shu said, "We're going to need a dozen beds in rehab facilities. As long as the donors and recipients are stable, I want them transferred no later than forty-eight hours after surgery."

"No problem. It only gets difficult when a procedure needs to be done at these places. Getting rehab space for recovery is easy. I'll set it up."

"Good. We're going to accelerate the plan."

"I'm ready."

"When are the other RVs going to be outfitted?"

"Two will be ready in a week."

"Make sure they're not late. I've authorized the New Mexico coyotes to supply six a week."

"Tay bought six RVs for transport."

"Did he spread the buy?"

"Yes. Two each from Minnesota, Michigan, and Ohio."

"I trust from different dealers."

"Yes. None from the same county. I double-checked the receipts."

Shu nodded. "Pick up another three. With more frequent trips, we'll have to rotate the units."

"I'll get them ASAP."

"I'd like you to head down to Arizona, by Lukeville. There's a national park called Organ Pipe Cactus."

"Interesting name."

"It's the only place that type of cactus grows. It's an excellent source of hydration and calories, making it a draw for illegals crossing by themselves."

"They go without a guide?"

"Many do. I'd like to see if we can cut the middleman out. We'd increase our margins and reduce our exposure to outsiders."

"I like that. We've got to keep an eye on the size of the circle."

"And remind everyone not to let their guard down."

"I'll reinforce the point."

"Gao is sending four new surgeons and six nurses over."

"At the same time?"

"It'll be staggered over a couple of weeks, but they'll need housing and transportation. The first will arrive on the tenth."

"We'll get on it."

"Don't base anyone in the city. Look at Southern and Central Jersey, Connecticut, and Pennsylvania. And no doubling up, it'll arouse suspicion."

"Can we still use working in tech as a cover?"

"Yes, but something different. Let's use an artificial intelligence start-up."

"Perfect."

"I'm going to be taking a trip to Beijing. I'll only be away for three days, but you're going to have your hands full. Get together with Tay. He'll have to take some of your responsibilities."

"We'll be fine. Enjoy the trip. When are you going?"

"Day after tomorrow. I don't want anyone to know I'm going."

"No worries. Can I help you prepare for the trip?"

"Just the standard arrangements."

34

Cory walked down Fifty-Third Street. He had never heard of Paley Park and Googled where it was. He knew there were no parks around here and thought he had made a mistake with the location.

There was an opening between two buildings, and he wondered if that was the park. He took another step, noticing a wall of a building covered in leaves.

It had to be the park, he thought, and picked up his pace. He turned into the small space, taking in the water that cascaded down the building at the rear of the park.

Black was in one of the white chairs scattered among a handful of trees growing out of the cement. He faced the water. The sound of the water covered the blare of the city.

Cory was a couple of steps from Black when Black turned and motioned to the chair beside him. Cory wondered how he sensed his presence.

"I never knew this place existed."

"It's a pocket park. Paley, the guy who ran CBS, built it. It's a good place to think."

"Yeah, the water drowns everything out."

"Eighteen hundred gallons a minute will do that."

"Wow. That's a crazy amount of water."

"How's your daughter?"

"Not so good. I mean, physically she's doing good, but she's depressed."

"Could be PTSD."

"Nah, nothing like that. I think she's just afraid."

"Good reason to be."

"This whole thing has got me crazy. I got to get back at these guys."

"You want revenge?"

"Damn right I do."

"The best revenge is one that's gone too far."

Cory hesitated. "All I want to do is bust those bastards up. They can't be swiping kids off the street and cutting them open."

"They changed tactics. They're using illegals, bringing them up from the border."

"Look, I thought a lot about what you said about taking them down from the inside."

"Infiltration works, no doubt."

"I got an idea how to do it."

"These guys are sophisticated; it's unlikely they'll trust anyone right away."

"I get that, but since they're bringing donors up from the border—why not use a donor? We'd get information on how they transport them and where they perform the operations. We let the police know, and they shut them down."

Black shook his head. "How are you going to get an illegal to cooperate? They're not going to trust you, especially if you're going to bring the cops in."

"What if I did it?"

"Did what?"

"Posed as an illegal willing to sell a kidney."

Black smiled. "You? Forget it."

"Why? Why can't I do it?"

"Look, I get you're pissed over what happened to your kid. It's natural. But this is dangerous. They find out, and you're a dead man."

"I know it's risky but—"

"Besides the fair chance of getting killed, you wouldn't get the goods on the higher-ups as a patient. You'd get the driver, some medical staff, but not those running it."

"The cops could lean on them, get them to turn."

"These guys have a couple of layers between them."

"But it would disrupt them. Make them back off."

"Until the heat died down."

"It's worth doing it."

"You tell your wife about your dream to go undercover?"

"It's no dream. I've thought this through."

Black shook his head. "It's too dangerous."

"You going to help me or not?"

"Me? What do you want me to do?"

"Your advice and contacts. I'm going to need to get in touch with the guys they use to supply donors."

"They're using coyotes to bring people over the border. All those guys give a damn about is money. You pay them enough, they'll do anything. Those guys aren't afraid of anyone, Chinese or whatever."

"So, becoming a donor isn't a problem?"

"You're whiter than milk. You'd stand out."

"There's plenty of skin tanning products that last two to three weeks."

"There's a risk someone will recognize you."

"I'll change my appearance, like the time I went on the run. You said it looked good."

"You've got this all figured out, don't you?"

"No. I need help with recording everything. You can get me the special equipment I'd need. You know, like, real small cameras and mics. You can get that kinda stuff, right?"

"This isn't a game of spy. These guys wouldn't hesitate to kill you. And you've got to make it out of Mexico first."

"I'm not looking to get killed. I just think it will work. Say it wasn't me but somebody like you doing it. Do you think it'd work?"

"It could."

"Just could? What are the holes in it?"

"You, to start with. But let's say you're a donor. How do you know you're not going to be strip-searched or drugged?"

"Can't you get information from someone who's gone through it?"

"We can track somebody back to their home. They are paid not to talk, but you can be sure, if it was a good experience, they'd spill some of it."

"Super. I'd know what to expect. Now, what can we use to document what's going on?"

"There's a couple of microscopic cameras and mics—"

"Microscopic?"

"Equipment the intelligence community uses. But it's all useless if you're naked or unconscious. Then, not only can't you film anything, but you'd also be light an organ when you wake up. You ready for something like that?"

"It won't happen. I'd bust out of there if it came to that."

"You think these guys aren't armed?"

"There may be a security guard or something, but the cops will be on standby. I'd signal them, and they'd save me."

Black scoffed. "Just like on TV, right?"

"I know this isn't a game, okay? If we work out the

details, nothing will happen to me, and we'll nail these bastards."

"No. I don't like it."

"Can you think about it? With your help, it could be perfect. I'll do it any way you say."

Black stood. "I'll roll it around."

"Thanks, man."

Black took a step and turned around. "I don't know anything about being married, but you'd better talk to your old lady about this."

35

SHU ROLLED HIS LUGGAGE THROUGH BEIJING CAPITAL Airport. He saw his name on a placard and signaled. The driver rushed over. "Mr. Shu, let me take your baggage."

"No. I've got them."

"You sure?"

"Where's the car?"

"Outside door ten."

Shu placed his suitcase on the back seat and sat in the passenger seat. "How's the traffic today?"

"The usual, sir."

"How long till we reach the Peninsula?"

"Uh, we're not going to the hotel, sir. I was told to drive you to Mama Xian's."

Shu smiled. Gao was making good on his promise to go to their old stomping grounds.

As the car slogged its way toward the world's most populous city, Shu looked at the skyline. He hadn't counted them but was sure there were ten more cranes than two months ago.

The sleek, modern skyscrapers were on the verge of

becoming the majority of structures. Shu marveled at the speed with which China was transforming itself.

More progress had occurred in the last twenty years than in the centuries before. Shu believed it was more proof the state-run economic system was superior to capitalism. He calculated it would only be a few short years before China took its rightful place as the world's leader.

A pang of emotion hit Shu as the car turned down a narrow street. The old neighborhood was changing. The sidewalks were crowded with people buying food from the carts that lined the street. He remembered shopping on this street with his mother.

Shu craned his neck and smiled. The candy wagon was surrounded by children. Shu's mother always bought him White Rabbit Candy and Haw flakes from the same stand.

Wondering whether he'd want to live in the area, the car turned and slowed. "Here we are, sir."

The red and gold lettering on Mama Xian's window needed a touch-up. Shu grabbed his baggage and walked into the eatery. The comforting smells reminded him he was home.

He searched the tables as the owner's son approached. They caught up quickly, and he showed Shu to the private room in the rear. The men seated around a table were chatting. Gao smiled and rose.

A man Shu recognized as an assistant took Shu's suitcase as Gao embraced his friend. "So good to see you."

"Same here, my friend."

"You've lost weight."

"Sometimes I work so much I forget to eat."

Gao turned to the table. "You all know my old friend and party stalwart, Park Shu."

As the group stood, Shu was given a glass of baijiu. Gao

raised his glass. "Ganbei." Everyone emptied their cups. Shu shook hands with everyone, and Gao led him to a chair. "Sit here, next to me."

"You didn't have to do this."

"I wanted to honor you. We're proud of the success of your operation."

"I couldn't have done anything without your support and guidance."

Gao nodded. "How is the expansion progressing?"

"The southern supply chain made its first delivery. The quality of donors was better than expected. I approved a second collection point."

"How many per week can we expect?"

"The plan is to transport six per week, from three locations, for a total of eighteen."

"Do you have the resources necessary?"

"We're in the process of securing more vehicles. I believe we have what we need."

"Operate for a month at that level, then add an additional run per week. That would double the volume. Can you handle that?"

"It's a bit too fast. I'd like to iron out what we have just set in place."

"But you have a month. That's more than enough."

Before Shu could speak, Gao stood. He raised his glass. "Another toast to Shu. He has brought much honor to the Party. Let's wish him continued success as he expands his operation."

Everyone knocked back their booze, and their glasses were refilled.

"You know, Shu and I grew up a couple of streets from here. We used to come to this very restaurant. Today, in honor of Shu, we will enjoy a special feast. I hope you're hungry."

36

———————

BEFORE CORY HIT THE SIDEWALK, HE WORRIED ABOUT WHAT Linda would say. She would never be on board with his plan. He wondered how to bring the subject up.

The thought hit him to disappear without telling her. He'd done that when he went into hiding. It had worked, but this was different.

Last time, Black had cautioned him about saying a word to anyone. Now, Black made a point of him talking to his wife about the plan. Was that because he believed she'd force him to abandon it?

Cory slipped through a closing subway car door. He considered whether Black would help him with his scheme. He realized if the operative said no, it was over. It was not only too risky, but Cory didn't have the contacts to get inside nor the equipment necessary to record the illegal activities.

Cory couldn't envision leaving the group free to continue with their off-the-grid transplants. He vowed to hound the police and his congressmen and continue raising the issue of becoming a donor if he couldn't bring them down.

CORY BOLTED INTO THE APARTMENT. Linda was in the kitchen. "Is that you?"

"Yeah, I'm late. The train stopped for, like, fifteen minutes. I thought they'd have to evacuate us."

"The subway is so run-down it's disgusting. And they'd better do something about the crime, or nobody is going to ride it."

"I know. How's Ava?"

"The same. She hardly ate anything for lunch."

Cory exhaled. "What are we going to do?"

"I called Dr. Bruno."

"What did she say?"

"She wants to see her and go from there."

"When is the appointment?"

"Day after tomorrow."

"Good. Bruno is the best. She'll help Ava get over this."

"I hope so."

"She will. Look, I got to get my guitar and run. I have three lessons."

"All right. I'll save you something for dinner."

CORY HUNG HIS GUITAR UP. The apartment was quiet. He went to Tommy's room. Linda was reading to him.

"Hey, little man. How are you?"

"Dad, I got a ninety-two on my spelling test."

"Super. You're a better speller than me."

Linda said, "Than I."

"Oops, a better speller than I."

"Hey, Dad, I scored over a hundred thousand points on the *Avenger* game."

"Wow. I'm gonna have to practice."

Linda said, "It's getting late. You've got to get to sleep."

Cory kissed the top of Tommy's head. "Good night, pal. I'll see you in the morning."

Cory knocked on Ava's door. "You up?"

He knocked again and cracked open the door. "Ava?"

His daughter was on the bed in a fetal position. "You okay?"

She shrugged.

Cory sat on the edge of her bed. She'd been crying. "What's the matter, sunshine?"

"I don't know."

He rubbed her back. "It's okay. You know, what you're feeling is normal. You'll get over it. Mom said she made an appointment with Dr. Bruno."

"I don't want to go."

"It'll be good for you."

"I'm not going."

"Do you know that I went to see her?"

"You?"

"Yes. I was having some problems, and she helped me work it out. It didn't take long. Why don't you give it a shot?"

"I don't know."

"Just think about it. I can come with you if you want. But you'll talk to her in private, and she can't tell us what you talk about. So don't worry."

"Okay."

"You want to watch a movie or something?"

"I don't feel like it."

"You want some ice cream?"

"I'm not a baby."

"I didn't say you were. I'm just trying to cheer you up."

"Just leave me alone. Okay?"

"Okay, sunshine. I love you. Good night."

He closed the door behind him and went into the family room. Linda was on the couch. He said, "Ava's a frigging mess."

"What did she say?"

"She was crying. I don't get why she feels like she does."

"Should I go see her?"

"She wants to be left alone."

"She can't keep isolating herself."

"Let's see what Bruno can do with her."

"She said she doesn't want to go."

"I know. She said the same thing to me. But I told her that she fixed me up, and it seemed to help."

"I don't want to force her, but we might have to."

"She'll come around. Don't nag her about it."

"When is this going to end? I want my daughter back."

"Those bastards did this to her, to us."

"How did this happen? How can these people do this?"

"Nobody is doing anything. I called Detective Grillo, but he had nothing to say."

"I can't believe it."

"Believe it. The police are going after killers and drug dealers. These animals are a low priority."

"That's nuts. They're letting them get away with it."

"I won't let them."

"What are you going to do?"

Cory explained his plan to infiltrate the transplant operations as a donor.

"Are you crazy?"

"I know it sounds out there, but it's the only thing that'll work."

"Then let the police do it."

"They're not doing shit."

"Keep pushing them. It's their job, not yours."

"I know but—"

"But nothing! You got us into this in the first place."

Cory leapt up. "You're blaming me for what happened?"

"They came after us because you were out there crusading."

"That's bullshit and you know it."

"Yeah? What about the threat they made to stop you from going to the press?"

"I had no idea they'd do something like they did. My kids mean the world to me. I would never put them in harm's way."

"I know that, and it's why I'm saying it's not worth the risk. Look at Ava, she's a total mess."

Cory hung his head. "You're right. If something more happened to them, I'd never be able to live with myself."

37

———————

Cory and Linda sat in Dr. Bruno's waiting room. They had to coax Ava to go see the therapist, but before she went in, her mood seemed to improve.

He wondered how Bruno would open the conversation. She was a world-class listener who somehow got people to spill their guts. Cory smiled at the thought of Black going to see the therapist. Would she be able to get him to open up?

Black was the most different person Cory had ever met. He was incredibly guarded, but Cory felt he'd loosened up with him. They weren't buddies, but they'd built a relationship.

Cory knew Black had been right. Again. Linda's reaction to hearing his plan to pose as a donor ended it before it began. Cory was torn over giving up, but Linda was right, he had to be super cautious.

He wracked his brain trying to come up with something else, but everything had downsides. There had to be a way to put a major hurt on these criminals, and he would find it.

Cory wanted to hear what other options Black had. There must be something they could do. He'd give it another day before reaching out to the operative. Cory needed time to think of an excuse as to why he was abandoning becoming an infiltrator.

He wanted to save face with Black. Though he acknowledged he had no marriage experience, Cory didn't want the operative to get ideas about Cory's makeup.

Cory was searching his mind for a way to mobilize Black into action when Linda put down her magazine. "What do you think they're talking about?"

"I don't know. Probably about how she feels about what happened."

"I never thought I'd be sitting in a psychologist's office, no less for my kid."

"Tell me about it. But at least we have a place to go for help."

Linda took Cory's hand. "I guess so. Let's hope she doesn't need to keep coming."

"It's going to take a couple of visits."

"I can live with that. It's been forty-five minutes already."

"We having fun yet?"

"We have to say something to Tommy."

"Just tell him Ava is going to a doctor. He doesn't need to know any more."

"You sure?"

"A hundred percent."

The door opened. Ava stepped out. Her eyes were red. Linda popped up and put her arm around her. "How you doing, honey?"

Dr. Bruno said, "She did wonderfully. I'd like to see her Thursday, if that's okay."

Cory said, "The day after tomorrow?"

"Yes. Will that work?"

Cory looked at his wife. "Uh, yeah. That's good, right, Linda?"

His wife nodded as Dr. Bruno said, "Can I have a moment, Mr. Lupinski? There's insurance paperwork that needs to be completed."

"Sure."

Linda said, "We'll head downstairs and get something to drink."

"I'll meet you in the deli."

Cory followed Bruno into her office. "Have a seat. I used insurance as a ruse. I'm concerned about Ava, and since she's still a minor, felt it necessary to convey some of what we discussed."

"What did she say?"

"She's experienced a traumatic incident. I believe she's suffering from PTSD."

"Like what soldiers get?"

"Post-traumatic stress disorders develop when someone undergoes a distressing event. Soldiers often experience it, as well as victims of sexual or physical assault."

"Are you sure that's what she has?"

"No diagnosis is completely accurate, but she's exhibiting symptoms."

"What kind of symptoms?"

"Quite a few, but she's having flashbacks, is unable to sleep, and doesn't feel safe."

"She hasn't left the house. How can she feel unsafe?"

"Ava is afraid whoever did it will do it again."

"She said that?"

"Yes. It's a common feeling."

"What can we do to help her?"

"Make her feel as comfortable as possible, at all times. We want her to feel things will improve over time. Ava must believe there is a path out of the darkness. We can't have her thinking the only way to end it is to take her life."

Cory leaned forward. "You think she'll commit suicide?"

"I don't believe so, but suicide rates among sufferers of PTSD are significantly higher than the general population."

"What did she tell you? That she was thinking of doing it?"

"No."

"So why are you saying that?"

"If I thought she was a danger to herself, I'd remand her into a safe environment. She's not, but I wouldn't be acting responsibly if I didn't alert the parents of the risk, no matter how small it may be."

"What do we do, Doc?"

"Act normally around her and support her as much as you can. Avoid putting her in a stressful situation. Try and make her surroundings as safe as possible."

Cory burst through the door. Linda and Ava were sitting in the waiting room.

"I thought you guys were getting something to drink."

"Ava didn't feel like it. She wanted to wait for you."

"All right then, let's get going."

When they stepped outside, Cory moved next to Ava's side. Linda said, "You want a drink?"

Ava shook her head.

"Okay, let's head to the subway."

Cory said, "No. Let's grab a cab."

"A cab?"

"Yep." Cory stepped off the curb and held his arm up. Ten seconds later, a yellow taxi pulled up and they got in. The cab turned west onto Twenty-Third Street. Cory hoped for traffic. He was dreading letting Linda know what Bruno said.

38

Back in their apartment, Cory locked the door and closed the blinds. Linda said, "You've got to pick up Tommy in an hour."

"Can you see if Joann can drop him off?"

"Why?"

He lowered his voice, "We should stay with Ava."

"What did Bruno say?"

"I'll tell you later."

"Tell me now."

"Make sure Ava is okay first."

Linda went into her daughter's room and a minute later came back. "She's going to take a shower."

"Keep her door open."

"Why?"

Cory pointed to their bedroom, and Linda followed him in. He closed the door and explained what Bruno said about the chance of suicide. Tears streamed down Linda's face, and Cory helped her sit on the bed.

She put her face in her hands. "Tell me this is a dream."

"We'll help her get over this. Bruno said we have to make her feel safe."

"She doesn't leave the house. How can she feel threatened?"

"Ava told Bruno she thinks the bastards who did it are going to get her again."

"But that's crazy."

"It's how her mind is working."

"Do you think Bruno can help her overcome it?"

"I hope so. But if they caught the bastards, she wouldn't be worrying about them."

"You should tell Grillo and that FBI lady how this is affecting Ava."

"They don't care."

"If they have kids, they will."

"While we're waiting on somebody to do something, our daughter is suffering."

"Call them. It's worth trying."

"Go check on Ava. I'll go in the studio and make the calls."

Cory hung up and dialed again. "I want to talk to Detective Grillo."

"Who's calling?"

"Cory Lupinski."

"Hold on, sir."

"I *was* holding, for ten minutes."

"I'm sorry, sir, but Detective Grillo is very busy. Why don't you leave your number, and he'll call you back?"

"Why? I'll tell you why. Because I'm still waiting for a callback from last week."

"I'll let him know you called again. Is this a good number to reach you?"

"Yeah, goodbye."

Cory made another call. "Detective Belfi."

"Hi, it's Cory Lupinski."

"Hello, sir, how can I help you?"

"That's easy. Catch the bastards who kidnapped and mutilated my daughter."

"I'm sorry, sir. But that investigation is being handled by Detective Grillo."

"He never calls me back."

"Sorry about that, but the department is overwhelmed. You can thank the mayor and city council for slashing our budget. We have twenty percent less manpower, and crime is exploding."

"So, the hell with finding the bastards who mutilated Ava?"

"No. It's just that we're putting out fires and trying to keep thugs from killing as many people as we can. We just don't have the resources we used to."

"That's bullshit."

"Tell that to city hall, not me. Now, is there something I can help you with?"

"What's going on with shutting down the illegal transplant ring?"

"I'm afraid there's not been much progress. We've had to back-burner it, but you've spoken to the Feds before. Give Knox a call."

Cory hung up. Everyone who lived in the city knew crime was rising and the police budget had been slashed. They were also dealing with the new no-bail policy, putting criminals back on the street hours after committing a crime.

Cory wondered if Linda was right. When she suggested the family move, he'd dismissed it. Scrolling through his phone for the FBI agent's number, he wrestled with whether it was time to move.

As he waited for the agent to answer, Cory tossed around whether leaving the city would help Ava.

"Agent Knox."

"Hi, this is Cory Lupinski."

"Yes, Mr. Lupinski. What can I do for you?"

"I want to know where you're at with taking down the transplant ring."

"There's not much I can elaborate on."

"Last time you told me the DEA was involved. Are they making progress?"

"There's been a pause in the investigation. The new administration has redirected their attention to an initiative tamping down the proliferation of fentanyl."

"So, these thugs are free to do what they want?"

"Of course not. You asked about DEA's involvement, and I answered your question. The FBI's investigation is ongoing."

"I don't care about the DEA, the FBI, or any other alphabet-soup agency. I want to know when you're going to catch the bastards who took my daughter's liver."

"As I said, our investigation is ongoing."

"What the hell does ongoing mean? What exactly are you doing?"

"I can't discuss an active investigation."

"You're hiding behind that bullshit?"

"Please don't use vulgar language, or I'll have to end this call."

"Vulgar? 'Bullshit' is vulgar? Give me a break, man."

"Goodbye, Mr. Lupinski."

Cory tossed the phone on his desk. "Damn it!" He brought his hand back to swipe the top of the desk clean and stopped in midair. He had to maintain control.

Cory leaned back, closing his eyes. He inhaled to a count

of three. He held it a beat and released it slowly. Cory repeated the breathing exercise he'd learned.

He felt his heart rate slow, and his mind cleared. His daughter was in trouble. It wasn't easy, but he had to shove his emotions aside.

Cory had to focus, not react. He opened his laptop. First item on the agenda was getting cameras and an alarm for the apartment. They'd think about moving, but there were several months left on their lease.

Cory looked at two listings and bought the cheaper package of video surveillance. He wasn't concerned with how well they worked. It was all about showing Ava she was safe. He paid with PayPal and went to check on Ava.

In her pajamas, Ava was curled up on the bed, and Linda was sitting next to her.

"How's it going?"

"She's tired."

"Hey, Ava, I wanted to let you know I ordered some cameras, and we're getting an alarm installed."

Linda said, "What? Why'd you do that?"

"It's time we got better security."

"Oh, that's a good idea, right, Ava?"

Ava shrugged. "It's up to you."

"I'm going to do everything possible to keep our family safe."

"Okay. I want to take a nap."

"You should do some of the schoolwork they sent home."

"I don't feel like it."

Cory said, "It's okay. You can do it after your nap."

As they left the room, Ava said, "Close the door."

"I'll keep it open a crack, in case you need us."

They retreated to the living room. Linda lowered her voice, "What's with the alarm and cameras?"

"Bruno said she didn't feel safe. This might help."

"I hope so. What did the police say?"

"Bunch of nonsense. With budget cuts, they don't have the manpower, blah, blah, blah."

"How could they—"

"It doesn't matter."

"What do you mean?"

"Look, it's up to us. I'm through depending on anybody else."

39

Cory and Linda were in bed. When Linda turned over for the fifth time, Cory said, "Relax. Try breathing in slowly and exhaling to a count of five. Concentrate on your diaphragm, expanding as it receives the air."

"You're teaching meditation now?"

"It's not meditation, or maybe it is, whatever, just clear your mind, or you'll never get to sleep."

"I can't sleep. I'm afraid she's going to do something stupid."

"I'll check on her every two hours and make sure she's still sleeping."

"She could be faking it."

"I can tell. You just have to watch the way she's breathing."

"You can tell?"

"Yes. I'll check every two hours. Go to sleep."

"You're setting the alarm?"

"I don't need it. All I have to do is tell myself to get up when I need to, and I will."

"Now you're a robot, too?"

"No. It works. Go to sleep."

Cory silently repeated a message to get up in two hours. Satisfied it had sunk in, he cleared his mind to concentrate on his breathing. A couple of minutes later he felt his eyes closing.

Cory rolled on his side and opened his eyes. He'd woken up in two hours. He tiptoed out of the room and slipped into Ava's bedroom. He watched her chest rise and fall. Satisfied she was in a deep sleep, he went back to bed.

FILLING the coffee machine with water, Linda trudged into the kitchen. She said, "I didn't sleep at all last night."

"You were super restless."

"Sorry for keeping you up."

Cory put a pod into the coffee maker. "You didn't. I slept good."

"You did?"

"Yep, even checked on Ava every two hours."

"She was okay?"

"Sleeping like a baby."

"I can't stop worrying about her."

"It's tough, but if you set your mind to it, you'll do it." He dug his phone out. "Here, look at these."

"A pool? What are you doing in a pool?"

"It was super cold. Just fifty degrees."

"When did you do that?"

"A little while back."

"Why?"

"To prove I could. You know, to control my reaction to my surroundings."

"You're talking like a teenager."

"I'm just trying to get control. It's like shutting out everything else so you can put your energy into what you're trying to do."

"I don't see how jumping into freezing water does any good."

"It's just training. If you stay in the water and not freak out, you can do anything."

"This is crazy, and it's not going to help Ava."

"It may not seem related, but it helps to focus on what we can do to help her. Less worry and more action."

"What kind of action? She won't even talk to us about what's bothering her."

"As long as she talks to Bruno, we'll find out what's going on with her."

"I never thought I'd be wishing it were tomorrow so we'd be going to see Bruno."

***

BRUNO WAS WEARING a navy-blue pants suit. She smiled. "Hello, Ava. How are you today?"

"Okay."

"Your blouse is cute. It goes beautifully with your eyes."

Ava shrugged.

"Come in. Make yourself comfortable." She waved at Cory and Linda and shut the door.

Cory dug into his backpack. He pulled out earbuds and a notepad.

"What are you doing?"

"Working on the lyrics for a track I just wrote."

"How can you do that here?"

"Easy. You have to focus, that's all."

"How can you focus while our daughter is in there?"

"Sitting around worrying isn't helping anybody. Why not make use of the time?"

"The only thing that counts is her well-being."

"Well, if I'm not earning enough to support the family, all our well-being is going to suffer."

"You know what I mean."

"It's not easy, but we have to stop spending energy on things that don't help and concentrate on doing what we can to help her."

"You sound like a self-help guru."

"I'll take that as a compliment."

"Ha, ha."

"No, seriously, hon, try to stop worrying and look for something to help her."

"Like what? I don't know what to do."

"What about reaching out to her friends. Maybe you can find a way to get them to accidentally pop over to see Ava."

"I've tried that."

"Try again."

"I can't do it."

"You can do anything you set your mind to. Keep trying. You'll see, it gets better. Try taking a couple of deep breaths."

She inhaled deeply. "Like this?"

"No. Breathe in through your nose. But do it slowly and exhale through your mouth."

Linda did as instructed.

"Good. Anytime your mind starts wandering, do the breathing."

"Okay."

Cory put his buds in and played the song he'd composed. He restarted it, playing the first four bars. Then he toyed with words, looking for a rhyme that fit the gratefulness theme he wanted to express.

He'd written a phrase and a half when the door to Bruno's office opened. Ava was staring at the floor. Bruno said, "We did some wonderful work today. If possible, it'd be a good idea to talk again on Monday."

Linda rose. "Sure. That's fine. We'll see you Monday."

"Mr. Lupinski, the insurance company sent a request for you to authorize payments. Can you sign them for me?"

Cory shoved his things into the backpack. "Sure."

He stepped into her office, and she closed the door. "We had an interesting session today."

"Interesting?"

"Yes. I'd like to suggest that when you speak with your wife about Ava that you ensure you're talking privately."

"I don't understand."

"She overheard you telling your wife the police weren't doing anything about apprehending those responsible for what happened to her."

"She did?"

"Yes, and it heightened her fears they'll come after her again. Her paranoia over this gang seems to have worsened."

"I feel terrible."

"Don't. Though it confirmed her belief, her anxieties are deeply rooted. She's afraid of these people."

"I know she has a right to be scared, but it's overblown."

"It's irrational because she's unable to define the threat they pose. The fact she doesn't know what they look like actually adds to the fear. In her mind, it can be anyone and everyone."

"Geez. It's terrible to be afraid. She say anything else?"

"She's been dreaming of getting retribution."

"Like what?"

"Dreaming she kills the people responsible for assaulting her."

Cory's shoulders sagged. "Oh boy."

"Subconsciously, she's acting out her desire for revenge."

40

———

Cory motioned with his hand to let Linda know he wanted to talk. He headed into the bedroom. She followed him, and he pointed to the bathroom. He closed the door behind them.

"What's going on that we have to talk in the bathroom?"

"Ava told Bruno she heard us saying that the police weren't doing anything to catch the gang."

"Oh my God. Poor Ava. I'm heartbroken."

"I know."

"She's terrified of them."

"It's crazy how scared she is. She told Bruno again that she thinks they're going take her again."

"I know you're against it, but we've got to move. It'll help Ava if we do."

"I'd do it for her, but I asked Bruno about moving, and she said being in new surroundings would make things worse for Ava."

"Really? Even if it was far away?"

"That's what she said. I get it, though."

"Mom? Dad?"

Linda pulled open the door. "Yes, honey."

"I didn't know where you were. I thought you left."

"We would never leave you alone."

Her eyes filled with tears. "I thought no one was home."

Linda put her arm around Ava. "There'll always be someone with you. You don't have to worry about that. Either Daddy or I will be home. All the time, you'll never be alone."

Ava's face crumpled and she began to cry.

"It's okay. You were scared. But we're here, there's nothing to cry about. Come on, let's go in the kitchen. We'll get dinner started."

TOMMY WAS IN THE SHOWER. Linda came out of Ava's bedroom. Cory said, "Come here, I need you to listen to this riff I just wrote."

They went into the studio. Cory said, "I never finished telling you what Bruno said."

"What else did she say?"

"That Ava said she dreams of killing the people who did it to her."

"Oh my God. That's horrible."

"Bruno said it's normal, that Ava is expressing a need for revenge."

"I don't like that. She has so much anger in her."

"Bruno said it's typical after what she went through. She said if they catch these guys, it will go a long way toward making Ava feel secure again."

"Why don't you call Detective Grillo?"

"They're useless. They're up to their eyes in murders."

"Then call the FBI."

"By the time they stop these guys, Tommy will be driving."

"We should go to the press and make a stink. They'll be forced to get on the case."

"But they'll come after us again."

"Yeah, yeah. Forget that."

"The only way to end this is to do it myself."

"Don't you dare, Cory. Stop with that nonsense."

"It's a good idea."

"Yeah, if you want to get killed."

"Don't be an alarmist."

"Alarmist? Going undercover to sell an organ, that's not crazy?"

"Not if you do it right."

"And you have experience at this?"

"Mr. Black has a ton of experience. I'd be working with him on it."

"He wants to do it himself, go for it. There's no way you're going to be some kind of spy."

There was a light knock on the door. "Dad? Can you help me with my homework?"

Opening the door, Cory said, "Sure, tiger."

CORY WAS DREAMING. Linda bolted out of bed. "What's the matter?"

"Ava's screaming."

The couple dashed to their daughter's room. Ava was going between wailing and moaning.

"Ava. Ava. Wake up."

Beads of sweat dotted her forehead. She opened her eyes. "I had a horrible dream."

"It's okay, honey. It's only a nightmare."

Ava gasped, "They were taking my heart. My chest was being cut open. And they, they were laughing at me. I couldn't move. My arms were tied. I couldn't stop them."

Linda embraced her. "Oh honey, I'm sorry."

Ava sobbed. "I'm so afraid. I know they're going to get me again."

Cory said, "No. That's crazy. They would never do that."

Ava shook out of Linda's embrace. "How do you know that?"

"I just do."

She shook her head and buried her face in a pillow.

Linda rubbed her back. "Honey, there's nothing to be scared of. We're here for you."

"No one can stop them."

"That's not true. It was just a bad dream."

Ava bolted upright, pulling her pajama top up. "Yeah? Then how'd I get this?"

"Dad?"

Tommy stood in the doorway. "Go to sleep, Tommy."

"What's the matter?"

"Ava's had a bad dream. It's nothing. Go back to bed."

"Again? She woke me up the last two nights."

Cory walked his son back to his room. "You got to tell me if something is going on with your sister. If we don't know, we can't help."

"She's afraid the bad guys are coming back."

"You don't believe they will, do you?"

Tommy shrugged. "I don't know. I guess I'm a little afraid too."

Cory tussled his son's hair. "There's nothing to be scared about. The police will get them."

"What's taking them so long?"

"They have a lot of crimes to deal with."

"They should get more policemen."

"They are. It just takes time to train them. Now, get back to sleep."

Crawling back into bed, Linda said, "She is getting worse."

"Tommy said she's been having nightmares. I wish he would've said something."

"I feel bad he has to see all this."

"Hate to tell you, but he's also afraid these guys are going to come after them again."

"Oh no. What are we going to do?"

Cory propped himself on an elbow. "I know you're against it, but we don't have a choice."

"What are you talking about?"

"Working with Mr. Black to infiltrate the gang."

"It's too dangerous."

"You don't know Black. He's super cautious."

"There's no way you're the one doing it."

"Don't worry, I won't."

"If he wants to go undercover, and it has to be him, and you keep your distance, I guess I'm okay with it."

41

Shu finished reading a research paper and closed the encrypted document. The confidential report, from Johns Hopkins Medicine, featured preliminary results of a clinical trial.

The latest hack contained valuable information. Hopkins had tested a regimen of immune-suppressing drugs, reducing organ rejection rates by 8 percent. Shu's operation was using the same drugs but with different dosages and combinations.

Shu smiled. He'd instruct his people to administer the medicines in accordance with the report. Obtaining the information before it could be widely adopted would give him an edge. He calculated the American bureaucracy would delay full-scale implementation for a year.

He opened a spreadsheet, putting in a password to gain access. He scrolled down the rows of countries to Argentina. Gao had secured inside information from Argentina's Ministry of Health.

Public records had understated transplant waiting times in the South American country. The true wait time exceeded a decade for livers and six years for a kidney. Authorities cited the poor recovery rate of donors for the increase.

Argentina's economic problems were covered by the news, but Shu knew there were plenty of rich Argentines. He'd target them, as he had the Canadians. It would bring a fresh stream of people willing to pay top dollar for an organ. Shu smiled at the thought of transplant tourism.

Operating on foreigners was a new focus for Shu. He believed it would help to keep the authorities away. While wondering what Gao would uncover about other nations' true wait times, Li knocked on his door.

"You have an update on the supply lines?"

"Yes, the Arizona line arrived an hour ago. Tay said the quality is excellent. He's sending a report to your QQ account."

"Good, and the New Mexican supply?"

"Approximately eleven hours out."

"Perfect. Tell Ling Ling to get the car."

"Uh, there is a problem I thought you should know about."

"And it is?"

"Dr. Zheng called in with a medical emergency."

Shu stiffened. "With a recipient?"

"Both. He said the donor has clotting issues and the recipient some kind of blockage."

"Some kind? How am I supposed to act if I don't have proper information?"

"Sorry, sir."

"Where are they parked?"

"Harrison, New York."

Shu stood. "Tell Ling we're going, and instruct Zheng to call me immediately."

Passing Yankee Stadium, Shu's cell rang. "Doctor Zheng, what is the condition of your patients?"

"The donor is generating an unusual number of clots."

"Have you administered an anticoagulant?"

"I was hesitant—"

"You do realize the risk of an aneurysm is high."

"Yes, sir. I was concerned about him bleeding out."

"If he has a stroke, bleeding is not going to be the problem. You must administer a low dose of an anticoagulant."

"We'll get it started immediately."

"What is the status of the recipient?"

"A blockage developed in the ureter."

"Did you attempt a flushing?"

"The patient is in his late seventies, and the walls of the tube are compressed."

"Is urine backing up?"

"Not materially."

"Slow the intravenous feed. It'll give us time to see if it resolves itself."

"I did that before calling."

"Good. I expect to be there in under an hour."

"It's not necessary, sir."

"It's my duty. These patients must fully recover."

Shu hung up and made a call. "Tay, find out what happened with Zheng's procedures. Talk to the nurses, in private."

"Will do."

"I don't recall the ages of the patients in the first two surgeries he did and their general health. I need you to check."

"No problem. Hang on."

"Text it."

"Yes, sir."

The car sped north, and the concrete gave way to greenery. Shu's phone pinged. There came a text from Tay: *1st - 28 and 68; 2nd - 31 and 64 Both sets of males in excellent health.*

Shu sat back. The patients had been much younger and in good health. Zheng had only a year of real-world surgical experience. Shu wondered if this would have happened with another surgeon.

Shu would have to be careful using Zheng. It was another reminder that the new bottleneck to growth was the supply of competent surgeons. He closed his eyes, considering options to solve the problem.

Exiting the New York State Thruway, Shu opened his eyes. He had an idea he'd discuss with Gao. They drove on a country road, turning onto a gravel driveway.

A half a mile off the main road, an RV sat in the cover of a dilapidated barn. Shu got out, rapping a knuckle on the door. The door opened. Shu stepped up into a small, plastic-curtained space.

He put on the disposable gown and mask he was handed and slipped into the main cabin. Two gurneys were at the head and two at the rear of the equipment-filled galley.

Shu nodded at the nurses sitting beside the rear beds. A man in green scrubs was bent over a patient in the front. He saw Shu, spoke to a nurse, and hurried over.

"Dr. Zheng." Shu picked up a clipboard off the end of a gurney. "How are the patients?"

"The donor seems to be responding. The X-rays and ultrasound aren't showing evidence of bleeding."

"Good, but we'll need to do a CT scan to be sure."

"But where? We can't bring him to a hospital."

"We can't have him die."

"Of course."

"We'll transport him to a surgi center we trust for the test. Write up a script using appendicitis for cover. Call Tay when we're done. He'll make the arrangements."

"But it may not be necessary."

"We can't take the risk to our operation. Now, the recipient's blockage?"

"It improved marginally."

"What about inserting a stent into the tube?"

"I was going to ask permission."

"Let's get going."

"You're going to assist?"

"Observe."

"Check the cystoscope beforehand. It's never been used."

Shu went to check on the other set of patients. He scanned the monitors. The vitals for both were strong, tamping down his fear.

42

———

Black was sitting on a curvy chair in another park Cory had never been to. This time it was Grand Central Plaza. He liked the bird's-eye view the second-story setting gave of the intersection of Fortieth Street and Third Avenue.

Cory sat next to Black. "This is another cool spot."

"A building this short is rare in Midtown."

"Yeah. Whoever owns it is passing up big bucks."

"Heard they made a deal with the city to leave this one alone in exchange for approving a project on the West Side."

"Figures."

"What's going on?"

"I want to go ahead with the undercover plan."

"You talk to your old lady?"

"She's on board."

"You didn't tell her everything, did you?"

Cory smiled. "She's on a need-to-know basis."

"It's your marriage."

"It's all good. You got contacts to hook me up as a donor?"

"Not gonna be a problem, as long as you're willing to pay."

"How much?"

"Eight grand."

"Done."

"Cash."

"That's okay."

"You really want to do this?"

"A hundred percent."

"You can get killed."

"I won't."

"I wouldn't be so sure about that. First, you've got to survive the border area. Life is cheap down there. The cartels will kill you if they don't like the color of your hair."

"I'll be all right. As long as you get me into the pool of donors the Chinese are pulling from, I'll be good."

"What organ you going to say you're donating? A kidney?"

"Originally, but I want to say it's a liver segment, like they took from Ava."

"What did I tell you about emotion? You're going to blow it if you start getting weepy."

"It's not emotion talking. Even though a liver regenerates, there are fewer people willing to donate because it's more dangerous for liver donors. I figure it'll increase the odds I'll get picked."

"A kidney is safer. They could force you to donate for real."

"I doubt it."

"What happens if they knock you out and really take a hunk of your liver?"

"Your contacts said they don't put them under until they do the operation."

"What happens if they change it up? What happens if help doesn't come soon enough? Then what?"

"I'll figure it out."

"This isn't a game."

"After what they did to Ava, I sure as hell know that. Now, aren't there some drugs to prevent someone from going under?"

"There are a couple of antidotes for the muscle relaxers they give before surgery."

"You can get them, right?"

"Of course."

"We can hide them in my sneaker or something."

"Got to be the anal cavity."

Cory squirmed. "Why?"

"You can't take the chance. These guys may strip you."

"You think they'll do that?"

"They're sophisticated. They won't take chances."

"But that's gross."

"Better than being dead. Besides, you use a little Vaseline and you'll be okay."

"But what happens when I gotta go number two."

"You'll figure it out, like you said."

"Not funny."

"None of this is. I'm concerned about you not speaking any Spanish."

"I can imitate broken English; the Chinese will never know." Cory began talking like someone from Mexico with limited English.

"It's good enough to fool the Chinese, but the problem is the other donors. They speak Spanish."

"So?"

"If you're posing as one of them, you'd be expected to speak Spanish."

"I can't just keep to myself?"

"It'd raise suspicion. It's better to claim to be from Belize. It's just south of Mexico, to the east. English is an official language there. You'd need to study the accented way they speak it, but it's not going to be hard."

"I didn't know they spoke English there."

"It was part of the British empire until 1981."

"I'll watch YouTube videos to get the accent down."

"You'll get it. But also put time into learning some Spanish."

Cory was confident with his ear that he'd pick up enough Spanish to get by. "I will. What about surveillance equipment?"

"The miniature stuff isn't cheap."

"Where do you get it?"

"A contact in Russian intelligence."

"Really?"

Black nodded. "The small stuff has a short battery life. You've got to record as soon as possible."

"Can it upload to the web?"

"Not without Wi-Fi."

"No problem, I'll ask them for the password." Cory laughed.

"But thinking about this, what you need is a GPS tracker."

"Why? We need proof, pictures of what they're doing."

"We'll know where you are. If the cops come, they'll nab the surgical RV unit."

Cory lowered his voice. "I don't know why I didn't realize that."

"Omissions and mistakes are deadly."

"I know."

"I'm inclined to focus on the transport end. It's just too

dangerous to have you in the surgical unit. They've got to have strict controls, and if they drug you, it's over."

"But—"

Black stuck his hand up. "You get chosen to come north, and we bury a tracker in a place like your shoe. That way, we can follow the RV. If you don't get made on the way up, they'll lead us right to the people doing the surgeries."

"Why not in the, you know, anal cavity? They'll never find it there."

"They scan for electronic devices, and it's game over for you."

"Man, you thought of everything. It's a perfect plan."

"No plan is perfect. Always remember what Mike Tyson said."

"The boxer?"

"Yep. He said, 'Everybody has a plan until they get punched in the face.' He's damn right about that. You have to be able to improvise."

"I know that. Playing music, I improvise all the time."

"That's another world."

"Maybe, but when you're playing in front of fifty thousand people, you don't think you get nervous? My hands used to shake when I started out, could barely hold the guitar, and my mind used to blank out. It wasn't easy, but I learned how to shut everything around me out."

"I get it, but playing music isn't life and death."

"I know, but I've been under a ton of pressure performing, cutting records, and yeah, I partied too much to blow off steam, but I always delivered."

"You think I didn't know that? I wouldn't be here if it weren't for that. But I'm telling you, this is another thing entirely. It's not like blowing a song. With this, there's no room for error. One screwup, and you'll never see your family again."

"You really think it's that dangerous?"

"Absolutely. You better be sure you want to do this."

"There's no doubt in my mind. I have to do it, but I need your help."

"Look, sit on this a couple of days. You decide you don't want to do it, no problem. It's like we never talked about it."

43

———————

Shu inserted the SIM card in his secure phone and dialed China.

"My friend Gao. How are you?"

"Other than busy, we are well. And you?"

"I can say the same. There are not enough hours in the day to accomplish everything."

"Is it too much for you?"

"Not at all. I'm not complaining. We are pleased with our progress."

"And the new supply lines? I hear they're going well."

"Yes. I can only wish I had come up with the idea earlier."

"The best time to plant a tree was twenty years ago. The second-best time is now."

"Yes, that proverb is certainly true."

"Indeed. The old masters gave us plenty of wisdom. Before I forget, we've passed word to our Argentina emissary to spread the message, discreetly, to drum up interest."

"Excellent. The margins are higher for organ tourism."

"Based upon the report, I'd expect a good deal of interest."

"Agreed. We have to be careful, as we're approaching our limits in regard to surgeons."

"Ask them to work extra shifts."

"That's an idea. However, we must be careful not to over-work them, or the outcomes will suffer. It would destroy the reputation we've built."

"Recruitment is the solution."

"Yes, and I have an idea."

"Go on."

Even though it was Shu's idea, he said, "It might have been something you said a while ago. Why not make acceptance into China's medical schools contingent on giving back something to China, who has given them so much?"

"Yes, I remember mentioning this. What do you propose?"

"Why not require two or maybe three years of service to their country. You decide what the particular service is, dependent upon China's needs, but one of them could be supporting our transplant efforts."

"There are many areas. Just yesterday, I was telling our deputies that we must ask our new doctors to serve in the countryside."

"That's an excellent idea. For us, we only need five or ten qualified surgeons to triple our business."

"I'll schedule a meeting with Mr. Jiu. He'll support the idea."

"Excellent. I'm wondering if you can ask the national health minister about progress in the artificial organ program. If I had one wish, it would be for China to lead the world in creating organs. It would reduce our costs and streamline our operation."

"I haven't seen a report recently, but I know there have been challenges."

"I've learned the University of Davis has been making progress growing human stem cells inside of pigs."

"I'll see what the Ministry of State Security can secure from Davis. We've obtained useful information from their viticulture program."

"If they get inside information, we can reverse engineer it. It would eliminate the need for donors, and we'd stay out of the American authorities' crosshairs."

"You are worrying needlessly. Remember, it is difficult to catch a black cat in a dark room, especially when it's not there."

"I haven't heard that in a long time. My mother said that when I had nightmares as a boy."

"It remains true. You give the Americans too much credit."

"You're right, but Confucius said, 'The cautious seldom err.'"

"He also said, 'A man who does not plan long ahead will find trouble at his door.' We have done the planning; relax my friend, relax."

"You know my tendencies better than most."

"We all have our weaknesses. But our system exists to provide support to those in need."

"No one does it alone. Behind every able man, there are always other able men."

Gao laughed. "You've been studying proverbs."

"One must, to keep up with you."

"Touché, my friend. Is there anything else?"

"I'd like to use some of the proceeds to see if we can get more qualified surgeons, maybe from Russia."

"We don't need Russia's help. They'd steal our idea."

"Wherever you think is best. We need help with the pipeline we have."

"The Venezuelans have many doctors in Cuba. We could force them. It would be cheap, and the surgeons would be happy to escape Cuba." Gao laughed.

"Indeed."

"How many you want?"

"I need to give it some thought. Do you mind if I get back to you?"

"Take your time, my friend. We'll talk soon."

Shu hung up. He needed help, but Venezuela and Cuba were medical backwaters. He didn't want their surgeons operating on his patients.

44

───────

Cory rushed into the apartment. He went into the studio, took his guitar out of the case and hung it up. He went into the kitchen.

"We got to get going."

"It's okay. She's going to do the appointment via Zoom."

"On video? That's crazy."

"Ava doesn't want to leave the apartment."

"Why not?"

"She's scared."

"But we're just going to Dr. Bruno. She was just there."

"I know. She called Dr. Bruno herself, and Bruno suggested Zoom."

"I can't believe this."

"It's a good sign that she took the initiative to call Bruno. It's the first thing she's done since it happened."

"We can't let her seclude herself. It will make it harder to get back out there when this is over. You shouldn't have let her change it."

"What was I supposed to do? She needs to see Dr. Bruno. We can't drag her there if she doesn't want to go."

"I know. But going there has been the only time she's left the house since she stopped seeing regular doctors."

"I don't like it. Let's see how the visit goes, and then I'm calling Bruno. I want to see what she says about all this."

"Tell her Ava doesn't even want to leave her room. I tried to get her to do the Zoom call in the studio, but she wants to do it in her room."

"This is no good. It's got to end."

CORY WAS ENTERING his handwritten composition into notation software when his phone vibrated. Dr. Bruno was returning his call.

"Hello, Mr. Lupinski."

"Hi, Doc, how did the Zoom call go?"

"She is making progress in some areas."

"What about the suicide thoughts?"

"I'm pleased that she seems to realize that doesn't solve anything. I believe it's not a threat at this time."

"That's super news. We were worried crazy about her."

"That's understandable. We'll continue our work together, and I believe she'll continue to progress."

"It's not going to be another Zoom, is it?"

"Yes. Why do you appear to be negative about it?"

"Because Ava never leaves the apartment. She barely leaves her room. It's not good."

"It's rooted in Ava's fear of her safety. She's fixated on what happened and the potential threat these people pose to her."

"But that's crazy."

"Not the best choice of words, Mr. Lupinski."

"Sorry, you know what I mean. It doesn't make sense."

"Not to us. However, the trauma Ava experienced has heightened the fears we rationalize away every day."

"If she stays locked up in her room all the time, it's going to get harder and harder for her to return to a normal life."

"It's a process, Mr. Lupinski. Isolating herself has tamped down her fears enough to take ending her own life off the table."

"That's good, that's great, but what about getting back to her life?"

"We'll continue our work; it may be slow going at times, but maybe we'll get lucky and the authorities will catch the perpetrators."

"You really think that would help?"

"Absolutely. Removing that threat, real or imagined, would go a long way toward making Ava comfortable in resuming her old life."

Cory thanked Bruno and hung up. He opened the studio door and motioned to Linda. She hustled over.

"What's the matter?"

"I spoke to Bruno. The good thing is, she said Ava's made progress and doesn't think there's a suicide threat."

"Thank God."

"I know. But she said Ava is still paranoid these guys are coming back to get her. She said that's why she won't leave the house."

"Poor thing. Can you imagine, a teenager afraid to go out? When I was her age, I wanted to be out as much as I could."

"Now you see why we can't wait for the police?"

CORY POPPED his earbuds in and hit play. He'd created an audio file of two men from Belize. Both had the same timbre voices. He listened closely, even visualizing himself imitating them talking.

Cory had transcribed scores of solos from players he loved, copying the notes and inflections of the soloist. He'd sung harmonies in all kinds of musical settings. He was confident he'd be able to memorize the accents quickly, internalize them, and speak as fluidly as a native.

Eyes closed, Cory listened to a loop for five minutes straight. He forced his inner ear to isolate the nuances in the accent. Before stopping the recording, Cory used another musical tool. He spoke the words in his head, hearing himself as he did notes when composing.

Believing he had it, he clicked on his mic. Cory repeated the words the men from Belize said. He looked at the sound waves the audio program recorded of his voice.

He compared it to those of the men. Cory smiled. They were a close match. He considered it a good sign and reached under the desk. Cory pulled out two boxes and carefully read the directions.

Two hours later, Cory put on his jacket. He cracked the door open. Linda was nowhere in sight. Cory slipped out of the apartment, walking to the subway.

He listened to the voice recordings as the crowded train made its way into Manhattan. At Cortland Street, a woman in her sixties got onto his car. Cory stopped the recording and stood, trying out his newfound broken English: "Ma'am, you can seat here."

"Thank you."

"No problem."

Cory smiled. The accent was perfect. He played the recording until the Fifty-Ninth Street station came up.

Exiting the subway, he looked forward to checking out the spot Black set to meet at. He never visited an indoor public space. Cory pushed through the revolving doors of a skyscraper into IBM Plaza.

A pair of birds flying overhead caught his attention. When he pulled his earbuds out, he heard other birds chirping and singing. Light flooded into the airy space. Cory guessed it was five stories tall.

Cory headed for a seating area by a clump of trees. He sat, eyes on the door for Mr. Black. Cory checked the time. It was ten minutes before two. The operative always arrived early for a meeting. Where was he?

45

———

A MINUTE LATER, BLACK SPILLED OUT OF THE REVOLVING door. He stepped aside, surveying the space. Cory waited until Black had his head turned and walked toward him.

Cory brushed by Black, and when he turned his head, the operative was looking right at him.

"Fooled you, huh?"

"It took me a second."

"Pretty good, right?"

He nodded toward a couple of chairs in the corner. "The accent is good."

"How about the skin color?"

"Not bad, if it holds up."

"They say it'll last two to three weeks."

"Who's they?"

"The manufacturer."

"You know them?"

"No. Why?"

"You want to put your life in their hands?"

"Of course not."

"Then test it. Make sure it lasts."

"How am I going to do that? What would my family say?"

"Work it out. You can't take chances."

"I'll tell them I'm doing an audition for a, oh no, I'm doing a music video. They'll buy that. We'll be stranded on a deserted island."

"Where'd you get the teeth?"

"Makeup-FX. They do all the Hollywood stuff. Looks good, right?"

"Yeah. But if someone like me is looking for you, they'd see through all this."

"But they're not."

Black nodded. "Still, I'd work on changing up your gait."

"Like a limp?"

"Nothing too obvious. A little bounce in your step is all you need."

"No problem. You talk to your guy at the border?"

"You sure you want to do this?"

"Do I look like I'm not serious?"

Black pointed to his temple. "I'm talking about in here"—he jabbed a thumb at his chest—"not here."

"Look, I can't deny what they did to my daughter isn't a factor. It's huge, especially since Ava's scared out of her mind that they're coming back for her. But don't forget, I was making noise about this from the beginning. It's why they came after us in the first place."

"There's a good chance you'll never see your family again."

"I know that."

"You have the eight grand?"

Cory dug into his backpack, pulling out a brown bag. "It's all there."

"Three weeks from today you need to be in Eagle Pass, Texas. It's a hundred and fifty miles from San Antonio."

"Texas? I thought I was going into Mexico."

"I wanted to avoid any problems with the border. Once you're in Eagle Pass, check into the Hotel Santa Rosa under Chester Musa."

"I got to write this down."

"Don't. Memorize it. And anyone asks, you're fleeing the George Street Bloods. A drug deal gone bad."

Cory repeated the names of the town, hotel, his alias, and the gang.

"I think I got it. What do I do there?"

"They'll come for you. You'll know it when they do."

"Anything else?"

Black stood. "That's it.

As he watched Black walk out, Cory cycled the names through his head, committing them to memory. He jotted a note in his phone to help him remember and headed to Donny's house.

His visit was twofold: wash off the bronzing agent and tell his friend he was going to be away for a week or two. Cory couldn't tell Donny what he was up to but needed him to reassure Linda that he was safe.

Donny would press for details, especially when he'd make him promise to take care of his family if something happened to him.

LINDA WAS SLEEPING on the couch when Cory came home. He put his guitar away and went to shut the TV when she said, "How was the session? It ran late."

"It was good, Donny was on it. This kid Gunnery has

some good ideas, but he likes to experiment a little too much."

"That gets expensive."

"The label is letting him do what he wants after his debut charted."

"Must be nice."

"Doesn't appeal to me anymore. I like going in, laying it down, and coming home. I couldn't imagine going on the road again."

"We're glad you gave it up."

"How was Ava today?"

"Pretty much the same. She came out, grabbed her dinner, and went back in. Said she was watching a movie."

"She's not going to get back to normal till those bastards are out of the picture."

"Maybe Dr. Bruno can make progress with her."

"I'm sick of depending on everybody else. Black and me are going to nail these bastards."

"This could backfire. They'll come after us, all of us."

"They won't know I'm even involved. Black's got contacts, and really, all I'm doing is paying to make sure we, I mean Black, gets inside."

"You should tell the police about this. They do undercover stuff all the time."

"I wish I could, but it would take them a year or more to get inside. We can't wait that long with Ava."

"But how is Black going to get in so fast?"

"He's got contacts with a guy who is supplying them donors."

"Tell the police then."

"I did, but they said they'd have to vet the whole thing and it would take just as long. This is a south of the border thing."

"They're smuggling people up for their organs?"

"Yeah. It means the cops have to get the State Department, Homeland Security, the FBI, and who knows who else in the mix."

"I can't believe all of them have got to be involved."

"You see what I'm talking about? We'd be lucky if they got anywhere in a year, and by then, the Chinese probably will have moved onto another supply point."

"They'll never catch these guys."

"We got a chance to get them now. We can't pass it up."

46

Cory backed up his phone to the cloud and looked through his backpack a final time. He wheeled his overnight bag into the kitchen. Tommy was playing with his phone.

"I'm getting ready to head to the airport."

"When you coming back, Dad?"

"Should be two to three days. If the shoot goes well, I'll be home before the weekend."

"Okay."

Linda said, "You got everything you need?"

"Yep."

"Where's your guitar?"

"They're going to provide one. It's just going to be a prop 'cause we're not really playing."

"You're faking it, Dad?"

Cory smiled. "You know what I say, fake it till you make it."

"Yeah, it's all in your head, right?"

"You're learning, Tommy." He kissed his son's head. "Let me say goodbye to Ava."

Cory knocked on Ava's door. After a second knock, he

swung the door open. The TV was on but the sound was muted. It didn't matter, his daughter was staring at the ceiling.

"Hey, Ava. How you doing?"

"Okay."

"Just wanted to let you know I'm going to be leaving."

"When you coming back?"

He studied her face, wondering if the look on her face was fear. "A day or so. Depends on how quick the filming goes. But don't worry, I'll get back as soon as possible, and Mom is not going to leave the apartment without you."

"You sure?"

"Absolutely. And Uncle Donny is going to come and help out."

"Isn't he doing the video with you?"

"Uh, no. He never played with the Coconuts."

"You said he did."

"I did? Maybe Donny did a session. Anyway, it doesn't matter, he's not on the gig."

Ava shrugged.

"You know, it might be good to get out of this room for a while and hang out with Mom when I'm gone."

"I don't feel like it."

"It's not good being cooped up in here. Can you try? For me?"

"Why doesn't everybody just leave me alone?"

"We want to help, that's all."

"You've got to go, so, go ahead then."

"Aw, come on, Ava, don't let me leave on that note. All I'm saying is we want the best for you. We're sorry if we overdo things at times, but it's because we love you."

"I know."

"Good. I'll see you as soon as I get back."

"Bye. Close the door."

Cory stood outside her room. He felt guilty for leaving. Did she think he was abandoning her? She should only know he was doing this for her.

Linda stepped into the hallway. "Everything all right?"

"Yeah, perfect."

"How was Ava?"

Cory raised his voice a notch. "Good. She's watching TV."

"She's okay with you leaving?"

"I think so. It's only for a couple of days. I told her you'd be here all the time, and Donny would come over too."

"All right. What time is your flight?"

"Just after two."

"You better get going."

Cory pulled his phone out. "I'll get an Uber now."

"How long is the flight to Barbados?"

"Uh, over four hours. I'll call when we land."

Linda gave him a quick hug. "Okay. We'll miss you."

"I'll miss you too."

"Hope it goes well."

"It will."

"Have fun."

"I'll try. Love you, bye."

THE DRIVE from San Antonio took Cory almost three hours. The border town of Eagle Pass was bigger than he imagined. Cory was thankful Black had arranged meeting the coyote on the US side. He dropped the rental car and got a ride to the Santa Rosa Hotel in a car without air conditioning.

Wondering how bad a thirty-one-dollar-a-night room

would be, he noticed a sign touting their free parking and lowered his expectations.

Using his accent and the name of Chester Musa to check in, Cory was handed a key. Shirt darkening from perspiration, he made his way to a second-story room. The only language he heard was Spanish. Everyone was talking at machine-gun speed, but he was able to pick out key words and it felt good.

He opened the door and surveyed the small room. A double bed anchored the room. Cory grimaced at the thin pillows and worn bedspread. He vowed to keep his underwear on when sleeping and stepped inside.

An ancient TV sat on a wooden console. It was older than the one he'd had in his first apartment. Cory put his backpack on a metal desk and switched on the air conditioner.

Wishing he'd brought flip-flops, he peeked into the bathroom. It was old but clean. He splashed water on his face and put the TV on. He flicked to a news broadcast in Spanish. He raised the volume to hear it over the noise from the AC unit.

Cory ate a sandwich he'd bought at a rest area while listening intently, trying to understand as much as he could. It was a tiring exercise, but he was getting better.

An hour later, Cory eased into bed. The mattress was thin but felt good. Though he was wired, exhaustion was coming on fast.

Closing his eyes, he recalled his conversation with Linda. He hoped she'd forgive him for lying. Every time she asked about Barbados and the hotel, he promised they'd visit one day and shifted the talk to the kids.

Cory tried to sleep, but the walls were so thin he could hear people changing their minds. He popped his earbuds in and focused on his mission.

Being on the ground in a border town was as real as it got.

But what made the fear rise was the reality that besides Mr. Black, no one knew where he was.

Being alone was dangerous. He swallowed his fear by acknowledging it was up to him to survive. Cory got out of bed and dragged the chair over.

He wedged it between the door and console and peeked out the window. Two guys were drinking beer in the parking lot, and a couple of teens were sitting on a car, passing a joint between them.

He tightened the drapes and hopped back in bed. Shutting his eyes, he concentrated on breathing. He needed to rest. He got off track when a motorcycle screeched by but fell asleep quickly.

47

CORY WOKE UP. A SLIVER OF LIGHT FORCED ITS WAY BETWEEN the drapes. The clock on the nightstand said it was 3:48 a.m. He took his earbuds out. The sound of a car racing faded.

He relaxed for a second before sitting up. Someone was outside the door. He slipped out of bed and knelt. The crack of light under the door had two interruptions.

Cory surveyed the room, looking for something to use as a weapon. He opened the nightstand drawer. Nothing but a beat-up Bible. Cory grabbed the plastic waste can out of the bathroom. Tiptoeing back into the main room, he heard someone slowly jiggle the doorknob.

Speaking in Spanish, Cory said, "I got a gun. You better get the hell out of here!"

The jiggling stopped. He heard footsteps. They were receding. Cory pulled the drapes open. He saw the back of a man taking the steps two at a time. He disappeared around the corner.

Cory sat on the bed. He tried to slow his heart. Had someone set him up? It seemed likely. He wondered whether they'd come back.

Black hadn't said how well he knew the coyote supplying the Chinese. Cory regretted not asking. He'd seen the news. They were filled with stories of the ruthless men who moved illegals across the border.

Many took the money and left their customers in the desert without enough water to survive. Others raped the women they were supposed to help. Just who was Black entrusting his life to?

Cory ran two scenarios through his mind. Assuming Black hadn't backstabbed him again, the only people who knew he was here were the coyote and the hotel.

He couldn't discount someone in the parking lot or another guest who'd seen him checking in, but settled on the coyote. Given their reputation, it made sense. Either way, he had to be careful.

He took a series of deep breaths. Cory looked at the chair squeezed against the door. He'd used his head. Was it the type of thing Black would have done?

Cory had to stay focused if he was going to make it out of the mission alive. He got dressed and lay back down. He checked the time, 4:35. Closing his eyes, he told himself to wake up in twenty minutes.

Cory drifted off to sleep, awakening twenty-one minutes later. He peeked through the window. Nothing threatening. He returned to bed, repeating the internal alarm for a short nap.

After three naps, he was ready to get up. It wasn't the time of just after six but a growling stomach that forced him out of bed. Cory took all the money out of his backpack. He split it into three parcels. Tilting the nightstand up, he snuck a third under.

He put the other third in his toiletry bag and split the last of it into two bundles. One he stuffed in his jeans pocket and the rest in his underwear.

Cory went through his backpack. He took the tiny GPS device out and stuffed it at the bottom of a pillowcase. Palming the burner phone, he surveyed the room, placing it under the tube that hung off the back of the TV. He took the fake teeth and placed them in the plastic cup on the sink.

He looked out the window, moved the chair out of the way, and opened the door. Cory locked the door, shaking his head at the flimsy doorframe.

Cory remembered seeing a Mexican restaurant a couple of blocks away when he was dropped off. Having an empanada wasn't his idea of breakfast, but he didn't recall any other options.

He skipped down the stairs, stopping when a heavily tattooed man blocked the landing.

"Disculpame." Cory said, excuse me in Spanish.

The man looked him in the eye, muttering, "Fucking gringo," before taking a small step to the side.

Cory nodded and hit the parking lot wondering if he should have applied the bronzing agent. He picked up his pace and headed down the main drag.

A block later, an old Chevy turned onto the avenue and slowed. The car had three males in it. Cory kept his eyes ahead as the vehicle crawled beside him.

He heard them speaking Spanish filled with curse words as they sped away. Cory wondered if he should have stared them down but discounted the idea. He was outnumbered.

Cory followed a man in baggy pants into Rosalita's Cantina. The smell of coffee and fried food engulfed him. Two of the handful of tables were filled with people sipping cups and arguing. Cory made out they were talking about soccer.

He smiled at the woman behind the counter and ordered coffee and two empanadas. Carrying his food to a table, Cory knew he was being watched. He sat, nodding to the tables before digging into the half-moon-shaped snacks.

The food began repeating on him as Cory paid for a coffee to go. Walking back to the hotel, he noticed everything was covered with a thin film of dust. Wondering why he hadn't noticed that before, he felt something press against his back.

It was a gun. Cory stopped. He knew what they wanted but asked, "Que quieres?"

"Dinero."

Cory swapped the coffee into his left hand and was about to reach in his pocket. He swung around, throwing the scalding coffee at the attacker.

"Hijo de puta!"

A pair of hands shoved him against the building. Cory screamed when another man kicked his shin. Cory collapsed onto the cracked sidewalk, staring at the cowboy boot that had caused the pain.

Going for the money, Cory said, "Perdon, perdon."

One of the men grabbed his arms, pulling them behind his back. Cory pleaded, "Take it easy. Por favor."

"Callatte."

Cory shut up as a hand reached into his pocket, pulling out the cash.

"Bonito."

Cory knew they didn't expect as much as he had and hoped they'd run off. Then he heard them say something. They weren't done with him.

48

———————

THEY FORCED HIM ONTO HIS STOMACH. A MAN TUGGED AT HIS sneakers, ripping them off his feet. A boot was planted on his back and someone peeled off his socks. Cory wondered if they were going to strip him naked.

"Quedate o martarte!"

Threatening him with death if he moved, he said, "Okay, okay. No problemo."

A car screeched to a stop, and Cory heard the men clamber in. As it burned rubber, the doors slammed shut.

Cory sat up. Trying to see what kind of car it was through the dust. It was red. He got to his feet, noticing two men sitting in the doorstep of an abandoned building across the street. They were pointing at him, laughing.

Leg hurting, Cory began walking. He kept his eyes down, dodging broken glass. He needed shoes. Taking his time, he saw a store with goods hanging from sidewalk racks.

A woman in an apron was shaking her head. She waved him over. Cory stepped around a sleeping dog and crossed the street. She said something to him that he didn't completely understand, but he knew the word *zapatos* meant shoes.

"No dinero, senora. Hombres steal."

She pointed to a rack of plastic flip-flops. "Para ti."

"Gracias pero no dinero."

She took a pair off and handed them off. "Bueno, yo espero."

"Gracias, gracias, yo returno."

Two blocks from the hotel, Cory saw a sign hanging off a building just off the corner. He stopped in his tracks. A second later he headed into Maverick Arms.

Cory looked at the guns hanging on the wall. He thought there must have been more than a hundred. It seemed crazy until he realized he was in Texas.

Behind a counter, a man put his newspaper down. "What are you looking for?"

"A handgun. Something small. Easy to conceal."

"Texas is an open-carry state. You don't need to hide it."

"Really?"

"Yep. Let me show you some."

He remembered the one Black had given him. It had gotten him in trouble, but it had something he needed. "I want one with a laser."

"What caliber?"

"Uh, something that would stop a man. You know, if I had to. It doesn't have to kill him but—"

"Let me see your hands."

Cory held them up.

He opened a drawer. "This here Bond is really popular. Got the Texas star right on the handle, and it's made instate."

Cory took the gun. It was cold. He regretted coming into the shop and handed it back. "Nah."

"That's right, you wanted a laser." He picked up another gun. It looked familiar to Cory.

"This here is a Smith and Wesson Bodyguard. It's thirty-eight caliber, so it'll do what you want, and this is the laser." He clicked a button and handed it to Cory.

It was the same gun Black had given him. "How much?"

"Three hundred."

Cory stared at it. He had to conserve his cash, but he could be robbed again, and having a gun when he met the coyote could be useful. The problem was Black had warned him against being armed.

"Tell you what. You buy it and I'll throw a box of ammo in for the same price."

Cory nodded. "I'll be back with the money."

Two doors from Cory's room, a shirtless man was leaning over the railing. Was he a lookout for someone robbing his room? The man reached behind his back. Cory froze.

He continued on when he saw it was a pack of cigarettes. Eyes on his room's door, Cory climbed the stairs. The man in the corridor didn't make a move, easing Cory's concern.

In the room, Cory sat and did his breathing exercises. He closed his eyes, concentrating on the air flow. He considered if he really needed a gun and when the coyote would make contact.

Black had cautioned him on a firearm. It was true that you couldn't pull a gun unless you were going to use it. Cory had shot his ex-manager during a fight. But the gun had gone off accidentally, hitting Stein in the leg.

Could he shoot to kill? The idea made him stand up. As he paced the room, he figured it would only be a day or so before he'd be on his way north. If he bought a gun, he'd have to get rid of it. Was it worth it?

He considered what Black would do. The operative always looked to reduce risk. Cory could hear him saying, 'You have to do what has to be done.'

Cory peeked out the window. It was clear. He tilted the

nightstand. Grabbing the money, he peeled off four hundred dollars and set it back down.

After paying for the Bodyguard, Cory stuck the gun in the small of his back. He walked out of the gun shop and onto the main street. Across the street, a Camino, with two men inside, drove slowly by.

Cory took his pistol out and jammed it in the front of his jeans. He made sure the handle was visible. He crossed the street. As he approached the general store, he pulled his tee shirt over the gun.

Back in his room, Cory took off the sneakers he'd bought. He examined the inner soles. Recalling the spot for it in the stolen pair, he peeled back the top layer.

Using the knife he bought, he cut out a hiding place for the GSP tracker. Cory recalled seeing the device when Black gave it to him. The third-of-an-inch device raised Cory's belief in the mission.

He put the unit in place, covering it with the inner sole. It looked perfect. Cory tried the sneakers on to be sure. He took a step and heard a rolling sound outside. He stopped.

There was a knock on the door. He tiptoed to the window. It was a woman with a tray of towels and a vacuum.

"Un minuto."

Cory took the gun off the bed and dropped it into the nightstand drawer. He opened the door, took two towels from the woman, motioned her in, and locked the door behind her. He let her give a quick cleaning to the room.

As the maid left, Cory spied a man who looked like one of the guys who'd mugged him. He squeezed the chair under the doorknob and went for his gun. Pulling the drawer open, an idea hit him.

49

———

Cory took the cans of toner into the bathroom. He undressed and stepped into the tub. He reviewed the directions and began applying the bronzing agent.

Examining himself, Cory touched up the areas around his eyes, ears, and genitals. He smiled, the white of his teeth appearing neon-like in comparison.

Cory made sure he was completely dry before getting dressed. He carried the gun back into the room and opened the drawer. Cory grabbed the Gideon Bible, flipping through a section of pages.

Cory set the gun on the book. He traced the gun's shape with a pen. Taking his time, he cut out a hiding place for the five-inch-long gun. It was just three quarters of an inch thick. The Bible was twice as thick, and when he closed it, you couldn't tell it was in there.

He picked it up with one hand, gauging if the extra twelve ounces was noticeable. There was a difference, but some of it was offset by the two hundred or so pages he'd cut the silhouette out of.

Cory would venture out to buy a cheap cross to wear. He

considered getting a religious tattoo but discounted the idea over infection fears.

He had to be healthy, or they'd pass him up as a donor. The head of transplants at Mt. Sinai had said donors were vigorously screened. Cory figured the gang had looser standards, but someone with an infection had to be off-limits.

When they did blood panels, he wanted the only point of interest to be his blood type.

PAYING close attention to what was said on a Spanish soap opera, Cory barely noticed the movement that blotted out the crack of light sneaking through the drapery.

Stiffening at the sound of a knock, Cory opened the drawer, palming the pistol. After a second knock, he asked who it was in Spanish.

"Senor Negro."

Black wasn't specific but said Cory would know who the coyote was. "Un minuto."

Cory pulled the drape back. Two men in tee shirts flanked a man in a cowboy hat. Cory slid the gun into his pants and opened the door.

The leader beckoned with his hand. "Vamos."

The seeds of doubt in his mind were being watered. Cory had practiced saying *who sent you?* in Spanish. "Quien te envio?"

"Senor Negro!"

"Okey."

Cory slung his backpack over his shoulder and went into the bathroom, placing the gun in the sink. He dropped his drawers, inserted the small tube, and squeezed his butt cheeks together. He pulled his pants up and put the gun back in place.

Cory pocketed his fake teeth and grabbed his wheeled overnight.

The man pointed at the luggage. "No. Uno."

"Un minuto." Cory pulled out a sweatshirt and jammed it in the backpack.

Cory trailed behind the men. Right before the stairs, he said, "Un minuto."

"No.

"I forgot. Perdon." Cory struggled for the word and held his index finger up as he ran back into the room. He reappeared quickly, holding the Bible in the air as he ran back.

The men looked at each other and laughed. Cory followed the men to a blue pickup truck. The boss pointed to the back of the vehicle. "Entra."

Cory climbed into the dusty cargo bed and was followed by one of the men. Back against the cab, Cory braced himself as the car lurched forward.

From the vantage point of sitting on one butt cheek, the town shrunk as the pickup sped away. He hoped the feeling to go to the bathroom would fade.

Slowing, the truck turned onto a street lined on one side with small cement homes. Four kids were kicking a soccer ball on a brown field on the other side of the street.

The pickup drove to the last house, parking by the front door. The man beside Cory said, "Vamos."

Cory jumped off the back of the truck and followed him. The pickup drove away. Gripping the Bible, Cory told himself to relax and be on guard as he stepped into the house.

It took a second to adjust to the darkness and the smell of body odor. The main room was littered with fast-food wrappers and cans. Tattered blankets were piled up in a corner.

The man motioned, saying something in Spanish. Cory understood aqui; it meant here. Cory stepped over a blanket, heading for a corner. If he was spending the night here, he wanted to be as comfortable as possible.

The man retreated to a chair by a card table in the kitchen. The counter was lined with plastic gallon jugs of water. Cory eased himself to the ground, pulling a blanket over him.

"Excusa. Bano."

The man hiked a thumb down a hallway.

Cory grabbed his backpack. "Gracias."

The top to the toilet was missing and the bowl was dirty. Instead of a handle, a rope hung out to flush. Cory forced the cylinder out of his butt and cleaned it. He took a leak. Eyeing the rough brown paper stacked on the floor used for wiping, he hoped he wouldn't need to use it.

Cory now stood outside the kitchen. He pointed, "Por favor, agua."

The man looked up from his phone and nodded. Cory grabbed a gallon, spying a stack of tortillas in a plastic garbage bag. He reached in. They were hard. He paused before taking two.

Cory retreated to the corner. Unsure where he was going or how long it'd be there, he guzzled the water. Not hungry, he tore a piece of tortilla off and ate it anyway.

Cory topped off the bottle of water in his backpack and stuck one of the tortillas in with it. Dusk was closing in. Using the rucksack as a pillow, he reclined, shutting his eyes.

Cory bolted upright. He heard a voice outside. The door swung open. A beam of light bounced off the walls. He reached for his Bible.

50

———————

Cory pressed his back against the wall as six men trudged in. It was hard to see, but their faces were dirty. The man who drove Cory here came in behind them.

He grabbed two jugs and held them out. "Beber y dormir."

The migrants guzzled and passed the water around. Cory could see the exhaustion on their faces. He wondered where they'd come from, when the man who brought them caught his eye.

"Ven aqui."

"Me?"

"Si. Subito."

Cory hustled to his feet, taking his backpack with him. The men walked outside. The truck's headlights provided the only light.

"Que pagar."

"Mr. Black paid you."

"No. Pagar."

"I told you Mr. Black paid for me already."

When the man smiled, Cory saw his mouth had more gold

than a small jewelry store. "Mr. Black? I don't see no Mr. Black. Do you?"

"Come on, man. You know I paid."

"Maybe you did, but this is a tax."

"A tax?"

"That's right. Pay or you rot here."

"I don't have money."

"Bullshit."

"I swear." He held up the Bible.

"Ah, a preacher man." He laughed. "Tell your God to give you money for the tax."

"I only have fifty dollars."

He stuck his palm out.

Feeling a surge of relief, having split up his funds, Cory dug out the money and handed it over. As the man walked to his truck, Cory reminded himself to prepare for the unexpected. It was the only way he'd make it out alive.

Cory stepped back into the room. A man was curled up in his corner. He saw Cory and scooted over. Hugging his Bible, Cory settled next to him. "Gracias."

He stuck out his hand. "Jesus. Cual tu nombre?"

As a dog howled, Cory said, "Chester."

"Soy de Allende. You?"

"Belize."

"We hear they have gangs there too."

"Yes. It is too dangerous to stay. My brother was killed, and I was next."

"Why?"

Instead of saying to flee the violence as he had practiced, he said, "Because I believe." Cory raised the Bible.

Jesus shook his head. "The cartels who run Mexico give money to the church. But no one is safe, not even the priests."

"What a shame. I tried to stay, but the Lord had other

plans. I resisted, but it was hard to resist God's will." Cory wondered if he was laying it on too heavy, but it made a good cover.

Jesus nodded. "After I settle in, my wife and son will come."

"Let's ask God to protect them while you are separated."

Jesus made the sign of the cross and reached for Cory's hand. "La oracion del Senor."

Cory struggled to remember the Lord's prayer in English as his new friend recited it in Spanish.

One of the other men in the room began chiming along, when someone shouted for them to shut up. Cory lowered his voice to a whisper, but Jesus didn't. When he finished, he said, "We need rest. We have a long journey ahead."

Cory reclined. Reaching into his backpack, he handed the tortilla to Jesus, bidding him good night.

Even with his breathing exercises, it took twice as long to force the images of his kids out of his mind and fall asleep. Cory bolted awake. What was that sound?

He realized Jesus had moaned, and closed his eyes. Cory considered whether Jesus or any of the men were getting paid to be donors. They were all about the same age as Cory. It was dark, but as far as he could tell, they seemed to be in good health.

Cory concentrated on clearing his mind and fell back asleep. He was startled awake again. Jesus had screamed in his sleep, and the other men were telling him to keep quiet.

He leaned toward him, whispering, "Jesus. Are you all right?"

"Bad dreams."

"You'll be okay."

"I hope so. My family is counting on me."

Cory surprised himself by saying, "God will see to it."

"I worry. God tells us our bodies are temples for the Holy Spirit, and I, uh, forget it."

"I understand. We have to do what have to do."

"Are you, uh, selling something?"

Cory looked around and nodded. "You too?"

"Yes. It's the only way out. I get the money to bring my family and escape the cartels."

"God protects those who protect others."

"I hope so."

Cory wanted to say he hoped as well, but said, "Don't worry. Try to relax, think about your breathing, it works for me."

A distant sound woke Cory. He concentrated. It was a vehicle. A truck. The sound was intensifying.

He stood. Pulling the sheet away from the window, he saw a pair of headlights illuminating a billow of dust. He looked left. A thin line of light sat on the horizon. To the right, complete blackness.

Cory watched the vehicle approach. It was a van. He considered whether it was another load of migrants who'd crossed over. He stepped back as the van came down the road. It backed up and stopped.

Two men got out. They swung open the rear doors. It was empty.

Cory shook Jesus. "They're coming for us. It's time to go."

The door slammed open. Two men in cowboy boots stomped in. "Arriba! Arriba! Vamos!"

The men scrambled to their feet. The watchman in the kitchen shook hands with them. They grabbed a jug of water and talked as the men assembled.

The watchman pointed at Cory, Jesus, and two other men. "Tu, tu, tu, tu. Vamos."

Cory climbed into the van. He welcomed the coolness of the metal floor but perched himself on one cheek to protect the anal capsule.

Jesus sat next to Cory, opposite the other two men, Oro and Tavio. He studied their leathery faces in the van's dim dome light. It was clear there was an endless supply of donors south of the border.

As the van bounced away from the safe house, Cory thought about the word, donor. It didn't apply. They weren't willingly giving up an organ to help someone. They were trading it to start a new life.

51

Cory peeked between the front seats and through the windshield. The road was deserted. He opened the Bible up, pretending to read, as he envisioned possible questions to be posed and situations to be encountered.

The van pulled off the paved road, bouncing along on a dirt road. As it slowed, Cory looked out the windshield, seeing the running lights of a dark RV.

"We're here." The van came to a stop and Cory crossed himself. Jesus followed, kissing his fingers after he did and offering it overhead.

The back doors opened. Bible in hand, Cory grabbed his backpack and was the first out. He was greeted by two Asian men. A small-framed man holding a clipboard and one whose shaved head reflected the rising sun.

The small man stepped forward. "Name, age, and where are you from?"

Cory pulled his shoulders back. "Chester Musa, thirty-eight, I'm from Belize."

He marked the clipboard and asked if Cory'd had a series of medical conditions. Cory answered no to all of them.

"Any allergies?"

"No."

"Good. You're donating a liver section?"

"Yes."

"Back against the van."

Cory moved into position, and they took pictures of his face and profile.

The man looked at the images and said, "Okay. Back in the van."

"The van?"

"Yes. Until I process everyone."

Cory waited in the vehicle as each man went through the same questioning and picture-taking. The Asian's Spanish was barely better than his. When the last man climbed into the van, the beefy Asian, named Chen, stepped forward with a large canvas bag.

He stuck his hand in and came out with four plastic packages. Each one contained scrub suits and flip-flops. Bile splashed the back of Cory's throat as Chen said, "Change into these."

"Now?"

"Yes."

He took his clothes off and, facing the wall, changed along with the others. Cory stuffed his clothes and sneakers into his backpack and stepped out of the van.

"Let's go." Chen led the men to the RV. He unlocked the door. Cory put his foot on the step and Chen grabbed his arm, pulling him back.

"Where do you think you're going?"

"On the RV."

"Not with that backpack."

"But I need my stuff."

"You'll have everything you'll need."

Chen spoke to everyone. "The only thing you can take with you is money. Put it in one of these baggies."

"But I need my sneakers. My feet, they're flat and—"

"Did you hear me? Money only."

Cory laid his backpack down, putting the Bible on top of it.

Each of them put their cash in the bags. Chen examined them and opened the RV's door. He took a wand out and turned it on. After scanning each bag, he handed the money back.

Then he scanned each of them. When he moved the wand toward Cory's crotch, Cory talked his heart rate down. He was worried Chen would wand his bag, finding the GPS device buried in his sneaker.

Chen swung open the door. "All right, let's get going."

"I'm sorry, but can I have my Bible?"

"No."

"Please, man. I need it. I don't go anywhere without it, for like thirty years."

Chen looked at his accomplice, who shrugged.

"No."

Jesus said, "Please, we need the Bible. We are afraid of what lies ahead. The only thing that helps is reading the Word of God."

Chen looked Cory in the eye. "What are you, some kind of preacher man?"

"No. Just a believer. What we're doing is scary, but through prayer, we know the Lord will protect us. Without it, I can't go forward with the donation."

"You want us to leave you here? In the middle of the fucking desert?"

"I'd rather be here with God than to be separated from his word."

Jesus stepped forward. "Me either. I won't go without God by my side."

Chen looked at his associate, who shrugged. "Okay, get on, preacher man."

Cory grabbed the Bible and hustled up the stairs. He went straight to the window, pulling the blinds aside. He hoped they'd load everyone's personal belongings into the cargo area below the RV's galley.

He kept his eyes on the back of the van until its doors were closed and it drove off. The GPS device was lost. His heart sank. The plan he'd thought was perfect had just blown up. He quelled the panic and started thinking.

He figured Black would know right away that something was wrong. Would he think Cory had failed to get chosen or that he'd been found out?

Cory was on his own. The question was, what to do next?

52

———

Cory watched the men climb aboard. Each of them smiled when they saw the inside of the RV. It wasn't plush, but considering where they'd come from, it was a Ritz Carlton on wheels.

Jesus plopped himself onto one of four gray leather recliners. "Bueno, no, amigo?"

"Si. Thanks for helping me take this." He held up the Bible.

Oro was opening the small refrigerator when Chen said, "Listen up! Everyone needs to shower. Make it fast. There's soap and towels. Put what you're wearing in the black plastic bag outside the door. Four sets of scrubs and slippers are in that cabinet." He pointed to a closet opposite the bathroom. "Hustle up. You've got five minutes each."

"Five minutes?"

"That's all. We've got to get moving, and if you want the first installment of cash, get it done in five."

Bible in hand, Cory stepped toward the bathroom. "I'll go first. I'm fast."

He'd never been on an RV before and was surprised the

bathroom was bigger than the ones he'd seen on boats. He pushed the shower curtain aside and stepped in.

Taking a shower had always given Cory a chance to think things through. Some of his best musical ideas came when water streamed over him. He didn't know whether it was the time limit or the fear of being on his own, but Cory couldn't make use of the time.

He opened the door to the galley. "Who's next?"

Chen was sitting on the bench in the kitchen area. He motioned to him. "Come here. Sit."

Cory sat and Chen grabbed his arm. He wrapped a rubber tube around his bicep. "Make a fist."

As Cory crossed himself, Chen shook his head. Chen took a hypodermic needle and two vials out of the bag.

Cory didn't flinch when Chen stuck the needle in. He watched the red blood pulse out, quickly filling the vial. Chen swapped it for another. It filled, and Chen removed the band and needle.

Chen wrote on the vials and placed them in a tray. "Next."

Hoping his blood panels would somehow eliminate him as a donor, Cory settled into a recliner. Closing his eyes, he visualized himself back in their Brooklyn apartment.

He and Ava were in the studio. She laughed at the way he mimicked the falsetto voice of Justin Timberlake. He missed her beautiful smile. It had been too long since she'd been happy and unafraid.

Chen finished collecting blood and put the tray in the refrigerator. He unlocked a cabinet in the front of the galley and removed four manila envelopes.

"All right. Here's your first payment. There's twenty thousand in cash in each. You'll get another twenty when you're released."

He handed one to Cory. He peeked inside: two fat bundles

of hundred dollar bills. It was good money, but even the full forty thousand wouldn't motivate most of the Western world to donate an organ.

He scanned his fellow donors. The look on their faces confirmed his guess they'd never seen so much money. Though it was exploitation, these men and hundreds of thousands of others would gladly subject themselves to this in their quest for a better life.

Chen said, "We're going to get moving. Rest up and keep it down. I don't want to hear you." He went up front and sat in the passenger's seat.

The RV lurched forward. Jesus was fanning a pack of bills. Cory whispered, "It's not enough. We should be getting ten times the amount."

"This is a lot of money."

"No, it's not."

"Are you crazy?"

"When I first heard about doing this, I thought it was life-changing, you know. But then I read in an American paper, they said paying people for organs was taking advantage of the poor."

"Maybe it is, but they never lived like we did. They know nothing of the fear, the poverty, the suffering we endure. What do they say about that?"

Cory shrugged. "We should pray for those in need."

"Praying to God is good, but sometimes we can't rely only on prayer, we need to act. Be an instrument of God in our own lives."

"God gave us free will. Let us pray that we use it well."

"Amen. I need to get some sleep."

"Me too."

Closing his eyes, Cory thought about free will. He wondered if being thousands of miles away on an RV with migrants qualified as using it well. He was sure his wife wouldn't think so.

The RV rocked after stopping. Chen came into the back and took the tray of blood out of the fridge.

"Where are we?"

"Shut up and mind your business."

Cory peeked out the window. They were in the parking lot of the San Antonio Strip Mall. He saw Chen disappearing into a Quest Laboratory with the blood. He caught himself wishing he had an infection of some kind.

It was hard to predict what Black would do in this situation, but Cory was sure that relying on wishes and hope weren't on the list. They were in San Antonio. If they tag-teamed the drive, they'd be in the New York metro area in a little over a day.

Cory was here to end the illegal operation, putting those responsible behind bars. Without Ava's fear that they'd get her again, she could resume her old life.

He was so close to the goal, but without the GPS to bring help, what could he do?

Chen stepped back on board. Cory realized if he couldn't come up with a plan, the only way to save himself would be to get off the RV when it made a stop.

53

———

The three men were sitting at the kitchen table playing cards. Cory had no interest in distractions. He had to figure a way out of the mess he had gotten himself into.

The RV slowed and Cory peeked out the blinds. They were on an exit ramp heading for the Meridian, Mississippi rest area. There were going to be other stops for gas, but at the last one, in Baton Rouge, Chen had stood by the door as they fueled.

Cory dug into the manila envelope of cash and pulled a few bills out of a bundle. He closed the envelope and motioned to Jesus. He whispered, "Here, hold this for me."

"Where you going?"

He handed him the manila envelope of cash. "Nowhere. Just hang on to it in case something happens to me."

"What are you talking about? What's going to happen?"

"If I don't make it through the operation or something."

"Nothing is going to happen. God is watching over you."

"I know, but you never know." Cory stood. "Go back to playing cards."

The RV pulled past the service building into the fueling

area. Cory figured if flight departure times aligned, he'd be with his family in under twelve hours.

The RV pulled up to a pump and Chen hopped out. Cory grabbed his Bible and, keeping his eye on the driver, went to the side door. He took a deep breath and put his hand on the doorknob. He pushed the door open.

Chen said, "What the hell are you doing? Get back inside."

"Uh, just wanted to get some fresh air."

Chen took a step forward and pulled his jacket to the side. Cory eyed the gun tucked in his band and leaned back. "Take it easy. I'm just feeling cooped up."

"I said get back inside!"

Cory closed the door, bumping into Jesus when he turned around. "Sorry."

"What are you doing?"

Cory whispered, "Chen has a gun."

Jesus shrugged. "It's normal. These guys deal with the cartels and coyotes."

"I guess so."

Jesus handed him back the money. "You were trying to leave."

"I don't know what I was looking to do. I'm confused, that's all."

"Pray on it. God will tell you what to do."

Cory smiled. "You're right. I'm going to do that. Go back to playing."

He sat down, swiveling the chair so he faced the front. Cory wanted Chen to see him praying. Cory opened the Bible and silently moved his lips.

Chen slammed the door after climbing back in the passenger seat. Cory looked up. Chen was staring at him. Cory smiled at him and went back to the Bible.

Chen walked over. "Preacher man, you a wise guy too?"

"Me? No. Not at all."

Chen stepped closer. Cory could smell coffee on his breath as he leaned over. "You better watch yourself."

"I don't want no problems."

Chen stepped on the instep of Cory's foot.

"Ow!"

Chen smiled and walked away.

Cory closed his eyes and concentrated on what to do. If an opportunity to run presented itself, he was going to take it. He thought about pulling his gun on Chen and the driver. The odds that the driver was armed were high.

He was sure that both had more experience with guns than he did. It was a huge disadvantage. Besides Jesus, he couldn't predict how the others would react.

Unless a situation where he could surprise them surfaced, using the gun in the Bible was too risky. He could end up dead.

He thought about the journey north. Maybe the RV would break down or get into an accident. Or someone could get so ill they had to make an emergency stop. Cory realized how pathetic it was hoping something would happen.

It was up to him. Black didn't know where he was, and he had no way to call for help. Cory was alone.

Change always brought opportunity. During the ride to New York, the scenery and weather would change, but that was it. Until they arrived, he'd be on the lookout but didn't expect an opening to exploit.

He focused on the information Black had given on the transfer point. His contacts said they used a large warehouse to unload the migrants off the RV. They'd undergo testing before being put onto the vehicles where the transplants were done.

Cory couldn't imagine an opportunity to run at their destination. There would be more gang members, and the handoff was likely taking place in a secure location.

He tried to envision what the surgi unit looked like. He'd heard there were forward and rear areas where the operations took place. What about the recipients? Were they already on board, or would they meet up elsewhere?

There were too many questions, and the words of Black, that knowing every detail eliminated risk, haunted him. He also heard his crooked lawyer, Tower, saying you didn't walk into a courtroom unless you knew what the outcome was going to be.

It was too late to learn more. Was it too late to save himself?

54

Cory looked at the migrants playing cards. They seemed relaxed. How could they enjoy themselves facing a surgery that could kill them?

Was it the cash that fogged their minds? They were poverty-stricken, looking for a new start, but Cory couldn't understand not being scared of what lay ahead.

He realized their ignorance presented an opportunity. He'd wait until they ate and settled down for the night.

The men had eaten with gusto again. Dinner was another protein-and-vegetable-filled meal. Chen dished out handfuls of supplements, and they washed it all down with a vitamin-filled drink.

"Hope you enjoyed that meal. It'll be the last time you eat until after the operation."

They sat around watching a Telemundo game show mirroring *The Price is Right*. Cory raised the volume and whispered to Jesus, "Listen, I'm getting scared. I don't know if I can go through with this."

"The transplant?"

"Yeah. It's too risky. I don't want to die."

"You won't. We know many people who donated, and everyone is okay."

"They never tell you about the ones that go wrong."

"I guess so. But what do you want to do?"

"I prayed on it, and I think we should take off. Get away from these people."

"But we need the money for a new life."

"We take the money and run."

"But that would be stealing."

"Not really. These people are trying to take advantage of us. Maybe God put us here so we could help ourselves."

"I don't understand."

"This is dangerous for all of us. What I'm saying is, why not take off before anybody gets hurt?"

"How can we do that? You said Chen is armed."

"There are four of us. We can overpower them."

"But he has a gun."

"I don't think it'll come to that. If we stick together, what are they going to do? They got to let us go."

"Look, I'll do whatever everybody else wants to do. If they say okay, I'll go with it. Talk to them."

"All right, but my Spanish isn't the best. Can you translate for me?"

"Yes, but my English is worse than your Spanish."

He was right, but Cory felt it would help if Jesus made the case.

"Let's do it now."

Jesus asked the men to gather and told them about Cory's plan to run.

The migrants looked at each other and Oro said, "But if we run, we don't get the other money. And where are we going to go?"

Tavio said, "Yeah, and how do you know they won't shoot us or track us down?"

Cory said, "What they're doing is illegal. They can't take the chance of hurting any of us or trying to find us."

"We need the other twenty thousand. I got to pay the coyotes to bring my wife and baby here."

As soon as he said it, Cory regretted it. "I'll get you the money."

Tavio said, "How you going to do that?"

"I don't know, I'll find a way."

"Yeah, right. You're just scared, man."

"That's true. I'm afraid to die, and you should be too."

"What's the matter, your God ain't going to protect you?"

"Just forget it, okay?"

The two migrants shook their heads and began whispering to each other.

Jesus said, "Sorry."

Cory felt Jesus was a good man. "It's okay. Tell them not to say anything."

"They won't."

"I hope not."

"Don't worry."

CORY HEARD a creak before feeling the heat of a migrant's breath. He opened his eyes. "What do you want?"

Tavio said, "Your money."

Cory sat up. There were two of them. "Leave me alone."

"You don't pay, we tell Chen you tried to get us to run out on them."

"Come on, man. You got to be kidding."

"This is no joke. You pay or we tell Chen."

"It'll be your word against mine."

"Yeah? You were the one opening the door at the rest stop."

"Screw you. I just wanted some fresh air."

"You think we're playing around? Just try us."

"Get out of my face."

"You don't pay by the time we get there, I'll rat your ass out."

Cory considered handing over the twenty grand. He had taken a few hundred out, enough to get him home, when an opening to run presented itself.

But he knew if he caved into the bullying, they'd be back. Who knew what they'd demand next? Cory quickly discounted paying them and asking for their help in exchange. Black had drilled in limiting the number of people who knew any plan.

He forced the new complication out of his mind and concentrated on observing his breathing. A few minutes later, he drifted off to sleep.

CORY WOKE UP. Jesus was filling the coffee machine with water. Cory tiptoed over. He put a finger to his lips. "Jesus, these two are threatening me."

"What? Why?"

"Said if I didn't give them the down-payment money, they'd tell Chen I wanted us to run."

"That's terrible. They won't do that."

"I can't take a chance. Chen might kill me."

"You think so?"

"These guys are bad. You know they kidnapped some kids that had Down Syndrome and took organs from them."

"That's disgusting. Are you sure? Where did you hear that?"

"Uh, somebody told me they saw it on the computer when I was thinking of doing this."

"These are bad people. You have to be careful, maybe I can talk to them."

"Don't say anything. I have a plan."

"A plan?"

"Yeah, let me tell you."

55

Cory reinserted the anal capsule, washed up, and came out of the bathroom. Tavio stopped him. "You better pay."

"I don't have any money."

"Don't bullshit me. We all got the down payment."

"I gave mine to Jesus."

"What?"

"Ask Jesus. I owed him money and paid it off."

"Hey, Jesus. Get over here."

Jesus said, "What's up?"

"He said you got his money."

"It's my money. He owed me. I fronted the money for the coyote, and he paid me back."

"That's bullshit."

"It's true. I got mugged and didn't have the money to pay to get across the border."

"Don't screw with me, man."

"I'm not. Jesus backed me up."

He shook his head and walked away. "You better sleep with one eye open."

Chen stepped into the galley. "What's going on over here?"

Cory said, "Nothing. Just a little argument that started last night over the card game."

Jesus said, "Yeah, Tavio accused Chester of cheating. It didn't happen. He's a sore loser."

"I don't want no fighting, you hear?"

"No problem."

"You too, Tavio."

Tavio nodded.

Chen went back up front and Cory whispered, "Thanks, Jesus. You're a lifesaver."

"I'll hold the money till this is over."

"No, it's yours."

"No way."

Cory put his hand on his shoulder. "It's yours. I'm good with the money we'll get later. Plus, I got family to lean on in the States."

TRAFFIC BUILT up as the RV made its way across the Pennsylvania border into New Jersey. Cory had settled on taking the drugs they would use to put them to sleep and instead use them to subdue Chen and the others if needed. He'd find a way to get some when they boarded the surgical RV.

He was debating whether to ask Jesus for help, when they pulled off the turnpike to get gas. The driver got out and went to a pump. Chen got out of the passenger seat and came into the galley.

Chen said, "We're going to arrive soon. Time is tight. Get off fast and do what they tell you."

Oro said, "Where we going?"

"Don't you worry about the where or what."

"But—"

"Just do what you're told, and you'll get the rest of the money." He pulled his gun out, waving it in Cory's face. "If not, it ain't going to end well for you, preacher man."

The driver got behind the wheel. As he pulled away, he got a call. He spoke two sentences in Chinese. He hung up and bantered with Chen as he merged onto the turnpike.

Fifteen minutes later, the RV slowed. Cory lifted the blinds. They were getting off at Exit Eight. He saw an access road for a state police station. Help was close, but there was no way to get it.

The exit sign said it was for Jamesburg and Cranbury. Cory didn't know anything about the area except it was filled with distribution centers for the largest retailers in the country. His buddy Donny worked at a massive Barnes and Noble warehouse before the company lost its footing.

It made sense. Black said the operation used a warehouse that the RV could drive inside of. The vehicle paid the toll and turned onto a road lined with warehouses that stretched out of sight.

After riding a couple of miles beside tractor trailers, the RV turned into a parking lot filled with cars. Seeing protective coverings, Cory figured a car dealership was using it to store their new inventory.

They drove along the long front of the building, turning left. The side of the building had twenty loading bays. All empty.

Slowing, the RV turned. Crawling, it climbed up a ramp. They were going inside the warehouse. For a second, Cory wondered what the person scheduled to get a section of his liver looked like. Was he a male? Younger or older?

The RV rolled to a stop and Chen said, "Get up. We're here."

Bible in hand, Cory stood. Their bluster gone, Oro and Tavio were slow to get up. The apprehension in their faces was clear to Cory.

Chen opened the door. "Come on, damn it! Get moving."

56

———

A RUSH OF DAMPNESS HIT CORY AS HE STEPPED OFF THE RV. His eyes adjusted to the grayness of the cavernous space. Three men in dark suits were standing outside an office area.

An Asian man in granny glasses approached. "Name?"

"Uh, Chester Musa."

"Welcome. What's that?"

"My Bible."

Chen said, "Musa's one of those holy rollers. Prayed the whole way here."

"It's the only way I can get through all this."

The man nodded. "Go see the physician assistant." He motioned to a room whose door was open. A woman was sitting at a table.

"Hello."

"Mr. Musa?"

"Yes."

She marked a sheet on a clipboard. "I'm going to check your eyes and ears." Picking up an ophthalmoscope, she peered into his eyes. Then she switched to a similar device and looked in his ears.

"Good. Everything is clear. Let's check your blood pressure, pulse, and oxygen levels."

The PA put a clip on his forefinger and wrapped a cuff around his bicep. She noted the reading and said, "Follow me. You need to get an MRI."

Cory followed the woman into a room with a white machine. He lay down on a bed that was attached to something that looked like a large donut. They gave him headphones to wear. Cory identified the classical music, composed by Wen-chung, as "Landscapes."

A technician made adjustments, and the bed moved toward the center of the donut. Cory was enjoying the layered sound of French horns when a loud banging began.

He concentrated on the music, shutting out the knocking sound as the images were taken.

At the end of the test, the nurse handed Cory a plastic bag with a fresh scrub suit and slippers.

"You'll need to change into these before boarding. Go behind the screen. Leave your old ones in the garbage can."

After Cory changed into the new scrubs, the nurse checked the sheet of paper. "You're on the black unit. It's the brand new one, on the left. The smaller vehicle."

"Thanks."

"You can't take that Bible with you. You want to leave it here?"

"No. I want to keep God with me as long as I can."

Cory headed for the RV. The vehicle was so clean, Cory saw his reflection on it. His heart dropped when he saw Chen step off, but realized, with Chen, he might be able to keep his Bible.

Cory nodded at Chen. "We're both on this one?"

"Yeah. Get on and don't give me any trouble."

"I didn't do anything. Tavio is a troublemaker."

The garage door to the ramp began opening. Chen said, "Hurry up. The boss is coming."

"Who's that?"

"Shut up and get on. And don't touch anything!"

Plastic sheeting protected the doorway from a galley that was split into three sections. The main living area had a small kitchen and just two recliners.

Clear plastic curtains separated rooms in the rear and front. Cory pressed his nose against the sheeting and did a double take; it was crammed with medical equipment.

Everything looked hi-tech and new. Cory had never seen an operating room, but it reminded him of an ICU unit. He took a step toward an entranceway.

"Don't go inside."

Cory froze. "Uh, I wasn't." He turned around. An Asian man in his forties with a buzz cut was dressed in green scrubs. "You a doctor?"

"Yes. Dr. Ho. You're Mr. Musa, donating a liver section?"

"Yeah."

"Don't be worried. You're in good hands."

Cory smiled, holding up the Bible. "I'm not. Between God and you, I know I'll be all right. Plus, you got all this hi-tech stuff here."

"Yes. This just came in hours ago. In fact, Mr. Shu is on his way to look it over. They shouldn't have allowed you on yet."

"I have to get off?"

"Yes. It should only be a few minutes."

Cory lifted the Bible. "Can I leave this here?"

"I don't see why not."

"Thanks." Cory opened a kitchen drawer and set it down. He felt naked without it.

Cory stepped off, and Chen said, "Wait over there." He

pointed to the front of the RV. Jesus was there, standing next to a woman in scrubs. Jesus introduced her as Nurse Jun.

Chen walked over to a black SUV. A man stepped out, and Chen approached, greeting him deferentially.

Cory said, "The boss is coming to inspect this place." He looked at Nurse Jun. "What's his name?"

"I don't know."

"You work for him and don't know his name?"

"Li hired me. I never met the boss."

Cory watched the boss put a stick of chewing gum in his mouth as he approached the RV. His purposeful stride contrasted with his thin hair and droopy eyes. Cory wondered if this thin man could really be the brains behind the gang.

Dr. Ho came out and met him. Cory heard him address the man as Dr. Shu. Cory turned to the nurse. "I'm pretty sure his name is Dr. Shu."

"Yeah. I've heard that name before."

Ten minutes later, Shu stepped off the RV. He went straight to the room where Cory had been examined. Chen stuck his head out the RV's window. "Hurry up! Let's get going."

Cory embraced Jesus, wishing him luck, and followed the nurse onto the vehicle. As the nurse stowed her bag, Cory cracked open the drawer. The Bible was there. And that meant the gun as well.

57

———

As the RV pulled out of the warehouse, Cory sat next to Nurse Jun. "You're knitting a blanket?"

"Yes, but I'm crocheting it."

"I always get that mixed up. How long is it going to take you?"

"Usually a couple of days."

"That's it? You're like a machine."

"I've been making things since I was a little girl. It's a good way to pass the time when I'm keeping an eye on patients."

The RV kicked into high gear. They were on a main road. "You have a tough job."

"It's not tough. I enjoy helping people."

"That's good. You know, I always thought nurses did more than doctors do."

"We get it done together."

"How many of these transplants have you done?"

"A lot."

"What kind of drugs you use to put us to sleep? I don't want to be waking up or feeling any pain."

"Don't worry. We use the same anesthetics they use in major hospitals, like propofol, morphine, and ketamine."

"Don't we need an anesthesiologist?"

"Not really. It's mostly a safeguard. Our supplies are finely calibrated."

"How much do you need to get put out?"

"Fifty milligrams of propofol will induce unconsciousness in someone your size."

"Isn't that the stuff Michael Jackson died from?"

"Yes. He took too much and overdosed."

"What's the quickest drug to put you out?"

"Ketamine."

"How much is in a needle?"

"There are different sizes, but the syringes we generally use hold sixty milligrams, more than enough to sedate someone."

"So, all you need is one to get zonked out?"

"Initially, but you'll have an IV line, and we'll administer bolus shots to keep you under."

"I'm not going to end up like Jackson, am I?"

"You have nothing to worry about. We monitor your respiratory system. We've never had a problem in a donor or recipient."

"That's good to hear. You sure we have the drugs on board?"

"They're in the cabinet with the red drawers. I checked as soon as I boarded."

"That makes me feel better. I don't like pain."

She smiled.

"Say, am I going to get to meet whoever is getting some of my liver?"

"Probably. But it would be after the transplant."

"Okay. I hope he or she is a good person."

"You're helping someone in need."

"Is that why you're doing this," Cory lowered his voice, "even though it's illegal?"

"Saving and extending lives is all I care about. Back in China, transplants are common."

"I guess they pay you pretty good."

Dr. Ho came out of the front section. "Nurse, we have to prepare. The rendezvous with the recipients and the other team is expected in forty-five minutes. Give Mr. Musa a Valium and prep him for surgery."

Cory's stomach hit the floor as Jun got up. "Yes, Doctor Ho."

Cory whispered, "How soon is the surgery going to be? I need to say my prayers."

"We'll begin removal as soon as the recipient is on board. I'll be right back."

Cory stood as Jun went into the operating room. He opened the drawer and took the Bible out. She came out holding a small paper cup. Handing it to Cory, she said, "Take this."

Cory stared at the orange pill. "Now?"

"Yes."

"How fast does it work?"

She handed him a glass. "It'll help you relax. We're going to start prepping you in thirty minutes."

Cory's hand shook as he raised the glass of water.

"Don't be nervous. You're going to be fine. Sit down and relax until we're ready." Jun went into the sterile area.

Mind spinning, Cory pulled open the red drawer. He grabbed a needle filled with ketamine. Clutching his Bible, Cory headed to the bathroom.

He closed the door and leaned his back against it. He set the needle and Bible on the counter.

There was no margin for error. He had to take every precaution. He put the Bible down and dropped his drawers. Cory squatted, forcing the container out.

He spilled the pills into his palm and swallowed them. He had to be as alert as possible. Cory looked at the needle sitting alongside the Bible as he pulled his scrubs up.

Envisioning plunging it into Chen, he realized he'd have to get close enough to do it. But Chen was armed.

It was too risky. Using the gun, he could keep his distance. That was safer.

Cory opened the vanity door, grabbing a six-pack of toilet paper. He made a hole in the plastic and slipped the needle into one of the tubes.

Cory grabbed the Bible. He opened it, peeling open the page that covered the gun. He took the pistol out. Finger on the trigger, he stared at the gun. His mind flooded with thoughts of his family and the fear he'd never see them again.

He shook them out of his head. As Mr. Black said, it was no time for emotion.

Cory chambered a bullet. He opened the Bible, placing the gun in its hiding place. Cory took a series of slow, deep breaths before stepping out of the bathroom.

He'd wait until the last moment before springing into action.

58

———

Chen was standing guard in the galley. He was in scrubs. "You're prepping in five. Come here."

"Are you assisting the surgeon?"

Chen grabbed his arm. "I keep an eye on things." He stuck an EpiPen into Cory's arm.

"Hey! What's that?"

Chen smiled. "A little something to make sure you don't give us any trouble. Sit down."

He considered pulling the gun on Chen and running for his life right then and there. But though he'd be safe, Ava would be living in fear, and his efforts would've been for nothing.

Cory thought about commandeering the RV. What would the police do seeing the unit and medical staff? Could they crack a staff member into exposing the gang? He wondered how they'd explain it away. Maybe they'd portray it as a mobile clinic offering free care.

It bothered Cory he didn't have enough proof to get the authorities to act. But what gnawed at him was the lack of revenge. He might be able to put this unit out of commission, but Dr. Shu would get off.

If he could wait until the recipient boarded, he'd have irrefutable proof of what the operation was. Cory tried to envision the sequences before surgery.

He'd be on a gurney and they'd hook him up to an IV. Then, they'd clean the area. He stiffened. What if the antiseptic they used cleaned away the bronzer he had on? He'd be exposed.

The nurse stuck her head out. "We're ready for you, Mr. Musa."

Cory had to use his arms to get up. The drugs had hit him. The antidote hadn't kicked in yet. Chen held the plastic to the side, and rubber-legged, Cory entered the operating area.

"Lay down here." Chen tapped a gurney that was surrounded by equipment.

Chen helped Cory up. "Give me the book."

"I need it."

"You'll be out in a minute."

"Just a little longer."

Jun said, "Hold still. You're going to feel a little pinch." She inserted an IV and hooked up a line.

He slurred his words, "That the drugs?"

"Not yet, just hydration." She cut the front of his shirt open and lowered his pants.

"Don't take advantage of me. I'm married."

Jun smiled and grabbed a bottle. She poured a brown liquid onto a swab and rubbed it on Cory's abdomen. The color was darker than his bronzed skin.

"How soon till the donor gets here?"

"Any minute now. I'm going to give you some medicine, so let me take this." She grabbed the Bible.

Cory pulled it back. "No!"

Chen stepped closer. "Take it easy."

"Back off." Cory was surprised at the strength he felt. The antidote must be working.

The RV slowed, distracting Chen. He said, "We're here. Get going." Cory gave a thought to pulling the gun but needed everyone on the vehicle.

Jun twisted the valve on the IV line as the RV came to a stop. He heard a vehicle door slam shut. His eyelids were heavy. Jun took the Bible out of his hands.

Cory tried to speak but nothing came out. Jun turned the overhead light on, but to Cory, everything went dark.

59

Cory heard sounds. He couldn't open his eyes. He couldn't speak. He realized something was in his mouth and fell back asleep.

"Mr. Musa. Wake up. Can you hear me?"

Cory tried to place the voice. He opened his eyes. The bright light stung. He shut them, wondering where he was.

"Mr. Musa."

It was nurse Jun. Cory squinted. Jun's mask-covered face was blurry. Cory swallowed. His throat hurt. He was thirsty.

"You did wonderfully." Jun swabbed his lips with a long Q-Tip. "How do you feel?"

Cory's voice creaked. "Where am I?"

"You donated a part of your liver."

Cory moved his hand toward the heaviness in his abdomen.

"Easy. It's going to be sore for a couple of days."

There was a wad of padding covering his stomach. "Am I going to be okay?"

"Yes. You donated to a child, so they only took your left lobe, the smallest one."

"A child? Are they okay?"

"Yes. Everyone is doing fine, and in a day or two you'll feel like yourself again. All you must do right now is rest. Okay?"

Cory squeezed his eyes shut.

"Do you need something for the pain?"

His incision wasn't bothering him, but he nodded. He needed relief, not from pain but from his failure to assure Ava she had nothing to fear. It went even deeper; he'd reinforced the danger the gang posed.

All Cory could think of was Ava. He'd come here to put an end to the torment his daughter was under but was lying as helpless as she had been.

CORY STIRRED. He woke up. It was the sound of an engine climbing uphill. He remembered being on an RV. He looked around, seeing Nurse Jun get out of her chair. "You're up. How are you feeling?"

"Okay. I guess."

"If you're able to drink a little water, I can remove the IV. That sounds good, doesn't it?"

Cory lifted his arm, looking at the tube. "Okay."

Jun brought a plastic cup to Cory's lips. He sipped and swallowed. "My throat hurts."

"It's from the breathing tube. It'll feel better soon."

Cory nodded. Reality crashed into him; they'd stuck a tube down his throat. "You said they took—the left part of my liver."

"Yes. It's only about twenty percent of your liver. You'll be fine."

"How big is the cut?"

"It's long. We need access to the bile ducts, but don't worry, Dr. Ho is a good surgeon. You take care of it, and you'll hardly notice it in a year or two."

Cory's stomach growled. "I need to eat. I feel weak."

"That's a good sign. How about some applesauce? If you can handle it, we can move to solids from there."

"Anything at this point."

"Let me take out the IV, then you can eat."

Cory closed his eyes, preparing for pain. But none came. Jun was gentle. "Okay. It's all out."

He bent his arm. As the nurse discarded the tubing, he said, "Feels good it's gone."

Jun peeled back the top of a small container and spoon-fed the applesauce to Cory. "Good. You feel okay?"

"Yeah. I think I can handle something else."

"Let's get you out of bed first. You need to get moving. It helps with healing."

Jun took the covers off. Cory said, "It's freezing in here."

"You'll warm up once you move around. Swing your legs around."

"Ow." Cory reached for his stomach. "It hurts."

"The first time you get up it'll hurt, but it gets better each time. Come on."

Jun lifted his legs and helped him sit up. "Ready?"

As Cory said, "Give me a second," Chen slipped in. In scrubs, he pulled his mask down. "Ah, the holy man is up."

Cory wanted to spit at him. "Where's my Bible?"

Jun said, "I'll get it once we do our little walk."

"All right." Cory grunted as he lowered his feet to the ground. He put a hand on the bed and nodded. "Okay."

Jun put a hand under his armpit, and Cory shuffled forward. Surprised by the effort it required, he said, "Hold on. I need a break."

"That's okay."

"How can I be so tired?"

"We had to administer a bit more anesthesia than usual, so you still have some in your system. Plus, your body is putting its resources into healing itself."

Cory cursed the antidote. It hadn't worked. "How long until I'm better?"

"Every day you'll feel better. After four days, you'll feel like yourself."

"So, I'm going be here at least four days?"

"That's up to the doctor, but usually we keep donors two to three days.

"That's it? Am I going to be all right?"

"Let's finish the walk. Dr. Ho was scheduled to come in after we're done. He can give you better answers."

Cory moved toward a cabinet. Sitting on top, next to a liver-shaped stainless-steel pan, was his Bible.

"There's my Bible. Get it for me."

Chen swooped in and picked up the book. "You know, I should read this. See what is so good in here."

"Give it to me!"

Dr. Ho entered. "What's going on in here?"

Nurse Jun said, "It okay, Doctor Ho. Chen was just kidding around, teasing Mr. Musa."

Cory looked at her and she winked. He said, "I misunderstood him. I'm very sensitive about my Bible."

Ho said, "You're recovering from surgery. I can't have you getting riled up."

Jun said, "Sorry, Doctor. I thought lightening things up would be good for Mr. Musa's frame of mind."

"Let's get him back in bed. I need to examine him."

Chen and Jun helped Cory onto the gurney. Ho asked

Chen to check on the recipient. As Ho pulled on gloves, he said, "I'm the surgeon who performed the section."

Cory wondered if he had also cut Ava open as he continued, "Do you have any pain?"

"It's not bad, except when I move around."

He took a penlight out and shined it in Cory's eyes. "Good. Let's take a look at the incision."

Ho peeled tape off Cory's abdomen, handing the old dressing to Jun. "It looks excellent."

He pressed his fingertips down. "Does this hurt?"

"A little, but not too bad."

"Good."

"How long until my liver is back to normal?"

"In the first six weeks, the liver regenerates rapidly, reclaiming most of what was sectioned off. It'll continue to grow over the next year."

"The kid who got mine, how's he doing?"

"It's a she, and she's doing fine."

"Oh, that's good. Will I be feeling like my old self in a couple of days?"

"Yes. It takes most donors four to seven days to feel good. You may have some pain, but it will subside. We'll give you a couple of days' worth of medicine to control it if it flares up."

"Okay."

"You'll need to see a hepatologist as soon as possible."

"A what?"

"A liver doctor. You'll need to be monitored by a specialist—"

"Something is wrong?"

"No. It's just a precaution."

"Oh. How long am I going to be here?"

"Another day and a half."

"Where am I going?"

"I don't know."

"Relax. You're doing well, Mr. Musa. Nurse, please dress the wound."

"Thanks, Doc." Cory realized it was ludicrous to thank the doctor who'd cut him open.

Jun said, "See, you're doing fine. Just stay clear of Chen and you'll stay that way."

"What do you mean?"

"He can be rough."

"How so?"

"He's dangerous. Just leave it at that. All right?"

"Okay, please give me my Bible. I need to say my prayers."

Cory made a show of opening the Bible. Eyes fixed on a page of Exodus, Cory tried to process what the doctor and Jun had said. He felt sore, but they had assured him he'd improve quickly.

Welcome news, but it meant he was going to be dropped off somewhere soon. He had only a day to act. He shifted in the bed to test the pain. It hurt, but Cory had the gun. He wouldn't need to get physical.

Chen was armed. Jun had made it clear he was dangerous. He had to find a way to surprise Chen. An opportunity to disarm him.

If he could neutralize Chen, he didn't expect a threat from either of the doctors or nurses on board. But what about the driver? He was a quiet, small-framed man. The driver never came into the galley, eating and resting in the driver's seat.

Cory gave up trying to figure the driver out, knowing Black would assume he was armed. A failure to do so could cost Cory his life.

Lifting his head, Cory surveyed the small space. He'd

need to get behind Chen. Cory would have to be in position beforehand because he couldn't move quickly.

Cory had an idea. When Chen went to use the bathroom, he'd get out of bed. Cory would keep his back to him, and when he passed by, he'd surprise him.

As unnerving as pulling a gun on Chen was, Cory looked forward to seeing the look on Chen's face when he did. It would be a role reversal like he'd never seen.

Cory wondered how many donors who'd gotten cold feet at the last minute were forced to go ahead by Chen. He didn't doubt Chen would've restrained them, jabbing them with a needle full of drugs to subdue their resistance.

It was the ugly side of humanity, but how much better was Cory if he pulled a gun to get what he wanted?

Searching for the moral high ground, Cory thought of Ava. The idea that Chen had swept his daughter and the Down Syndrome kids off the street solidified his resolve.

These people had to be stopped. It was up to him to put an end to this rogue gang.

60

Cory woke up. They had started the RV. The vehicle lurched forward. They were on the move. He propped himself up as Jun was heading into the bathroom. Chen was leaning against the kitchen counter.

"We going somewhere?"

"Yep."

"Where?"

"You'll find out when we get there."

"You dropping me off at a rehab place?"

"Stop with the questions."

"Just one more, okay?"

Chen stared at him.

"How long until we get there? I want to know if I have enough time to do my morning prayers now or if I should wait till I get there."

Chen turned his back on Cory. He filled up the coffee maker with water. Cory lay his head down. How was he going to do this? He'd just been sliced open. Was he crazy enough to think he could get past this thug?

Chen was big. Maybe he should jab him with the ketamine. He'd aim for the jugular. But if he missed, who knew how long the drug would take to disable him? Sticking a needle in Chen was too risky. He had to use the gun.

Seeds of doubt continued to get fertilized when he remembered what Black had said. Cory couldn't recall the exact words, but it was along the lines that once you make your plan, be open to change but always maintain confidence.

The other part of Black's sermon he could still hear him say was, 'Doubt causes mental chaos, and chaos leads to demise.' Cory took several deep breaths, focusing on his goal.

Cory dug under his pillow for the Bible.

Chen said, "You looking for this?" He held up the Bible, and Cory's heart began pounding.

"Give it to me."

Chen tossed it onto the bed. Cory picked it up. It was too light. He looked at Chen. He was smiling. "You think you're smart, don't you?"

"I don't know what you're talking about?"

Chen came to his bedside. He pulled Cory's gun out of his waistband and pressed the muzzle against his temple. "I should blow your goddamn head off."

Jun came out of the bathroom. "Put that gun down!"

"This bastard carried a gun on board."

"It was for my own protection. I didn't mean—"

"Thought you had God watching over you. You're full of shit. I should put a bullet in your brain right now."

"Chen, put that away, or I'll get Dr. Ho."

"He's a threat."

"No, I'm not. I could've done something if I wanted a million times."

"He's right. Besides, he'll be getting off soon."

"He's been a troublemaker since day one."

"No, I haven't. I did everything I was supposed to. You took my liver."

"Leave him alone, Chen."

"Bastard had a bullet in the chamber. He was ready to do something."

"I swear I wasn't. I forgot to take it out, that's all. I had to be ready when I was crossing over."

"I'm keeping an eye on you. One wrong move and you're a dead man. You hear me?"

Cory nodded. Chen backed off to a corner. Wearing a scowl, he stared at Cory. It was unnerving, but Cory knew he'd be safely out of reach at a rehab place soon.

The relief from getting away with bringing a gun on board faded. Cory hadn't accomplished his mission. And worse, he'd had part of his liver taken on top of lying to his family.

He'd go back home with his tail between his legs. He couldn't imagine facing his kids. He was not only a failure but one who'd gotten his ass handed to him like a bigmouth in the schoolyard. How had everything gone wrong?

Feeling sorry for himself, Cory closed his eyes. It was embarrassing enough with his family, but telling Mr. Black would be worse. He wondered how to soften the story when he remembered another thing Black had said: feeling sorry for yourself was a waste of energy. He said you had to play the hell out of the cards in your hand. Reviewing the situation, Cory felt like he had a handful of jokers.

Cory had an idea. It was risky but if executed right might work.

Testing his condition, Cory brought his knees toward his chest. A dull pain splayed across his stomach. He stretched his legs out.

It hurt, but he didn't think it was bad enough to stop him

from controlling his reaction. He remembered the cold pool he'd forced himself into. `

He pulled his legs in, focusing on how he'd get around Chen. He moved his knees to one side. He winced but pushed through it. Cory swung his legs over the edge of the bed.

"Where you going?"

"Gotta take a dump."

Chen nodded as Cory's feet hit the ground. "Make it fast."

Arm supporting his abdomen, Cory shuffled to the bathroom. Once inside, he opened the door to the vanity. Reaching in carefully, he pulled the full pack of toilet paper out. He tilted the pack, and the needle he'd hidden slid out of a tube.

He sat on the bowl for a minute, then flushed it. He held the hypodermic needle against his abdomen with his hand. Cory took a deep breath and opened the door. It was showtime.

61

Cory stepped out of the bathroom. Chen was sipping a coffee. Stitching needle in hand and bolt of yarn in her lap, Jun was crocheting. Shuffling slowly to the bed, Cory kept a grimace on his face.

He slipped into bed, placing the needle alongside his thigh. Cory said, "Hey, Jun, how's the kid with my liver doing?"

"Doing well."

"She getting off with me?"

"No."

"Oh, where is she going?"

Chen said, "Shut up! It's none of your business."

Jun said, "There's no reason to be nasty."

"It's okay, Jun. He's right. I should mind my own business."

Chen scoffed.

Cory groaned as he propped himself up.

"You okay?"

"Bad pinching in my gut."

"Take it easy."

"I feel like I have to stretch it." He grimaced and swung his legs off the bed. He pressed the needle against his belly and stood.

Jun stood up. "Feel any better?"

"Yeah. It's crazy, but it went away."

"It makes sense. It could have been an adhesion loosening."

"Adhesion? Is that something to worry about?"

"No. They're just fibrous bands that form between organs and tissue. Basically, it's just internal scar tissue."

"You know, I'm real grateful for how well you took care of me."

"Thank you. It's my job."

"And you, Chen. I know we had our moments, but I appreciate everything you both did for me."

Jun said, "That's sweet of you."

Cory took his free arm and wrapped it around Jun. "Thanks."

Jun returned the hug. Cory stepped away. "Come here, Chen, give me a hug."

"You're nuts, preacher man, you know that?"

Arm outstretched, Cory stepped closer to Chen. "We're all God's children."

Chen turned away. Cory took the cap off the needle. He reached, aiming for Chen's neck. The needle sank into Chen's flesh. "What the fuck?" Cory pushed the plunger in as Chen reached for his neck.

Chen pulled the needle out. He looked at it. "You mother-fucker." Chen reached into his holster. Cory pushed him back. Chen stumbled. He raised the gun.

Cory rushed him. The gun went off. "Ahhhh!"

Ears ringing and midsection ripping with pain, Cory hit the floor. He heard voices, but everything sounded like he was underwater.

62

—————

CORY ROLLED ONTO HIS SIDE. CHEN WAS CLUTCHING HIS knee. His hands were covered in blood. Jun rushed over as the RV skidded to a stop.

The pistol was inches away from Chen. Cory got on his knees. Chen reached for the gun. Chen's hand wrapped around the butt of the weapon.

Jun moved into his line of vision. Cory flattened onto the floor. Jun shifted positions. Chen was unconscious.

Cory crawled over and grabbed the gun as the driver appeared, saying, "What the hell?"

Cory and the driver pointed their guns at each other. Two shots went off. Cory grabbed his thigh. The driver crashed into a cabinet.

Dr. Ho stormed in. He surveyed the damage and froze. Cory pointed his pistol. "Help the worst first."

Jun said, "Chen's bullet wound is just below the knee. I'll put a tourniquet on." She motioned to the moaning driver. "He's been hit in the shoulder."

Ho said, "Give him twenty milligrams of morphine."

Cory said, "I got hit in the thigh, on the side. Hurts like hell, but it's not bleeding bad."

Ho knelt by Chen. "He's unconscious."

Jabbing the driver with the morphine, Jun said, "Chen was stuck with a needle of ketamine."

"Who did that?"

Cory held the gun up. "I did. I'm in charge now."

Ho said, "How large a dose? His heart rate needs to be monitored."

Tying the tourniquet, Jun said she would. She cut away Chen's pants. "It's superficial. I'll clean the wound."

Ho was putting pressure on the driver's bullet hole. "The bleeding is slowing. But he needs surgery to remove the bullet."

Cory said, "He in real danger?"

"Not especially. But the wound needs to be cleaned and dressed."

"Hurry up and do it. Then look at my leg." Cory waved the gun. "But first, give me your phones."

Jun and Ho handed over their phones. "Good. Now, get me Chen's and the driver's."

Cory crawled over and picked up the gun the driver shot him with. He pointed a gun at Jun. "I'm sorry, but I need you to check Chen's waistband for my gun. Please don't do anything stupid. I don't want to hurt you."

Jun found it, handing it over as if she were passing over a dead mouse. Cory held it in his lap. "Thanks. I'm really sorry about all this, but I had no choice."

The nurse's lip quivered.

"Don't worry. You're not going to get hurt. Please look at my leg."

Jun cut away Cory's pant leg. A hunk of flesh hung like a

flapper. Cory sucked in to keep from vomiting. The pain intensified as Jun cleaned the wound.

"Ow!"

Jun lifted the flap of flesh, putting it in position, and wrapped a roll of gauze around it. A phone in the pile next to Cory began vibrating. "Give me a bag."

Cory loaded the phones and one gun in and said, "Help me up."

Dragging his leg, Cory made his way to the driver and Ho. "He in any condition to drive?"

"Certainly not. We just gave him morphine."

"All right. Listen up. There's been a change of plans. We're going to see your boss, Dr. Shu."

Ho said, "You can't do that. We have a patient, a child, who needs medical attention and men with gunshot wounds."

"You're a doctor, a surgeon to boot, and Jun is a nurse. Deal with it."

"But—"

Cory raised the gun. "You got people to take care of." He pointed at the driver. "He okay to talk?"

Jun said, "He should be."

Cory made sure the driver saw he was armed. "How you feeling?"

He shrugged. "Okay."

"Where is Shu?"

"I don't know."

He pointed the gun at his face. "Tell me."

"I swear, I don't know."

"I don't have time for this." Cory pushed the muzzle of the gun against the wound on his shoulder.

"Ow! Stop it!"

"Tell me where Shu is."

"I don't know."

"Then we're going to drive right back to that warehouse near Cranbury where we started."

"He's not going to be there."

"We'll wait until he shows up."

"They'll kill you."

"Not before I expose this entire operation."

"You don't know what you're up against."

"Tell me then."

He shook his head.

Cory pressed the wound. "Tell me!"

"Fuck you!"

Dr. Ho said, "Stop torturing him. It's immoral."

"And paying for organs isn't? And what about snatching kids off the street and taking their organs? You want to lecture me about morality? Look in the goddamn mirror first!"

Ho whispered, "I'm not proud of my participation, but I didn't do it willingly."

"Don't make excuses now."

"You don't understand."

Cory walked away from the doctor. "Damn right, I don't. Go check on the kid."

He dug a phone out and went to Google Maps. They were on a road outside of Hopewell Township, twenty miles outside of Cranbury. Just a half an hour away, but could Cory find the warehouse he'd been examined and transferred in?

It was flying blind. And leaving things to chance was unacceptable. He had an idea. Cory checked for a hospital. Capital Health Medical Center was a few miles away, in Pennington.

Cory stuck his head in the rear compartment. Ho was entering data on a laptop. Cory was struck by the little figure hooked up to the machines. He said, "How's she doing?"

"Fair to good. She needs to be closely monitored, but I expect she'll fully recover."

"She was going to be transferred to a rehab place?"

"Yes. That's what they normally do."

"A hospital would be better, wouldn't it?"

"Of course."

"You want to make a deal?"

"What kind of a deal?"

"We'll drop the kid off at a hospital so she can get the care she needs."

"That would be excellent, but what's the rest?"

"You tell me where Shu is."

"I don't know. I really don't."

"You know where the warehouse is."

Ho hesitated. "Yes, but he's not there all the time."

"You call him and tell him to meet you there."

"He'll ask why?"

"You tell him you have confidential information on another surgeon and, uh, Chen."

"If I lie to them, they'll kill me."

Cory pointed the gun. "Tell them I had a gun to your head."

"No. It's too dangerous."

"I'll let you go with the kid. Jun too."

"You're going to the authorities, aren't you?"

"I want to shut this operation down. They don't have to know you even exist. Or we can say they forced you to participate."

"They did. They threatened my family in China if I didn't cooperate. I told them no, but they kept pressing and making threats."

"Don't make excuses for what you did."

"It's not as bad as you make it out to be. We helped people who would have died without a transplant."

"You think it's okay to kidnap kids and cut them open for their organs?"

"I have no idea what you're talking about. I never did anything like that."

"Look, at this point, you either help me get Shu, or you go down like the rest of them. I don't care either way."

"Okay, okay."

"Where is the warehouse?"

"At the end of Dayton Boulevard."

Cory handed him his phone. "Call Shu. You better talk in English. One word in Chinese and I'll put a bullet in your head."

"I should call Li then. I speak Cantonese, and Li speaks Mandarin."

"Who's Li?"

"Shu's right-hand man."

"Call him. But take a couple of breaths. Make sure you're relaxed; I don't want him suspecting anything."

Ho inhaled deeply three times. He tapped on the phone, and Cory said, "Put it on speaker."

Li answered, "Wei."

"Hello Li, it's Doctor Ho."

"Is something wrong?"

"Not exactly, but I must see Shu immediately."

"Why?"

"I'm afraid we have a leak."

"Who is it?"

"It's rather complicated, and uh, in fact, there are two informers working against us."

"Tell me who!"

"I'm sorry, but this is highly sensitive, and I must tell Shu personally."

"Where are you?"

"Dropping the donor off in a few minutes. We can meet at the warehouse if that works."

"We just left there. We'll turn around."

"See you later then."

Ho hung up and Cory asked, "How did he sound to you?"

"Pretty normal."

"Good. Now, about Chen and the driver, are they stable enough to stay on board?"

"It's not optimal, but you don't want to release them?"

"They're criminals. Unless they're going to die, I want their asses behind bars."

"Let me examine them, okay?"

"Let's go."

Ho looked over the men, and Cory spoke to Jun. "Look, I don't know how involved you are with this illegal transplant garbage."

"I only did it to do help people. I—"

"Spare me. You've been good to me, and my way of saying thank you is releasing you before I get the authorities involved."

"What do you mean?"

"I want to get the kid to a hospital, and you and Ho can go along and disappear after you get her there."

"Really? Oh, thank you, thank you so much."

"Take a look at my leg. Change the dressing if it needs it."

"Sure, sit down."

Cory eased himself into a chair, keeping his leg straight out. Jun knelt and unwound the gauze.

"Ow."

"Sorry. It looks pretty good, but it needs to be stitched up."

"Not now."

She applied an antiseptic and wrapped it back up. "You're good to go, but I wouldn't let it go more than a day. You're susceptible to an infection."

Cory stood. Exhaustion was coming on. "Jun, can you do me a favor and make me a coffee?"

"Sure."

Dr. Ho said, "In my medical opinion, both men should be hospitalized."

"But they'll make it a day without going in."

Ho nodded. "There could be internal bleeding or an infection brewing."

"All right. Get the kid ready to get off."

"Here?"

"I'm not taking the chance of driving to a hospital. We'll call Lyft for a ride. Capital Health is a hospital just a few miles away."

"All right."

After giving Chen and the driver another dose of sedatives, Ho and Jun lowered the collapsible wheelchair to the ground. The Lyft driver helped, and within minutes, Cory was looking at the car's taillights as it pulled away.

Cory limped to the RV's driver's seat. Chen and his associate were both out. Cory put his hands on the wheel. The large steering wheel reminded him of the bus they'd toured half the country in.

He started the engine and put it in gear. The RV hesitated before lurching forward. Though the journey ahead was short, it was completely uncertain.

63

Cory estimated he was a couple of minutes away from the warehouse. He pulled the RV over and took out Dr. Ho's phone. He opened the screen to the last number called.

Cory panted like a dog. On the verge of hyperventilating, he hit redial.

"H-h-hello?"

"Who is this?"

"Uh, the donor, Chester Musa. We need help."

"Where's Dr. Ho?"

"He's been shot."

"What? By who?"

"Chen shot him, and the driver got shot too. We need help, please help us."

"Where are you?"

"Close by. Dr. Ho told me where to go."

"Okay."

"Do you have doctors? They're bleeding all over, and the kid isn't doing good."

"What kid?"

"The one who got my liver."

"Hurry up and get here."

"Okay." Cory hung up.

Li turned to Shu, saying, "There's been an altercation on the unit. Chen shot Dr. Ho."

Shu asked, "What about the patients?"

"The donor seemed all right but said the recipient was in trouble."

"What kind of trouble? She wasn't shot, was she?"

"He didn't say."

"How did this happen?"

"Chen must have overheard Ho telling me he'd been exposed and—"

"Where are they?"

"They'll be here any minute."

"Open the door."

"Okay."

"Call Dr. Wan and get him here. And notify Holiday Rehab we may need a couple of beds."

"I'm on it."

Shu pulled out his phone and dialed Dr. Ho's number. It rang five times before Cory answered it.

"Hello?"

"Who am I speaking to?"

"Chester Musa, the donor."

"I understand there has been an event."

"Yes. A shooting. It was scary and people are hurt."

"Are you all right?"

"Yes. I'm good. But—"

"I need to speak with Dr. Ho."

"He's hurt. Real bad."

"I understand. What is the condition of the recipient?"

"I don't know, but the doctor, Dr. Ho, he said she wasn't doing good."

"I need you to read me her vitals."

"I, I don't know how."

"I'll walk you through it."

"But we're just pulling into the parking lot."

"Okay. I'll make sure the door is raised. Drive straight in."

"Okay."

Shu hung up and said, "How long until Dr. Wan gets here?"

Li said, "He's visiting his daughter in Hawthorne."

"That's more than an hour away. Depending on the condition of the recipient, I may need help caring for the others."

"Get a medical bag from the PA and tell her to be ready to assist."

CORY TOOK his foot off the gas. Idling, the RV crept through the parking lot. He saw the entrance ramp. The door was open.

Cory palmed Dr. Ho's phone. He'd bounced around who to call. The natural call was to FBI Agent Knox. But Cory couldn't take the risk bureaucracy would slow down a response.

The NJ State Troopers had a station just off the Cranbury exit, and calling 911 should get them here in five minutes. If he made the call too early, he risked tipping off Shu before he boarded.

He'd call as soon as Shu climbed on board.

64

Li left, and Shu paced the floor of the warehouse, asking himself what could have gone wrong. Dr. Ho had mentioned a leak, claiming that Chen was a snitch.

It didn't make sense. Chen had been with Shu from the beginning. Why would he turn against the operation? Chen was rough around the edges, but his loyalty had never been questioned.

Shu felt something was off. It didn't make sense. All of Chen's family were in China. He had to know the Party would punish them for his traitorous behavior.

Had Chen been in America too long? Was he becoming self-centered like most Americans? Shu tried to figure what the Americans could promise Chen in return for turning against the operation.

They may have dangled citizenship and a new identity, along with financial support. But did Chen believe he could avoid the long arm of the Party?

Shu smiled at the thought. China played the long game. If Chen was a turncoat, they'd wait. Let Chen get comfortable, believing he was safe. They'd use their contacts and hacking skills to locate him and exact revenge when he least expected it.

Chen was injured, the donor had said. How badly, he'd find out soon. Shu would make sure he was pressed for a confession, but not until the recipient was stabilized and safe.

Li came out of the office holding a bag. "Is this good?"

Shu opened the valise and looked in its compartments. "Yes. We should be all right with this. As soon as I examine the recipient, I'll know whether we can stabilize her on the unit."

"I don't like the way this came about. If she wasn't doing well, why didn't Dr. Ho advise you?"

"These cases can turn quickly, but this is strange."

"Are you armed, sir?"

"No. You know I have an aversion to firearms."

"Given the circumstances, I think you should be prepared."

"You'll be there if anything goes astray."

"I think I hear them."

They trained their eyes on the open garage door.

Shu said, "Why aren't they coming in?"

"I don't know. Let me take a look. Stay here."

Li walked to the door and stepped onto the ramp. He waved to the RV, but it didn't budge.

"They're just sitting there."

Shu started in his direction when Li's phone rang. It was Cory. "Tell Shu to come on board."

"Drive inside."

"No. Get Shu out here."

"He's not coming alone."

"You got twenty seconds, or we leave."

Li watched the RV slowly back up. "Hold on a second—" The line went dead.

"They won't come in. They don't want me on board, only you, and they said twenty seconds, or they'd leave."

"Okay." Shu opened the medical bag.

"No. Don't go. It's some kind of trap."

"Dr. Ho said there were gunshot wounds, and the recipient was not well. I have to go."

"I don't like it. You're not armed."

Shu took out a vial and needle. He stuck the needle in the vial and withdrew the plunger. "Give me five minutes, then come on board."

65

———

Cory watched Shu step out of the warehouse carrying a bag as he headed down the ramp. Li was a couple of paces behind.

Shu paused when he hit the parking lot. He surveyed the area. He said something to Li and started for the RV.

Li hung back. Cory hoped he'd stay there. With each step Shu took, Cory's heart rate quickened. He took his eyes off Shu. He reminded himself to focus and stuck the gun in his waistband, covering it with his shirt.

Shu put his hand on the doorknob and paused. Cory looked out the window. Li had begun walking toward the RV.

The door swung open. Cory said, "Hurry. She's in pain."

Shu stepped in and surveyed the galley. "Where's the recipient?"

Cory dialed 911 and pulled the gun out. "She's safe."

"What are you doing?"

"Shut up!" He pointed the gun at Shu. "I need help. There's been a shooting, and two men are shot. Hurry!" When Cory gave the police their location, Shu made for the door.

Cory pulled him back. "Get back here."

Shu swung his arm and jabbed Cory with the needle.

"What was that?"

Cory knew what it was by Shu's smile.

Cory pointed the gun at Shu. "You bastard."

Cory pulled the trigger. Shu fell to the ground and cried out.

Cory hurried to the driver's seat. Wondering how long he had, he heard Li firing at the locked door.

Cory put the RV into drive. He hit the gas. He felt serene. He knew it wasn't focus but the drugs.

A shot was fired, and the RV swerved. A tire had been shot. He turned out of the driveway.

On the main drag he opened the window and put the air conditioning on. He approached the toll barrier. The RV bounced off the curb at the toll booth.

Out of the side-view mirror, Cory saw sparks flying. He was riding the rim on one of the rear wheels.

Cory's head bobbed as he steered the RV onto the turnpike. The building he saw off the turnpike was blurry. Was it the rest area or the state trooper station?

Cory put his head back. His hands slid off the wheel. Horns blared, waking him. He hit the divider and bounced into the center lane. He yanked the wheel to the right.

He blacked out. The jolt from sideswiping a car woke him. The RV bounced onto the grass. Cory tried to hit the brakes but lost consciousness.

Bam! Cory slammed into the steering wheel. The searing pain in his abdomen forced him awake. The RV had slammed into a building. Everything went black.

66

Cory heard a voice. "Dad. Dad, open your eyes."

He thought he was dreaming until a hand enveloped his. "Cory, can you open your eyes? Try. Just for a minute."

It was Linda. But he couldn't wake up. She said, "Come on. You can do it. We're all here."

Cory had to think. Who is we? Then he heard another voice. "Dad, you're the bravest person in the whole world. Ever. I can't believe you got them. Thanks, Dad, I love you."

Cory mumbled, "Ava? Is that you?"

"Yes. It's me. Open your eyes, Dad."

The bright light stung his eyes. "Ava, you're okay?"

She smiled, "Yes, Dad. How are you?"

His son got in his face. "Tommy."

"Hey, Dad. You're a superhero. Everybody is talking about you."

"I'm no hero." He reached for his wife's hand. "Oh, Linda. Thank God. Am I going to be all right?"

"You're going to be fine. You just need to rest."

"I don't remember what happened."

"You crashed into the police station."

"What happened to Shu? Did they get him?"

"Yes. He's in the hospital too."

"You shot him, Dad. I can't believe it."

Cory looked at Linda. "I'm sorry about all this."

Ava said, "Don't be sorry, Dad. You got them. They deserved it."

"I should've said something to you, I'm sorry."

"Don't worry about that. Just get better so you can come home."

<hr>

CORY OPENED HIS EYES. A ray of light spilled into the room from the hallway. It was as quiet as a hospital could be. His gut hurt and his leg, hanging in a sling, was throbbing. Reaching for the call button, Cory gasped.

"Oh my God. You scared me. How long you been there?"

Mr. Black said, "A couple of minutes. I didn't want to wake you."

"What time is it?"

"Two in the morning."

"How'd you get in here?"

Black shrugged. "How's the leg?"

"Pretty good."

"And the liver thing?"

"All's good."

Black pointed to an IV bag. "What's that for then?"

Cory touched a forefinger to his temple. "It's all up here."

Black smiled. "I had my doubts you could pull it off, but I never doubted your motivation."

"Couldn't have done it without you."

"What happened after you lost the GPS?"

Cory filled him in. Black grinned. "You really adapted."

"I tried. But I got to be honest, if the antidote would have worked, I think I would've ended up running."

"Sometimes bailing out is the best option."

"I'm glad I didn't. You should've seen Ava. It looks like she's back to her old self."

"That's good."

"I still can't believe it all worked out."

"You could've been killed, you know."

"I still haven't processed it."

"You talk to the cops yet?"

"No, my doctor wouldn't let them today."

"Don't give them too much. They kidnapped you, just like they did with your kids."

"But they got Chen and others who'll say I was there in Texas."

"You went there to try and get some info on what they were doing. They got wise and grabbed you and put you with the others. They were armed, right?"

"Oh yeah."

"With all the media attention on you, I doubt they'll charge you with anything, but if they do, it'll be self-defense."

***

Cory came out of the studio smiling. Linda said, "Good call?"

"That was the national registry for organ donors. Guess what they said."

"There's been an increase in people signing up?"

"How about a five hundred percent jump. They said they had never seen anything like it."

"That's fantastic."

"And they said it's not slowing down."

"All the publicity really helped then."

"Yeah, I never understood why the government never pushed people to sign up like they do in other countries."

"We don't like being told what to do."

"I know, but you're helping someone in need, and you're going to be dead anyway."

"We don't like talking about death. We're going to live forever, right?"

"Maybe one day. You know, I was thinking of doing a press conference, possibly with the girl who got a section of my liver. It's not for everybody, but giving up a slice of my liver really wasn't that bad."

"It might help convince people to consider donating."

"That's what I'm thinking."

Linda reached for her phone. "It's Ava."

Linda answered, speaking for a minute. She hung up smiling. "She's staying out late, again."

"Thank God, she's back to normal."

"Thank God and you, Cory. You're the one who saved her."

Author's Note:

I enjoy the research required to write a story. Though I go down many rabbit holes, I like learning and uncovering interesting information.

This story was no different, however, one fact I found unsettling; there aren't enough donors to satisfy the demand.

I'm not sure why the huge imbalance between those

needing organ transplants and donors isn't common knowledge or why a larger effort to bridge the gap is not being undertaken.

The sad reality is many waiting for an organ, die before their name reaches the top of the list.

Please consider becoming a donor. It's an easy way to help those in need. More information can be found here - www.organdonor.gov

---

I hope you enjoyed reading this book as much as I enjoyed writing it. If you did, I'd appreciate it if you would write a quick review on Amazon or your favorite book site. Reviews are an author's best friend and even a quick line or two is helpful. Thanks, Dan.

Have you read these other books by Dan Petrosini?

THE LUCA MYSTERY SERIES

Am I the Killer

Vanished

The Serenity Murder

Third Chances

A Cold, Hard Case

Cop or Killer?

Silencing Salter

A Killer Missteps

Uncertain Stakes

The Grandpa Killer

Dangerous Revenge

Where Are They

Buried at the Lake

The Preserve Killer

No One is Safe

SUSPENSEFUL SECRETS
Cory's Dilemma
Cory's Flight
Cory's Shift

OTHER WORKS BY DAN PETROSINI
The Final Enemy
Complicit Witness
Push Back
Ambition Cliff

YOU CAN KEEP abreast of my writing and have access to books that are free of discounting by joining my newsletter. It normally is out once a month and also contains notes on self-esteem, motivational pieces and wine articles.

It's free. See bottom of my website: www. danpetrosini.com

ABOUT THE AUTHOR

Dan is a USA Today and Amazon best-selling author who wrote his first story at the age of ten and enjoys telling a story or joke.

Dan gets his story ideas by exploring the question; What if?

In almost every situation he finds himself in, Dan explores what if this or that happened? What if this person died or did something unusual or illegal?

Dan's non-stop mind spin provides him with plenty of material to weave into interesting stories.

A fan of books and films that have twists and are difficult to predict, Dan crafts his stories to prevent readers from guessing correctly. He writes every day, forcing the words out when necessary and has written over twenty-five novels to date.

It's not a matter of wanting to write, Dan simply has to.

Dan passionately believes people can realize their dreams if they focus and act, and he encourages just that.

His favorite saying is – "The price of discipline is always less than the cost of regret"

Dan reminds people to get the negativity out of their lives. He believes it is contagious and advises people to steer clear of negative people. He knows having a true, positive mind set makes it feel like life is rigged in your favor. When he gets off base, he tells himself, 'You can't have a good day with a bad attitude.'

Married with two daughters and a needy Maltese, Dan lives in Southwest Florida. A New York native, Dan has taught at local colleges, writes novels, and plays tenor saxophone in several jazz bands. He also drinks way too much wine and never, ever takes himself too seriously.

He puts out a twice-a-month newsletter featuring articles, his writing and special deals and steals.

Sign up at www.danpetrosini.com

www.ingramcontent.com/pod-product-compliance
Lightning Source LLC
Chambersburg PA
CBHW071938210726
48293CB00001BA/233